MURDOCK CRACKS ICE

ROBERT J. RAY

A DELL BOOK

Published by
Dell Publishing
a division of
Bantam Doubleday Dell Publishing Group, Inc.
1540 Broadway
New York, New York 10036

The trademark Dell® is registered in the U.S. Patent and Trademark Office.

ISBN: 0-440-21413-0

Reprinted by arrangement with Delacorte Press

Printed in the United States of America

Published simultaneously in Canada

June 1993

10 9 8 7 6 5 4 3 2 1
RAD

This book is for Margot,

who works at a real job
so that I may play
in the vast vineyard of words.

ACKNOWLEDGMENTS

Thanks go to:

Jean Femling, ace writer, ace critic, for reading a rough draft and beaming a bright light on the darkness therein.

My Seattle NWC critique group: Larry Zuckerman, Rick Myers, Candice Fulton, and Melinda Johns.

My Seattle Freelances critique group: Kerry Wilke, Susan Oatis, and Dick Dickenson.

John Pettit and Connie Miller, who gave me access to northwest locales dripping with mystery.

Chief of Detectives Roy Skagen and Sergeant T. D. Augerson, both of the Seattle Police Department, for valuable tips on crime and crime fighting in Seattle.

My agent, Ben Kamsler, who finds markets for my words.

My editor, Jackie Farber, who has a sharp eye for character and nuance.

The ice was here, the ice was there,
The ice was all around:
It cracked and growled, and roared and howled,
Like noises in a swound!

SAMUEL TAYLOR COLERIDGE
The Rime of the Ancient Mariner

Prologue:
To Die in Newport Beach

THROUGH HIS NEW EUROPEAN SHADES, $285 FROM Les Optiques de Newport Beach, Rollie watched the kid on the skateboard snake his way past Biff's, past the gay bars and the T-shirt shops and Sid's Blue Beat, threading a figure eight through a clot of tourists and making a flirty circle around two twinks, fifteen going on twenty-five, wearing those black butt-hugger biking shorts.

Sweet meat.

The kid on the skateboard was teen lean, neon smile, a cap that said RAMS, and flowered jams that hung to his knee-caps. Rollie watched him make the turn onto the Newport Pier, crouching, knees flexed, elbows tucked in tight like an Olympic ski hero on TV. The kid gave the high sign when he saw Rollie, a cool nod, and zoomed on past him up the pier.

Headed for Hawaii, that kid.

The time was 3:47 on a Saturday afternoon in October. Rollie's meet with the dealer, a rat-face named Joel, was set for 4:00 P.M. Rollie stretched, feeling the strength flow from his ice high. Seven hours into it, twenty hours to go before the smoke wore thin, forcing him back to earth and reality.

The sun felt fine on his face, on his shoulders and arms. The sea breeze had blown off the smog, another day in paradise, and Rollie was dressed southern California to blend with the natives—white chinos, rugby shirt by Izod, white Reeboks, a jacket from Neiman's on Fashion Island.

The kid slid to a stop in front of Rollie. "How's it hanging, dude?"

"It's hanging." Rollie handed him half of a fifty-dollar bill. "See you in twenty, dude. Now split."

"Balboa Boulevard," the kid said. "Next to a gray Volvo with California plates, right?"

"You got it, dude."

"Mondo." The kid shoved his board at Rollie and walked off, passing the two twinks, a blonde and a brunette, who were onto the pier now, heading this way, heads shaking as they argued. The brunette wasn't much. The blonde, however, was your archetypal California beach sweetheart, golden hair, a Valentine face, legs so sweet you could taste the honey.

Twinks made great mules.

"Ladies." Rollie flashed a roll of bills. "A moment of your time."

"Let's go, Phyl." The blonde tugged at Purple Hair's sleeve.

"Wait, Cin-dee. Let's listen, okay?"

"Little job for you, ladies. Twenty dollars now, twenty later. Easy little job." His knee nudged the REI rucksack that leaned against the pier railing.

"Let's go, Phyl."

"Cin-dee, wait." Purple Hair swung away from the blonde and looked at him. "What's the gig, mister?"

"Easy gig. Take this rucksack. Deliver it to a dude inside

Sid's. He'll give you one exactly like it, a twin, like. Deliver it to me, get the other twenty." Rollie swept the blonde with his X-ray vision, ankle to knee to thigh to Mecca.

She turned away. "I'm going, Phyl."

"Make it sixty, mister, and you've got a deal."

Rollie put the roll in his pocket. "You don't want the gig, say the word."

"What's in there? In the sack."

"Baseball cards."

The blonde was twenty steps away, heading off the pier.

"Fifty," said Purple Hair.

"Deal."

Sly look as Purple Hair held out her hand. Rollie gave her a twenty and a five and the rucksack from REI, brown, with black straps. Purple Hair had a gold filling on the left upper incisor. She nodded, yeah, yeah, yeah, as he repeated his delivery instructions.

"Got it?"

"I got it, sheesh."

Hips swinging, Purple Hair walked off carrying $205,000 in newly cooked ice. Her pal, Little Miss Touch-Me-Not, was climbing the stairs to a second-story apartment above the surf shop. Sweat on Rollie's palms as Purple Hair crossed the Quad, disappeared into the door of Sid's Blue Beat. He adjusted his shades. To his right, the blonde had reclined on a chaise. Jacket off, arms raised for a stretch, shadowy armpits thick with sex.

He felt eyes on his back, digging in, turned to see a guy on a ten-speed, white jacket, white shorts, shades, a white cap. The biker looked away, kept going.

A minute on the sweep hand. Ninety seconds, sweat oozing under his arms, sun hammering at him, and Purple Hair was out of Sid's, and Rollie on the board, zipping down the pier with the wind in his face, grind of plastic wheels on the

concrete sidewalk, Purple Hair's eyes open wide as she saw
him zooming right at her, his arm out, the bills clamped
between his index and middle fingers, tourists falling aside,
this was the moment of truth and he felt safe and high and
alive.

"Hold it out!" he yelled.

Purple Hair held the rucksack at arm's length. In slow
motion, Rollie traded her, a wad of bills for the rucksack,
and then he was rolling again, skating south along the sidewalk between California palms and beachfront bungalows,
and way back there the biker in white, fading as Rollie hung
a left, and there was the kid, his arms folded, leaning
against the gray Volvo.

He paid off the kid, gave back the skateboard.

"See you, dude."

"Anytime, man. Anytime." The kid zoomed off, at one
with the board, the sidewalk, the barren beach.

Behind the wheel of the Volvo, Rollie divided the cash,
$100,000 into an overnight delivery express mail carton,
preaddressed, prestamped. He kept $5,000 for mad money.
He put $100,000 into a manila envelope. Humming a Ma-
donna tune, he dropped the express mail carton into a
curbside box on Balboa Boulevard then headed on down
the Peninsula to the Inn of Cortez. He parked next to Val's
Beamer, a navy blue 735. That feeling again, eyes on his
neck. He turned, swept the boulevard. No one there.

Inside the Inn, Val Smith waited at the bar. Val was Rollie's real estate broker, a lady jock who jogged and played
volleyball and worked out. The workouts worked. Tight
body, weight 129, age thirtysomething and holding. They
kissed and she rammed her tongue in his mouth. Her eyes
glistened, a sign she smelled money.

"Chick," she purred. "Hello again."

"Captain Kirk here." He handed her the manila envelope. "And here's the green light on my California escrow."

Val hefted the envelope. "You're serious?"

"Sirius is the Dog Star. It's a go."

"You're high, damn. You're way out there."

"Get high," he said. "And you dialogue with God."

She checked her watch. "The escrow office is open until five. I'll call from the room."

"While you strip," he said.

"I hate it when you're ahead." Red fingernails, fingers tight on the envelope. "Damn."

In room 203 on the second floor of the Inn of Cortez she made her call while he undressed and watched her from the bed. Finished with her call, she raised her skirt to show him what she wore, a garter belt and dark stockings. Pale bikini line against the brown thighs.

"Ready to fly?"

"Ready."

He packed a pipe with ice crystals, tamping them down into the little bowl, handed her the pipe, watched her light up. Her eyes widened as the smoke hit home, yes oh yes, and he climbed on, nestled in, and sent her into orbit. Way out there, spinning and spinning, Rollie gave Val a green pill.

"Is this it?" she asked. "What we've been waiting for?"

"This is it," he said. "The old Chick Dickens ice antidote."

"Now?"

"Take it now."

She popped the green pill.

"Where did you get them?"

"Connections."

She held out her hand. "How about a couple more, for when you're not around?"

"Sorry."

"Hey! Come on."

"One to a customer," he said. "Supply and demand."

That ticked Val off, not getting her extra green pill, so she huffed away to the bathroom and Rollie ordered pizza from Domino's and white wine from room service. Juiced from the ice, he felt no fatigue, felt nothing but up, Rollie soaring, thrusting at the eyeball of the sun.

The pizza came, but no wine. Val was still sulking in the shower when the phone rang. Rollie answered, some guy.

"Yeah," he said. "Hold on a minute." He opened the bathroom door. Val was out of the shower, patting her body with a towel.

"Did you change your mind? About the pill?"

"No," he said. "Phone call for you, some yakety-yak about a property." Raising the mattress, he tucked Val's $100,000 away.

Val spoke from the bathroom. "It's my broker, dear, a cool property in Bluebird Canyon. Been on the market a year, a real downer."

"Real estate sucks," Rollie said.

On her way to the phone, she flicked him with her towel. "Not all my buyers pay cold cash, Chick."

When she was dressed and out the door, munching a slice of pizza, Rollie checked his black book. This was no good, Val deserting him for business. So who's in the book? There was *J* for Joanne, 213 Los Angeles area code, a girl with a sexy overbite. He'd met J in August, on the flight from Sea-Tac. There was *F* for Frederika, 818 area code, a hot smile, from La Chinoise in September. He made two calls and talked to machines. The third call hit pay dirt, *C* for Carla, 714 area code, Disneyland in June. Carla remembered him. She wasn't busy tomorrow. They made a date for tennis at the John Wayne Club and were rapping about strokes and spin when there was a knock on the door.

"See you tomorrow, on the courts." He hung up and opened the door. Saw a guy in a white coat standing beside a room service cart. On the cart was a white tablecloth and on the white tablecloth was an ice bucket, chrome-plated, beaded with frost, and a bottle of bubbly, its top swathed in a white tea towel.

"Your wine, *señor*." Room Service had an accent. He was forty, bald, thickset. Looked familiar. They all did.

"I ordered white wine. Not champagne."

"*La señorita, señor.* The young lady is ordering."

"Wheel it in."

Rollie opened the door and stood aside and Room Service wheeled in the cart and as Rollie turned to get a buck tip from his wallet he heard a crunch at the base of his skull and the room tilted and he must have been out because he woke up lying on the floor near the bed with his nose screaming from smelling salts, and then he opened his eyes and saw Room Service, sitting on the floor with his legs crossed in the yoga position. A gun was in his left hand. The gun was an automatic with an extra barrel screwed on the front. Silencer.

Trying to sit up, he felt the bite of leather on his wrists and he looked down, disbelieving, saw his belt tight around his flesh. A bad situation here.

"You're him," Rollie said. "The guy on the bike. From the . . . pier."

Room Service nodded. "Where is the money, *compadre*? Where is the *laboratorio*?"

"What?"

"The place for making the ice, *compadre*. In *inglés*, it is called cooking."

"I don't know any—"

Room Service rapped Rollie's ankle bone with the pistol. There was a pop, a small bone snapping, and pain screamed up his leg. "I have little time, *compadre*. I have a small patience. I am waiting."

Rollie Nielsen stood six feet two inches in his stocking feet. He weighed 192 pounds. He'd played football in high school. His reflexes were fair until he smoked ice and then he turned into a speeding bullet. He outweighed this bald dude with the automatic and he was high from smoking ice. Ice controlled pain. Ice gave a guy an edge. Rollie was an action guy. He'd been around. He was safe because he was high and when he was high he was Superman. To wiggle out of this, he needed a distraction. Maybe Val would come back.

"Who are you, guy?"

"The money, *compadre*. The *laboratorio*."

"How did you find me, anyway?"

Again the rap on the ankle. Inside Rollie's head, blue lights of pain sprouted like star shells over Lake Union on the Fourth of July. Tears came to his eyes. He could feel the envelope through the mattress. "Okay. You got me. The money's in a backpack in the trunk of that Volvo. It's gray, south end of the lot. The keys are in my pants pocket. There."

Room Service nodded as Rollie fished in the pocket and came out with the car keys. "And the *laboratorio, compadre*?"

"It's out of town."

"Where? How far?"

"Near Loma Linda. A town east of here, in the desert."

"Loma Linda." He pronounced it with a Spanish accent. "In my language, it means pretty hillock. Where is this Loma Linda *laboratorio*?"

"It's pretty far out. I'll have to show you."

Grinning, Room Service motioned with the pistol. "You may get dressed, *compadre. Muy rápido, sí?*"

Rollie got to his feet. Room Service backed away, giving him space. The phone rang. Room Service looked at it, turning his head, and Rollie chose that moment to act, swinging his arms up for a double-fisted whammy, slamming Room Service on the side of the head, going for it, the pistol falling away and the phone still ringing now as he took a foot in his stomach, the guy was good, a pro, but Rollie was safe because of the ice, which gave you an edge, and then Room Service, down on one knee, bringing up a second pistol, his trouser leg up, a holster strapped on, and Rollie trapped in the middle of the room as the gun went off, soft pop, like a balloon crushed under an auto tire, and Rollie still fighting with one slug in him, safe and sliding for home, a second pop and then a third, black snakes coiling inside his skull as he hit the floor, and seeing Room Service, bald head gleaming in the light, his eyes sad, where is the lab, *compadre,* where, and Rollie kicking out, going for his balls as a white light exploded.

The phone, ringing and ringing and ringing, was the last thing Rollie Nielsen heard.

1

I WAS MAKING CHILI WHEN I FELT FEET SHAKE MY stairs and the red warning light blinked above the door. The red light was part of my new security system, Insta-Gard Alert, the autumn special, $79.95, from Home Club in Irvine.

Handel played on my stereo, a tune from *Israel in Egypt*, voices galloping in chorus, and I hummed along, slicing the bell pepper, cutting the lush green flesh into one-inch squares. The chili had cooked seven hours. It was Wednesday. My dinner guest was here, Miss Cindy Duke.

My apartment sits above The Saintly Silver Surfer and Leo's Cafe on the southwest corner of the Quad at the beach end of the Newport Pier. From my cooking island I can look out the big kitchen window, across the deck and past the palm trees waving above the public toilets and across the sand-strewn sidewalk that skirts Punker's Strip—gay bars and T-shirt joints and E. Gads Saloon and the Shrimp Factory and Sid's Blue Beat and La Belle Epoque where the swells munch their nouvelle cuisine—and then along the beach where sea gulls swoop down for bread bits tossed by tourists.

My recipe today was for Murdock Chili—three pounds of chili grind, four onions, one bell pepper, garlic and chili powder and cayenne and Ortegas and pinto beans—the recipe printed on an index card in my mother's careful hand and kept in the tin file box she'd used when I was a kid and we moved from army post to army post, following the Sergeant and his career.

The tin box sits on my kitchen cabinet. It's olive green, with U.S. ARMY stamped on the front and under that a rectangle where my mom had taped her name. The tape peeled off after she died, leaving only bare tin.

I tasted the chili just as Cindy came onto the deck in her biking outfit. Black racing shoes, black biker's shorts, a pink windbreaker still zipped. In her right hand was her crash helmet. On the back it said DUKE VII. On the front it said ADIDAS. Cindy waved at me and then turned to speak to someone on the stairs and then Phyl Murphy came into view, a cigarette hanging from her lip.

Phyl was Cindy's pal, best friend, and roomie. They were both fifteen. Cindy's dad was dead. Her mother was in drug rehab. For a year now she'd lived at Phyl's house in Eastbluff, inland Newport Beach. They both went to St. Luke's, a private school. I added a dash of cayenne and a pinch of salt. Better.

Cindy and Phyl were arguing. Nothing new there. Teens always argue. Using a German-made knife, I sliced into a yellow onion, white juice oozing out as I peeled off the yellow bark. Eyes watering, I split the onion in half and razored the blade against the grain, nine cuts, ten, then turned it forty-five degrees and crisscrossed against the slices, dicing and slicing. As I scraped the onions into a bowl, I checked the deck. Still arguing.

In her biking shorts, Cindy Duke was a sylph. Cute legs and blond hair that glowed in the setting sun and ten million dollars waiting in mutuals and money markets for her to turn twenty-one. Phyl, chunky, with a style borrowed from cheap teen magazines, didn't like walking in Cindy's shadow.

Phyl had lost weight. Tonight she wore basic punker black. Leather hip-huggers snug to the butt and slung low to display her navel. A black halter that resembled a brassiere. Black bomber jacket, festooned with silver chains. Black boots and black headband. In the center of the headband was a fake gemstone, Swami Ananda green, that glowed dully from her forehead. The right side of her hair was upjutting spikes dyed purple. The left side was shaved close to the skull, then plowed bone white, with a precise chevron of corporal's stripes above the line of the headband. Look in the mirror, fling yourself into orbit.

I stuck my head out the door and they broke off their argument. "Hi Cindy. Hi Phyl. I've got chili for three, Phyl, if you're staying."

"It's rad, Mr. M." Phyl blew smoke my way. "Gotta go gig out." Puffing her cigarette, she blew smoke at Cindy. "Bye."

"Phyl!"

"It's mondo, Cindee-rella. See ya around."

With a toss of her spikes, Phyl flounced down the stairs, high heels going clickety-whack.

Arms crossed, Cindy watched her pal descend. A shake of her head before she turned away, closing that chapter, to join me inside. Quick hug, smell of perfume mixed with clean biker's sweat, and a long look.

"Where's Uncle Wally?"

"He phoned. He's into a grudge match over at Le Club. Fifty bucks a set riding on it."

"I love Uncle Wally," Cindy said.

"He loves you too." I kept on slicing. "The Planet Mondo, isn't that where Flash Gordon hangs out?"

"That's Mongo, Matt." Cindy giggled. "Mondo means cool, very now. In Italian, it means clean. I looked it up at school. Can I change those candles? They're down to mere nubs."

Mere nubs. Mondo and Mongo. Cindy liked words. One of her dreams for the future was to write books, follow in the footsteps of her dad.

"Candles in the bottom drawer."

She knelt down in front of my entertainment center, hunting for candles.

"What was the argument about?" I said.

"The usual."

"What's the usual?"

"Oh, sex and drugs. Guys. Stuff like that. Your candle supply is low, Matt."

We stood back to back in the kitchen while she dug the burned-down candle nubs out of the holders. They were brass, a gift from a lady antiques buff. Stooping to check the vertical alignment, Cindy bumped me with her hip. "I love you, Matt."

"Mondo," I said.

She bumped me again, harder, a bump with purpose, and then carried the candles in their brass holders to the table. She struck a match and lit the wicks and soft yellow light bloomed in her hair. Her cheeks were hollowed like a starlet's as she looked at me over the candles. "You don't think I'm serious, do you? You think I'm just a kid. You think I'm kidding."

I ladled the chili into soup mugs. Mine was red, Cindy's was brown. They are ceramic mugs, with handles so you can get a grip on your eating. I used to have eight of them, but now, with breakage through the years, I'm down to five. The right soup bowl turns good chili into great chili, memorable chili. "Sure I do."

"You're not listening. You think I'm too young."

I carried the steaming chili mugs to the table. Cindy filled my wineglass with Mondavi red.

"Can I have some wine, Matt?"

"No."

"Mother used to let me have it."

"When she cooks, you can ask her."

"Don't be mean."

I grinned. "Nice try, Lady Mondo. No wine."

"Phyl drinks. Beer and wine, even booze. She's a smokestack."

"What Phyl needs is a hairdresser."

Cindy giggled, unzipped her windbreaker, took it off. Underneath she wore a white pullover, sleeveless, with a V-neck. She had the Duke family eyes, pale blue with a silvery sheen, and her mother's electric good looks.

"How about a Pepsi then?"

"Help yourself."

She went to the fridge, came back with a Pepsi. A lull in the Handel, only one lone trumpet now, singing sweet across the grooves, as she popped the tab top. "Can I live here, Matt? With you?"

"No."

"Hmm," she said. "Thanks so much."

I was sitting with my back to the kitchen, Cindy on my left. She got the view through the window across my deck. She ate slowly, her gaze locked on something I couldn't see. I finished a bowl, savoring the aftertaste, cayenne against minced onion and bell pepper. She was still eating.

"Are you in some kind of mood, Matt?"

"No. Are you?"

"I thought it might be your work or something. How is old Ella, anyway?"

Ella Steinberg was a novelist, poet, and professional rabble-rouser who'd hired me to control the rabble while she promoted her book in southern California. For that service I got $300 a day and expenses. I liked Ella. Her books were over my head. I liked her views on women's rights, the environment, the Arabs, pro-choice. On gun control, we split. "The tour's over," I said. "Ella's back in Boston, typing another tome. I am unemployed."

"I liked her," Cindy said.

"She liked you."

"She asked me to phone if I ever got to Boston." Cindy dragged her spoon around the bottom of her bowl. "Can I turn the music down?"

"Sure."

She left the table and turned down the Handel. "Phyl's really bugging me. She's cutting classes, not doing her homework. Her clothes reek of smoke. She brags all the time about doing it with this guy, Johnny. Having sex, I mean. She's doing drugs, Matt."

"That's what you thought in September."

"It was just pot then. Now she's bragging about doing coke and there's this new stuff, ice."

"Does her mother know?"

"Janice? She smokes pot herself. And she's never at home, always out on the great husband hunt. I can't live there, Matt. I did drugs. I don't want any more, ever."

"Don't blame you for that, kid."

"So let me."

"Wouldn't work. Not here."

"Why? Why wouldn't it work?"

"Twenty reasons."

"Name one."

"Too dangerous. You know the kind of work I'm in."

"You should try biking along PCH. The whole cosmos is dangerous."

"They burned me out last Christmas. Remember? Burned my house up. Took two months of work to make it livable again."

"I remember. I also helped fix it."

I took a deep breath, let it out. "The bad guys could still come after you."

"You'd protect me."

"The answer is no. N-O."

"You don't have to shout, okay?"

"Sorry."

She pushed her chair back with a sharp scrape. "How about a refill?"

I felt full, bloated, guilty. "Okay."

At the stove, she ladled in more chili. "So what are we, Matt?"

"We're pals," I said. "Buddies."

"Pals?"

"Right."

"Buddies," she said.

"Yeah. Buddies."

"There's a show on TV called *Body Buddies*." Cindy was grinning now. She liked watching me sweat. "Maybe we could try that?"

"Eat your chili."

"Next Wednesday, let me cook something."

"What?"

"A casserole. I have this recipe. I've tried it out on Phyl and her mom. They like it. Her mom's new boyfriend liked it too."

"Okay. Sure. Next Wednesday, you cook."

She set down my chili bowl. She held out her empty Pepsi

can and we clinked. She clinked again, bumping my glass with the soft metal. "That's only two. Come on, Matt. Do six."

"Why six?"

"Jane says you clinked with her five times. I didn't want you to get your ladies confused."

Jane Blasingame was a Texas state senator, a woman from my past who'd lost a runaway daughter in sunny California. She and Cindy had become pals. "You hear from her lately?"

"I got a letter Saturday. Hello to you, she says, and why don't you ever write? You owe her three letters."

I said nothing. Writing was not my bag.

"She's invited me for Thanksgiving."

"Turkey Day in Texas," I said. "Nice."

"You just want to get rid of me," Cindy said.

"You like Jane. You like her ranch. You can ride horses. It will be a real Thanksgiving."

"Away from Phyl," she said. "Away from you." Tears now in Cindy's eyes, another whirligig turn on the roller-coaster ride through Cynthia Duke Teenage Moodland. She slid off her chair and came close. "I feel awful, Matt. I feel weird. Would you hold me, just for a minute?"

I stood up and put my arms around her and her shoulders shook and she started crying, brave Cindy Duke, her dad dead, her mom in drug rehab, her home with Phyl on tilt, no place to run.

With a shudder, Cindy broke away. Her eyes filled, brimmed over. Bright tears trailed shiny tracks down her cheeks. A choked sob as she ran into the bathroom. Teen legs, teen elbows, the soul of an anguished woman yet to be.

The bathroom door closed with a slam. Water ran. I stared around the room. Empty wine bottle, Cindy's pink windbreaker, candles guttering in the slight breeze. My mouth tasted sour, all that wine. I blew my nose.

I was grinding coffee for Murdock Blend when the red intruder light came on. No music now, so I could hear the footsteps on my stairs. In the full California dark, the Insta-Gard security light, activated by a motion detector, flooded my deck with a white blaze. Cindy arrived in the bedroom door as someone with weight and authority came up onto the deck and at the same time the teakettle whistled.

Cindy Duke, her face fresh, her hair neatly combed, marched past me to answer the door.

2

THE MAN WHO STOOD IN MY DOORWAY, BACKLIT BY my double spot, was tall and rangy, with a shock of gray hair down over his left eye. He wore a tweed coat with elbow patches, a blue shirt with a tie, heavy-soled shoes, and rumpled chinos. Seeing Cindy brought a smile to his face. He stuck out his hand, big and square, and said: "Howdy. I'm Thor Nielsen, from Elliott, Washington. Fella downstairs at the cafe says Murdock lives here."

Cindy introduced herself, stepped aside prettily. Thor Nielsen, holding his hat, came inside. The hat was an Indiana Jones prototype, new, without a mark or sweat stain. Seeing Thor Nielsen, I thought of my father, the Sergeant, coming home after a tough day with his platoon, sniffing the air to see what was for dinner.

Cindy, her balance restored by a quick trip to the bathroom, beamed as she introduced us. Thor Nielsen's handshake was strong, the pads of his fingers callused from work.

"Would you like something, Mr. Nielsen?" asked Cindy the hostess. "We have coffee, beer, red wine?"

He looked at Cindy. He looked at me. "You sure?"

"How about some chili," I said.

"Smells good. Sure I'm not intruding here?"

"You two men sit," Cindy said. "I'll get it."

"Thanks." He sat down in the spare chair. I poured the wine. We toasted and he took a sip and nodded. "Like to hire you, Murdock."

"What's the job, Mr. Nielsen?"

"It's my boy," he said. "He came down here and—"

Cindy arrived with the chili and hot garlic bread, fresh from the oven. Thor Nielsen nodded and dug in. "Been dancing around with the police all day, not what you would call fun." He ate two bites, shook his head, put his spoon down. "Damn." He blew his nose. Then he dug into his pocket and brought out half a dozen photos wrapped with a red rubber band. In each photo, the subject was the same guy. A blond Viking type, late twenties. He had pale eyes, a chiseled face, a high Scandinavian forehead. I went through the photos. There was one college boy shot, Thor's son wearing a mortar board and black grad gown. Two lumberjack shots, plaid shirt, boots, the Viking son swinging a double-bladed ax. Two jock shots, one football, one helmeted biker. In the last photo, the son posed on a yacht, champagne glass in hand. He wore a blazer and a tie and dark glasses.

Cindy, leaning over my shoulder, let out a gasp that was pure melodrama. "Can I see that one?"

"Sure." I handed it to her. She moved away.

I knew the son was dead. I asked anyway. "What about your boy, Mr. Nielsen?"

"He's dead, Mr. Murdock. I need your help."

"Tell me about it, okay?"

He coughed, blew his nose again. "Feels like they're giving me the royal runaround, your local cops. They got me down here to identify the body. I did that. It's him, all right. It's Rollie. I'd like to take him back, but the police won't give him up yet. Won't tell me when they might." He gulped some wine, shook his head. "Seems what they're after is his address. Rollie lived close to campus, liked to walk to class, he said. I wanted to know why, they got huffy on me. His damn telephone's unlisted. They say the university's only got a P.O. box. It's all Greek to me. The police here, they want the Seattle police to search his place, mess through his books and stuff. Why? They won't say. I'm all at sixes and sevens here. Can't follow the game plan. Think you can help me?"

In the kitchen, the sound of glass breaking. "Damn!" Cindy said.

"You okay?"

"Just a glass. Sorry."

"What about it, Murdock?"

"What would you want me to do?"

"Get me some answers. Find out what happened. Find out what my boy was into that got him . . . killed."

"How did he die?"

"They're not saying. Not coming right out with it, anyway. But I can smell it." He emptied his wineglass. The chili remained untouched. "He was murdered. Some damn California sonofabitch murdered my boy."

From behind, Cindy tapped me on the shoulder. "Matt? Can I talk to you a minute?"

"Be right there, kid." I turned back to Thor Nielsen. "Did they say where he died?"

He pulled out an envelope with notes scribbled on it. "A place called the Inn of Cortez. I was down there today, checking it over. Fancy place. Rooms start at a hundred seventy-five a night. My boy was a graduate student in chemistry, Mr. Murdock. I helped him out with tuition, books, lab fees. What the hell was he doing in a ritzy motel room?"

"Did you know he'd come to California?"

"Hell no. Is there more of that dago red?"

I filled his glass. He drank. He showed me a name written on the back of an envelope. The name was Gaspard, Rolande.

"See that?"

"Yes."

"My boy was in room 203, registered under that name."

"Tale of Two Cities," Cindy said. "We just read it in school."

"What?"

"Gaspard," she said. "One of the characters in the book."

"Was your son a reader, Mr. Nielsen?"

"Sure. Reads that science stuff. Chemistry textbooks, he read them on the john."

"How old was he?"

"Twenty-nine."

"What degree was he working on?"

"His doctorate. In chemistry."

"At the university?"

"Right. The old U-Dub."

"How far along was he?"

"He finished up with his course work last summer, had some experiments to clean up before he got his degree. I'm a farmer, Mr. Murdock. I came to you for help." Thor Nielsen brushed at a tear with the back of his hand.

Cindy tapped my shoulder again. "Matt?"

"Yes?"

"I need to talk to you. . . . Would you excuse us for just a minute, Mr. Nielsen, while I speak to Mr. Murdock?"

"Sure."

Cindy topped off Thor Nielsen's glass. She led me into the bedroom. She closed the door.

"What?" I said.

"That guy, the one in the photos, I think I saw him. I think he's the one who gave Phyl money. Only . . . I'm not sure."

In the other room, a client waited. My patience was thin. "What money?"

"On the pier, on Saturday! I'd have to look at it again. The photo with the shades clued me. He wore different clothes, but the hair was the same. And the teeth when he smiled. It was . . . oily."

"The hair?"

"No, the smile."

"How much money?"

"Seventy dollars. Phyl hid it from her mom. She kept flashing it in my face all weekend."

"What was he buying? Her wardrobe?"

"No. A couple minutes of her time, was all."

"What did she do?"

"He gave her this rucksack. To take to a guy. It was brown, like a book bag."

"What was in it?"

"Baseball cards, Phyl said. But she was joking. She traded the rucksack for another one, exactly like it."

"Then what?"

"Then she handed it back to the guy and he gave her money and split on a skateboard. Phyl told me later that it had been a drug buy—she was excited about it, really wired —and that made her a mule. Did you see how she was dressed tonight?"

"Hard to miss that," I said.

"She's thinking maybe that guy will be back. Being a mule really turned her on."

"Phyl wants to do it all over again?"

"Um. She really felt wired after. Couldn't stop going over it, every detail. She's bored with being a kid. You know?"

"Where were you while this went down?"

"On the deck." Cindy pointed outside. "Catching some rays."

"Saturday, you said?"

"Um. I came to see you. Phyl had had a fight with her boyfriend, so she tagged along. When we got here, she dragged me out to the pier, where that guy came on to us. I split."

"Okay, tell me straight. What are the chances that this is the same guy? The one on the pier, the one in the photo? When you really think about it, what are the odds?"

Cindy blinked. Her lip trembled. I saw tears coming. "You don't have to be mean, okay?"

She took a step away from me, her confidence gone. I sighed. In the next room, a paying client was getting drunk. "Okay. I'm sorry. Tell me what went down. Just the facts, okay?"

"You don't believe me." She shook her head. "Why should you want to hear this?"

"Remember how he was dressed?"

"Sure. You trained me, remember?"

"I remember."

Cindy took a deep breath, then launched into her description. "Okay. He wore white pants, a striped pullover, a white windbreaker, very snazzy, and Reebok Air Soles. The rucksack was brown. I think it was from REI, but I'm not positive. He acted weird, like he was on something."

"So you split and came up here?"

"That's what I said. Phyl walked into Sid's. She came out a couple of minutes later and this guy rode at her on a skateboard. He grabbed the rucksack and gave her money and skated away."

"Which way?"

"South." Cindy pointed down the beach.

"Anyone follow him?"

"It was jammed down there, the Saturday crush. I don't know."

"Okay. Then what?"

"Phyl came up here. She showed me the money. Fifty for the trip, twenty for a tip. When the other guy came out of Sid's, she pointed him out getting into his car. He was a dealer, she said, and really connected. I laughed, told her she was blowing off."

"Had she seen this other guy, the dealer?"

"She'd seen his car."

"What kind of car?"

"A red Isuzu."

"What about it?"

"Phyl said she's seen it around the school." Cindy paused. "She knows a guy who knows him."

"Did you see him?"

She shrugged. "Sure."

"Did you recognize him?"

"No. But he did drive off in a red Isuzu."

"With the second brown rucksack?"

Cindy nodded. "I think so."

"There are lots of red Isuzus. Loads."

"That's what I told Phyl."

"Anything else?"

"No. It's not much, is it?"

"You did great, Cindy."

Kids see things. They live in a world of MTV where sex gyrates on the screen in three-minute fantasy bits. Kids make stuff up. If they read, they read fantasy and sci fi and teen romance. Kids eat fast food and smoke pot and maybe ice if they can get it and try sex too early. Maybe Cindy was right. Maybe the guy with the switchable rucksacks was Rollie Nielsen. Maybe not.

Back in the main room, Thor Nielsen was pouring himself a fresh glass of wine. The bottle was down to an inch. When he spoke, he slurred his words. "So, Murdock. You're a private eye. You gonna help me, or what?"

"A couple more questions."

"Shoot."

"What was your boy wearing when he died?"

Cindy looked at me, hard.

"Cops wouldn't say."

"Who did you talk to over at the station?"

"Two cops talked to me," he said. "One was named Giordano. Didn't like him much. The other was named Daggett or Doggett, looked like an old wolfhound I used to run. They tried to seesaw me, that bad cop, good cop crap." He drained his wineglass. "There was another fellow in the background, kind of slick-looking. Didn't get his name."

"Mind telling me where you got my name?"

"Didn't I already?"

"No."

"Goddamn mind must be going. Ever since Rollie's ma died, I've had a hole in my head and the stuffing just leaks out. Fellow named Chen gave it to me. Louie Chen."

"Who's Louie Chen?"

"Chinese kid. He and Rollie were roommates at the university. They call it the U-Dub up there. Anyhow, when I heard about Rollie I phoned up Louie Chen. He used to come out to the farm with Rollie for a weekend now and again. Nice kid, a worker who doesn't mind a little dirt. Serious."

"How did he get my name?"

Thor Nielsen scratched his head. "Beats me. I told him about Rollie and he gave me your name. Said you hung out at the beach. I asked around. They seem to like you around here."

"Where does Louie Chen live?"

"Seattle. Runs a home security business."

"And he and your son are close now?"

"Not like in college. Said he'd seen Rollie last summer."

"Have you got Louie Chen's number?"

"Sure." He hauled out another envelope and another. He put on a pair of reading glasses and moved into the light and ran a thick finger slowly down the writing on the envelope. He read out a number with a 206 area code.

I wrote Louie Chen's phone number on the back of my own envelope. Inside was a reminder from Southern California Edison that I was two months behind in my payments for power. If I didn't pay up, they'd shut off my juice. No more lights, no more bathroom heat, no more Handel on the RCA stereo.

Watching me, Thor Nielsen grinned. "I like a man who keeps his notes on the back of an envelope."

"Thanks. So do I."

"Do we have a deal now?"

"Yes. I get three hundred a day, plus expenses. I keep a log for phone calls, travel. I may have to pay for information."

He plunked a wad of money on the table. "There's nine hundred. How long you think this will take?"

"A friend of mine is a cop. I'll phone him tonight, ask him to nose around. I'll give you a call after I've seen the police reports."

"Great, Murdock. Great." He shook hands with Cindy and then with me. "Call me Thor, okay?"

"Okay. I'm Matt."

"And I'm Cindy."

He had a motel in Irvine, he said, right between a strawberry field and the freeway. Holding his new hat, wobbling from the wine, Thor Nielsen left us alone.

3

I TOOK CINDY HOME TO EASTBLUFF. I WATCHED HER wheel the ten-speed up the driveway. I thought of Phyl in black leather. Had she really made $70 for transporting a controlled substance across my Quad on a sunny Saturday? How much was fact? How much was real? With teens, it's tough to tell.

Back at my place, there was a note from Wally St. Moritz: "Sorry to miss your chili. We murdered them, seven–five, four–six, seven–six, seven–six. See you on the morrow."

I stood on the deck sipping coffee. String of lights along the beach, fuzzy through the haze. Not much of a breeze, a sour smell on the air. You come to California for the promise of a promise, gold in the hills, escape from your past, a new life. You wind up in a smog-smudged nightmare with crazed gulls crying.

Rollie Nielsen, the grad student from Seattle, was dead. The cops wouldn't say how he died. Thor Nielsen smelled murder. The cops wanted access to Rollie's place in Seattle. Thor was puzzled about the unlisted phone number. When he died, Rollie had been registered under the name Rolande Gaspard. The Inn of Cortez sported ritzy rooms. One reason for a ritzy room was to get laid. How was Rollie with the ladies? My mind whirled. Unlisted phone, false name.

My coffee was finished. I went inside to make some calls. Louie Chen first, then Webby Smith.

Louie Chen's answer machine clicked on. A serious voice answered: "This is Mr. Chen, of Perimeter Control Home Security. If you are calling for a bid on securing your home, please leave your name, your telephone number, and a convenient hour to return your call. Thank you."

I left my number and asked him to call. Then I phoned Webby Smith at his home in Laguna. When I told him what I wanted, he grunted.

"You want it yesterday, I bet."

"You feeling okay?"

"Sure. Just great. I'm feeling just terrific."

"What's up, Webby?"

"It's Jeannie."

Jeannie was Webby's current lady, mid-twenties, a grad student working on a Ph.D. in kinesiology, the science of muscles.

"How is Jeannie, anyway?"

"She's gone. She left me."

"Uh-oh. When?"

"Last night. She left after midnight and now I'm hurting. I'm dizzy, I've got these abdominal pains, I feel like dying."

"What happened?"

"She woke me up, crying, wanted to get married, she said. Drive up to Bakersfield, meet the folks. Make some plans, set some dates, get things going. I said things were already going. Something made her mad, I can't figure what, so we argue half the night and then she packs a bag and leaves me there."

"Where did she go?"

"What?"

"Where did she go at two in the morning?"

"A friend's place. By then it was three."

"Did you call her?"

"I wanted to. I didn't."

"Do you want to get married?"

"I've been married."

"Do you love her?"

"I thought so. Now I'm not so sure." Webby sighed. At his end of the phone I heard the TV going, a sports announcer with the nightly scores. "So who are you working for on this Nielsen thing?"

"The father. Can you help me out, Webby?"

"I'll try. Since Leon Book's been away, it's tougher getting through to Newport Beach." A pause. "Drop by my office tomorrow. I need to work, get her off my mind."

"You thought about calling her, talking it over?"

"No. And no advice, okay?"

"Sorry. Just trying to help."

"See you tomorrow." Webby hung up.

Just before getting to bed, I read the newspaper story about the death of Rollie Nielsen. It was buried on page 8 of the Metro section of the Monday edition of the *Orange County Tribune,* two inches of copy, no byline. An Anglo male had been found dead at the Inn of Cortez on Sunday morning. Cause of death was unknown at this time. Identity of the dead man was being withheld until the family was notified. An investigation by the Newport Beach PD was under way. No names of cops on the case. No time of death. Nothing.

Hmm.

I checked the *Trib* for Tuesday and Wednesday. Zip on

Rollie Nielsen, aka Rolande Gaspard. The cops had the case buttoned up. I wondered why.

The Laguna Beach police station shares a building with the Laguna Beach fire department. The building is stucco. Last year it was Laguna beige and you could park at a meter for a dollar an hour. This year the building is Puerto Vallarta orange. Parking at the meters in Laguna Beach has jumped to a buck-fifty an hour. Webby hates the color. Me, I think it fits the town.

The air was still as death as I parked my pickup at a meter three blocks down the street. I chunked in six quarters and strolled through the hazy October air to the station. A roller-skater passed, a girl with a ponytail, wearing a pink halter and Levi cutoffs that showed a white rim of bottom. Youth is the only constant in California, the only true stability.

Webby Smith has a glassed-in office in the far corner of the police department's assigned sector of operations. When I rapped on the glass, he looked up from a jungle of paperwork and gave me the evil eye. Webby is a couple of years younger than I am. He stays healthy by training for the Iron Man—that's where you swim, run, and bike your way to athletic fame all in one day in scenic spots like Arizona and Oregon and Hawaii. His face this morning looked bleak as the Gobi Desert.

I opened the door and went in. "Hey, Iron Man."

"I told you," he said.

"Told me what?"

"The report on that Nielsen kid. With Leon out of town, I have to work with L. Robert Archer, Lieutenant Bureaucrat with the three-piece suits. Archer glad-hands me and passes me to Giordano, a turkey if I ever saw one."

"From back East," I said. "A real charmer."

Webby tossed his pencil down. It rolled off the edge of
the desk and fell to the floor. He swore at the pencil. His
uniform, black with regimental piping, looked slept in. He
opened his desk drawer and hauled out a file. "So I went to
the sheriff. And I checked with Sacramento. I checked with
CHP and the DEA and the Bureau and a liaison from the
CIA. You're lucky I know people. I'm a good guy to know."
He picked up the pencil. The point had snapped off. He
tapped the eraser end on the file folder. "I love her smell."

"Whose smell?"

"Jeannie's. She smelled like fresh-baked bread. I'd lie in
bed and inhale her smell, Jesus heck I feel bad."

"Did you call her?"

"No." He shoved the file at me. "Want some coffee?"

"Your coffee?"

"The department's."

"Pass."

At the hot plate, he spoke to me over his shoulder.
"You're a coffee snob, Sherlock. You know that?"

I was reading the Nielsen file, a murky fax from Newport
Beach. It wasn't much. Two pages of routine stuff: 1) Nielsen died of gunshot wounds from a small-caliber weapon,
three slugs in the body and one behind the left ear, full
ballistics report to be forthcoming. 2) The autopsy showed
traces of methamphetamine hydrochloride, a controlled
substance. The street name was ice. 3) Time of death, between 8:00 P.M. and midnight. 4) No identity documents had
been found. No driver's license, no credit cards, no address
book, no business cards, no keys, nothing. 5) Victim registered at the Inn of Cortez using the name Rolande Gaspard. I looked up from the file. "Vietnam did it to me on
coffee, Iron Man. Legacy of the departed French."

"I was there, old buddy, fighting the good fight. Why
didn't I discover Frog coffee?"

"Women," I said. "And those weekends in Bangkok."

"I could use a weekend in Bangkok right now." Webby sat down heavily. "So how do you read Nielsen's dad?"

"You want me to read this or you want to bug me so I can't?"

"Want to bug you. Bugging you's the only thing left, Sherlock, my only pleasure, bugging my nosy PI pal." He set the mug down. He tapped the side of his head. "Also, I got stuff in the Webster Smith memory bank that's not in the fax file."

"How do we access the Webster Smith memory bank?"

"Lunch," he said. "On you. Tomorrow."

"Deal."

"Right. How do you like this? Nielsen, Roland S., was number nine in a string of hits with the same MO."

"Serial hitter?"

"That's the scenario, according to my DEA guy."

"When did they start?"

"June. Eight hits, up and down the coast, from Portland to San Jose to Santa Barbara to San Ysidro. Victims are all ice cookers. They die Mafia style, twenty-two slug behind the ear. Place of death is a hotel or motel, no identification left at the scene. Nielsen is the sixth victim with a college degree. Did you know he was a chemist?"

"Yes." I jotted notes on my envelope. "Any female victims?"

"No."

"Can we conclude that Nielsen was cooking ice?"

"A user for sure. There was meth in his bloodstream." Webby sipped his coffee. "Cooking is a strong maybe double plus."

"Is that it?"

"There's more. After the hit, the local PD gets a call that

tells them the location of the ice lab. As of last night, no call had come on Nielsen's lab."

"I have the feeling you're leading up to something."

"Your feeling is correct. My pal at the DEA asked me to ask you for the address of Nielsen's pad in Seattle. The phone's unlisted. No Roland Nielsen. No Rolande Gaspard."

"They ID'd him pretty fast. What did they use, a DNA swatch?"

"Oh, sure. Wonderful DNA, fancy futuristic forensics. But he's got a record, this guy."

"What kind of record?"

"Our boy Nielsen was a campus radical during his wild college years. Protest marches, handing out inflammatory leaflets. He got fingerprinted during a sweep of a student rally at the university."

I made a note to ask Thor Nielsen. "Was he alone when they found him?"

"Yeah. But there'd been a female on the scene. Forensics found pubic hairs on the sheets, dark blond, along with traces of face powder and eyeliner. And the call about the dead body came from a female."

"What time was the call?"

"Sunday morning around ten. Do I get the address?"

"I'll ask the dad. After meeting Giordano, he's not feeling cooperative. Do they think the ice lab's at this address?"

"Leads are thin on this one, Sherlock, so they'll go for whatever."

"What about transport? Did they check the airlines? How did he get to the Inn of Cortez?"

"An airline check showed no Nielsen or Gaspard on flights from Seattle to John Wayne or LAX. How he arrived here, they don't know."

"Great police work, as usual. Did Giordano and his people query the employees over at the Inn?"

"Yeah, and that reminds me." Webby took his feet off the desk.

"I feel a lecture about to happen."

"This is it. Don't motor your ass over to Balboa and start asking a lot of questions of those selfsame employees. This is cops only. There are Feds with fingers in the pie. The DEA's keeping a low profile, working through the Newport Beach PD. No one talks to the media. They know you're on the case and your reputation has preceded you. They don't want you snooping around."

"Who says?"

"Detective Giordano, who else? He's in charge of the case. He's pissed at you for getting in his way last summer and he's asked me to speak on his behalf. And now let's talk about lunch. Friday at one, the Rusty Pelican."

"What's her name?"

"Who?"

"Your next conquest. What's her name?"

"How'd you know?"

"Radar. Also, you go there to ogle the waitresses."

"Her name's Wanda." Webby, on his way to falling in love again, took a deep breath. "She just might save me."

I stood up. "Could this be a turf war?"

"What?"

"A hitter, a pro, knocking off ice makers. DEA guys lurking around. Giordano acting testy."

"What turf?"

"The international drug marketplace," I said. "Ice versus coke, dealers competing for customers. You cook ice in the garage, in your handy basement lab. It's smokable stuff, no needles needed, so your customers avoid the AIDS problem, no chicken tracks on their arms, and the ice high lasts what, a day?"

"Or longer. Where you getting this, Sherlock?"

"Just thinking out loud. Let's say you're an ice dealer. You avoid the hassle of U.S. Customs, nasty Coast Guard cutters, smugglers who rip off your product. So, thinking out loud, who would lose market share if the cokeheads of America became iceheads?"

"Coke dealers."

"And they are located in?"

"Colombia."

"You get a gold star."

Webby scratched his chin. "That might explain it."

"Explain what?"

"There's CIA people nosing around the case. I didn't understand until you presented your Turf War scenario. Then something clicked. There's CIA and they're working some South American angle."

"You want answers about the wide world, the one outside the Orange Coast, I've got 'em."

Webby waved me out. "I got work to do. Get that address for me, okay?"

"I'll try." I paused at the door. "I'm really looking forward to watching you girl-hunt tomorrow. Upwind from a perfumed female, you are poetry in motion."

"The reason I want you along, Sherlock, is for protective coloration. A guy your age, gray in the beard, crow's feet, lines in the face, you make me look so good."

"Hey, I needed that."

"The Nielsen address," he said. "So I can feed my favor- ite Fed."

4

THE SUN CAME OUT AS I HEADED DOWN BALBOA Boulevard to the Inn of Cortez where Rollie Nielsen had died. I parked in the lot. Nice breeze today, two Balboa belles in tennis clothes strolling along the promenade, tanned legs and tight tennis tushies, a wonderland scene, skaters and bikers, gulls swooping, a volleyball game starting on the beach, and a room at the Inn where Rollie Nielsen had been murdered.

The night man for last Saturday was named George. He came on at eight. The day man, his name was Rip, would not give me George's address or home phone. George had already been closeted, Rip's clever way of saying it, with the police. No, I could not look at the guest roster for Saturday.

I strolled to the bar.

The bar at the Inn of Cortez was dark as a cloister. Leaded-glass windows, shards of California sunlight, a row of copper mugs that hung on hooks along a slender curved rack that was attached to the curved mantel above the bar. A waitress, blond, wearing a green blouse with a deep V, took my order. She wore tight pants and spike heels. The time was eleven in the morning. Could she make it to the end of her shift in those heels? A dozen drinkers in the place, warming up for lunch. In the far corner, an old party in a blue blazer and a red ascot was coming on to a redhead in a shimmery dress while she laughed and blew smoke in his face.

The bartender eyed me as he drew my draft. He was a longhair with horn-rimmed glasses and a scholarly look. I tipped the waitress a ten and flashed the Rollie Nielsen photos.

"The cops said to keep quiet," she said.

I added another ten. She looked at it, checked the room for new customers, and sat down, fingers on the money. "He was here with a date. I remember because she'd been waiting an hour, so I identified, you know? A girl hates to be kept waiting, all these horny guys. The place was packed on account of the game—Saturdays and Monday nights we got three screens going—so I didn't have time to catch their conversation, if you catch my drift?"

"What time were they here?"

"Fourish. Maybe closer to five. Like I told the cops."

"How was he dressed?"

"Him I don't remember. Ask me about her."

"Okay. How was she dressed?"

"Sharp dresser. Silk jacket, gorgeous creamy blouse I would have killed for. Two strings of pearls—to my eye, they looked real—and a skirt that did not hide her figure."

"Hair?"

"Blond, a natural. Shoulder length. She was a workout type."

"Did he give her anything?"

Broad grin from the waitress. "You have a dirty mind."

"A gift, a package."

"I didn't see anything."

"Did she talk to anyone before he got here?"

"She used the phone. I passed her on my way to the ladies'. She had her Filo fax out. I had one of those for a while, trying to organize my life. It didn't help." She looked past me toward the bar. "Uh-oh, signals from on high. Gotta go." She tucked the bills into her pants pocket and hurried back to work.

I finished that beer. It tasted fine. I thought about one more. I raised my finger to signal the waitress. I had $500 in my wallet. The rest was in my hidey hole in a secret compartment behind my fridge. Detecting is a mind game. Wally St. Moritz says I should think things out. I could sit here in this pleasant bar with the fat cats of Balboa Island and drink beer and think my way through the maze, left turn, right turn, another right turn, two quick lefts, and then slide down a striped barber pole to the dark cave where the killer waited.

Thinking is hard work. Beer oils the brain. The second beer tasted fine. I was on my third, making a lot of mental progress on the Rollie Nielsen case, when the bartender joined me. He took off his glasses so he could polish them with a handkerchief. The handkerchief had a monogram, GAL, sewed in red. His smile was neon bright. Maybe he was a used-car salesman picking up a second trade. He reached into his hip pocket so he could show me his ID, plastic-encased, in a leather case. Flip it open, flip it closed. His name was Loomis, Gerald A. He was not a moonlighting car salesman. He was an agent of the CIA. Loomis leaned close, a conspiratorial wink. Was there a place where we could talk?

We sat facing the sea in my Ford pickup at the edge of the parking lot. Sun at high noon, clouds billowy here in paradise as Agent Loomis got right to it. "They're talking about you down at the station. Bad-mouthing, you could call it."

"Who's they?"

"Detective Giordano, people from the DEA. They say you'll muck up the case."

"Why tell me?"

"Because Lieutenant Smith says otherwise. I checked your history, some old Pentagon files. Excellent service record, serving your country, and some impressive detecting on that Soames drug bust in San Pedro."

"Just trying to save a client."

Agent Loomis made a tent of his fingers, tips pressed to tips, then brought the index fingers close to his lip so he could blow on them. "As an entrepreneur, Murdock, you have a certain freedom of movement. Because of that, I'd like to woo you over. To my team."

"What's the game plan, coach?"

"I put you on a retainer and we trade information. I tell you what we've got. You tell me what you've got. That way, we cover both sides of the street."

"How much is the retainer?"

"Five hundred."

"A week?"

"A month."

"Intelligence on a shoestring, right?"

"Sorry. Congress keeps cutting us back. So what have you got?"

"When's payday?"

"I can have the money tomorrow."

"That's when I start trading. Tomorrow."

Loomis was young, a real eager beaver with ladders to climb. "How about if I begin?"

"Your deal."

"All right. This Nielsen thing is hit number nine. It's been established that—"

"I know that."

"The victim used an alias. It was—"

"I know that too. The name was Gaspard."

He frowned. "We've got a sketchy profile of the killer."

"Shoot."

"A European male, late thirties, early forties. He's educated, multilingual. Speaks English with a slight German accent. Witnesses—these are few—think he's upper-class. His MO suggests familiarity with weapons, probably some heavy military training. Our guess is that he's German or Swiss. He's a professional, very slick, very thorough. We were slow on this because of the lack of reporting by regional law enforcement."

Cops love blaming other cops.

"Your turn, Mr. Murdock."

I didn't have much to lose. "How about an alleged eyewitness who saw the victim making an alleged drug buy a couple of hours before he got iced?"

His eyes popped. He couldn't help it. Maybe it was the word *alleged*. "Where?"

"The alleged drug deal took place on the Newport Pier," I said. "Saturday, midafternoon."

"Nice piece of work, Murdock. I want an eyeball-to-eyeball with your eyewitness."

"Alleged is alleged, Agent. Not until I check it out."

"Why?"

"Client privilege."

"Of course. That entrepreneurial edge, awfully American. How long will it take to check?"

"A day. Maybe two. Where can I reach you?"

He handed me a business card. Gerald A. Loomis, Central Intelligence Agency, 305 area code, a P.O. box in

Miami. On the back, printed in block letters, was a phone number with a 213 area code, Los Angeles. They could patch through to him, he said.

We shook hands. His grip was fishy. He climbed out of the pickup. California sunlight flashed off his glasses. I watched him walk toward the stucco building. I yawned. The dashboard clock said 12:01. I needed a nap.

The phone was ringing as I unlocked my front door. It's a Uniden touch tone, with a speaker and a red Hold button. You can program in those fourteen numbers you dial a lot. You can redial with the press of a button. My local phone company, Pac Bell, calls me once a month with suggestions for updating my service. Next week, they say, you can talk to Mars. I grabbed the phone before the machine started.

"Wait," I said. "Be right back."

I punched in the code to disarm my Insta-Gard Alert. The code is 8642676, the phone pad equivalent of *unicorn*.

"Thanks," I said. "This is Murdock."

"Louis Chen, from Seattle, returning your call."

"Mr. Chen," I said. "Thanks for the recommendation. I owe you one."

"My pleasure. When I heard of Mr. Nielsen's destination, your name came to mind. What can I do for you?"

"You and Nielsen were college roommates, right?"

"That is correct."

A long pause, then Chen said: "We haven't been in touch much since our college days. What exactly did you have in mind?"

"The usual. Habits, friends, patterns of behavior."

"Hmm."

I waited. Nothing happened. "When did you see him last?"

"It was July."

"Mind telling me the occasion?"

"I installed a system for him."

"Home security, right?"

"That's correct."

"Mind telling me what it cost?"

"I'd rather not disclose that. It was top of the line, however."

"Did you do the work?"

"Yes. Rollie insisted on it."

"What's your training for that?"

"I was a physics major. Voltage presents certain interesting problems."

"This was at the University of Washington?"

"That is correct."

"How did Rollie seem in July?"

"Ebullient."

"Ebullient?"

"It's the opposite of reserved."

"Any reason for his . . . ebullience?"

"I suspect it was a woman. Perhaps more than one. Rollie always liked the ladies."

"Any idea who it was?"

"None."

"Tell me about the security system."

"It's top of the line, as I said. Manufactured in Germany, it's a perimeter control system that lays down a laser grid. The price was higher because Rollie wanted a remote."

"Tell me about the remote."

"It's a beeper device, worn on the belt or tucked away in an attaché. Businessmen like it because it alerts you in the car or the office if an intruder breaks the laser beam. There's an alarm, a digital readout. It comes in a handy size, like a pack of cigarettes, and is operated from the cellular phone frequency."

"Where else does it ring?"

"I'm sorry?"

"Does it alert a security company? The police?"

"That's the usual procedure. Rollie wanted something different, however."

"Mind telling me what?"

"It only alerted his personal beeper."

"What was your opinion of that?"

"We disagreed. He was the customer. He prevailed."

So Rollie Nielsen had something to hide. "Any idea how political he was?"

"Rollie was . . . politically active, I suppose you'd say."

"Could you describe that for me?"

"He joined Greenpeace. He also fought the lumber interests." There was a pause. "Can you hold? My other line is buzzing."

"Sure."

Commotion out my window on the Quad as two marines in uniform argued with a guy on a skateboard. Hard to tell what they were arguing about. The skateboarder—he seemed too old for his transportation—had a ponytail secured in back with a black ribbon.

"Mr. Murdock?"

"Still here."

"Were you thinking of coming to Seattle?"

"No. Why?"

"From your questions, I thought you might be interested in inspecting Rollie's condominium."

"Near the university, right?"

"No. This one is on Queen Anne Hill. Quite a fashionable neighborhood. Rollie had it decorated as the quintessential bachelor pad, complete with Jacuzzi."

I wrote it down. I checked my other envelope. "Thor Nielsen said Rollie's place was near the university."

"The place where I installed the system was on Queen Anne, a penthouse with a view. Very posh."

"I'll check with Thor. Maybe I wrote it down wrong."

"Mr. Murdock?"

"Yes?"

"If you do come up, I'd be pleased to show you around."

"Thanks. But the case is here."

"I'm quite interested in detective work, you see."

"Great," I said. "Thanks for your time, Mr. Chen."

"I was serious about my offer."

"I appreciate it."

"My regards to Mr. Nielsen. I am sorry for his loss."

"I'll tell him."

"Good-bye."

"Good-bye."

I stared out the window. The skateboarder was gone. The marines were talking to two girls in shorts and halters. Louis Chen had given my name to Thor Nielsen. I'd forgotten to ask him where he got it.

I phoned Thor Nielsen at his motel in Irvine. His room did not answer.

5

AT MIDAFTERNOON, WITH THE SUN BEATING DOWN, I sat with the Ford parked in precious shade, watching the kids leave St. Luke's School in Dana Point. Cindy Duke was with me. She wore a white blouse, jeans with a calculated rip in the right knee, and a heap of Mexican jewelry from Texas.

The kids of St. Luke's looked well fed and cared for. Tuition was three arms, a leg, your teeth, your house, your job, tough on parents who wanted their darlings out of the public system. There was no sign of the red Isuzu dopemobile, so we settled for lesser game, a fat-assed kid named Bernie Dodds. According to Cindy, Phyl had seen Bernie hanging out with the driver of the red Isuzu. Mr. Isuzu's name was Joel.

"Is that a real name, Joel?" I said. "Or is it fake?"

"Phyl says it's real."

"Bernie Dodds looks too old for St. Luke's."

"He got held back, Phyl said. The teachers had it in for him."

"How well do you know old Bernie?"

"Just well enough to avoid him."

Across the hot street, Bernie Dodds was in conversation with a skinny kid wearing black shorts, black sneaks, and a T-shirt with a monogram. This was Johnny Teegarden, Phyl's sweetie. Phyl Murphy, wearing a miniskirt and knee boots and a black blouse, came out of the building and walked toward the two guys. When she got close enough, the skinny kid gave her bottom a squeeze.

"Jesus," I said.

"It gets pretty steamy in the car on the way home," Cindy said. "You don't want to ride with the wrong people."

"You trying to tell me something?"

A pause. Then she said: "Bernie Dodds."

"What about him?"

"Sometimes he, well, you know."

"No, I don't know. Sometimes he what?"

"He puts his hands on me. Tries to kiss me. Don't worry. I don't let him."

"Why didn't you tell me?"

"I knew it would make you mad."

"It does."

"Thanks. He also offered me pot."

"You didn't tell me that either."

"It's my world, Matt. I can't come running to you every time something happens. It's my world and I've got to live in it."

Through the windshield of the Ford I watched while Bernie Dodds and Johnny Teegarden slapped hands, the first step in an elaborate good-bye handshake, wrists crossing, ending with double thumbs up. Johnny walked off with Phyl. Bernie headed for a fire-red Trans Am.

"There goes my ride," Cindy said.

"Better catch it."

"I'd rather come with you."

"No. You've done enough. Better scoot on home."

"I hate it there." The Mexican beads clicked as she opened the door and slid off the seat. Her face was a mask of sadness. I watched her until she went out of sight behind the building. Then I followed Bernie Dodds.

He took the Crown Valley Parkway to Interstate 5. We drove north past Mission Viejo and El Toro to the Jeffrey off-ramp, where he exited. Together, we headed northeast, orange groves on the right, construction to the left, dozer blades flashing in the sunlight. Four lanes of traffic clotted the roadway here, Volvos and BMWs and Jags, America's middle class hustling along the mythical fast lane toward gridlock on the freeway.

Bernie parked his Trans Am in a driveway of a house in Northwood. Quiet street, posh homes. On the lawn next door, a sprinkler spouted water in wasteful jets, another jerk ignoring our southern California water problem.

Bernie looked at my Ford, looked away. He went inside. I climbed out and walked to his Trans Am. I opened the door and got in. The wheel had a leather cover that smelled of palm sweat. I opened the glove box. Kleenex. A package of condoms, ribbed for giving "Her" ultimate pleasure. A pair of brass knuckles. A switchblade with the blade broken halfway up. Cassette tapes with catchy names like *Dr. Feelgood, Detonator, Liquidizer, Slaughter, Repeat Offender.*

The driveway had a slight incline. I released the emergency brake, pushed with my left foot, got us moving backward. I guided the Trans Am down the driveway into the middle of the street. I put on the hand brake. Then I nosed my Ford up against the skin of Bernie's car. Looking serious, I rang Bernie's front-door buzzer. No answer. From inside the house, I heard the planetary beat of music from other worlds. I knocked on the door. No answer. The door was unlocked. I walked in.

Middle-class house, that fleshy suburban look, walls crowded with framed paintings, rooms crowded with cushy furniture. *Architectural Digest* on the coffee table, next to a novel by Anne Rice. The music was louder here, deafening. It came from the second floor. I called hello. Did not expect an answer. I took the stairs two at a time, walked down the hall, pushing against the sound, to a closed door. Music pumped here, bursting the very air. I opened the door. Posters on the walls, life-size, of guys with guitars and skinny, big-mouthed gals in wet T-shirts. Bernie Dodds sat in a swivel chair facing the windows, his back to me. Speakers on both walls, trapping him in between. I found the power switch on his stereo. I punched the button. The sound died like a duck full of buckshot. In the silence, Bernie Dodds stared at me as he jerked his hand away from his crotch. Red-faced, he stood up, an ugly kid with an ugly mouth. His zipper had stuck in the up slide.

"Who the fuck are you?"

"Your car," I said. "It hit my car."

"Whaaat?"

I pointed to the street. "The police are on the way. Hope you have insurance."

"Police? Where?" Eyes wide, he bungled his way past me to the balcony. From there, he could see into the street, his Trans Am butted up against my pickup. He swung back to me. "You followed me here! I saw you when I got off the freeway. Who are you?"

"I'm the guy who wants a connection with Biff in the red Isuzu."

"You mean Joel—" He stopped. He realized he'd made a slip. Guys like Bernie Dodds, their life is one long slip. "You better get out before my mom—"

I stepped close. He moved backward until his butt

touched the railing of the balcony. His eyes darted to the left. He wanted his mama to come home. Now.

"Tell Joel I want a meet. On the Quad."

"Why?"

"A guy died just after he saw Joel. The cops are on it. Tell Joel if he comes clean I might save his sorry ass. He's got to reach me first, before the cops reach him."

"He'll want a name."

"Santa Claus." I wrote my number down. I left him there, quivering, his back to the railing. I wanted to warn him to keep his hands off Cindy. I decided against it. No need to involve her.

The music started up again as I reached the front door. Heavy metal followed me out. I was nowhere with this case. I was following a thread so thin, it cut my fingers. I drove the Ford to the end of the block. I parked in the shade and waited. Bernie Dodds walked down the driveway. He climbed into his Trans Am. He drove it back into the driveway. This time he locked his car doors.

I hate surveillance. You sit there. You wait. Your mind plays games. Your bladder sounds false alarms. I waited thirty minutes before driving back to the beach. No action from Bernie Dodds. My roust had not sent him flying out to squeal to the driver of the red Isuzu.

I spent what was left of the afternoon showing photos of Rollie Nielsen to denizens of the beach. A waitress at Sid's thought she remembered him. A waiter at La Belle Epoque thought Rollie had been at table number seventeen on Saturday night, around midnight, he said. Since Rollie had died between eight and midnight, I hoped his ghost had enjoyed the show.

As I headed away from La Belle Epoque, a skateboarder tried to run me down. He was muscular and lean, no fat anywhere, and he wore his cap on backward, like a baseball pitcher. He looked Chicano, mid-twenties. On the cap it said DODGERS.

Back at my place, I listened to my messages. Two different clicks told me two someones had called without leaving messages. There was no message from Bernie Dodds saying he'd set up a meet with Joel. My roust had failed.

At dusk, I showered. I went over the case in my head. I didn't like breaking the news to Thor Nielsen that his boy died with dope in his veins. Your boy was selling dope, Mr. Nielsen, maybe cooking the stuff. That information will cost you $300.

Two homes in Seattle might mean a double life. Might just mean two homes, an investment in Seattle real estate, a hot market. Some of the best people have two homes. Maybe the U-District place was rented. Maybe Rollie Nielsen, like a lot of kids, didn't tell his dad everything. I finished my shower and dried off. My face looked tired. How long since I'd had a physical?

With the towel wrapped around me, I sat on the edge of the bed and phoned Seattle information. No listing for Rollie Nielsen. One listing for Gaspard. I called it. A woman answered. In a creaky voice, she said she did not know any Rolande Gaspard. I was hanging up when a voice called: "Knock knock."

Cindy Duke appeared in the doorway, her hair tousled. She wore biking clothes.

"Oh wow," she said. "A skin show."

"Let me get dressed, okay?"

"Mind if I watch? Woo woo. This is better than Chippendale's."

"Out."

She left the room grinning. Through the door, as I dressed, I heard music. *Pictures at an Exhibition,* a gift from

Senator Jane. I checked my face in the mirror. The beard needed edging, but I didn't take the time. I phoned Thor Nielsen, but his room didn't answer.

Cindy was sitting on the deck in a chaise, drinking a Pepsi. I got a beer and joined her. There was no sea breeze now to freshen the air. The sky hung on the horizon like a red-orange ball. Down below, the skateboarder with the Dodger cap zoomed by.

"I think Phyl's worried, Matt."

"What about?"

"About that dead guy."

"You told her?"

"We talked about it, sort of. She didn't like hearing the fact that he was dead."

"Jesus, Cindy."

"She's my friend, Matt."

"I know."

"So we talked and I think she's coming over."

"Here?"

"Yes. She wants to see those photos."

"When?"

"Later," she said. "Can she see the photos?"

"Sure, now that you've told her."

"You'd never get to Phyl. She doesn't trust anyone over twenty." Cindy grinned at me. "Watson and Holmes, Matt. That's us. Duke and Murdock, Inc."

"Has a ring, all right."

"How about a glass of wine, to celebrate."

"You never give up."

"No." She faked a yawn. "And I still want to live here."

Before I could answer, I heard Thor Nielsen's voice calling up from down below. "Hey, Murdock? You home?"

I walked to the railing. Thor Nielsen came up the stairs. He wore the same clothes he'd worn yesterday. In his right hand was a paper sack. In his left was a large pizza box from Domino's. "Dinner," he said. He set the stuff down. He shook hands with me and then with Cindy. Looking tired and old, Thor took a director's chair, put his heels on the railing. Cindy tested the pizza, found it too cold for her taste, and walked inside to zap it with the microwave.

The sun slid behind a cloud, the air crowded in around us, making it tough to breathe. Thor and I opened beers and I told him what I'd learned about his boy.

When I finished, he didn't say anything. Just sat there, his face heavy and sad, while the silence built. Down below on the Quad, a photographer was unloading camera gear out of a Jeep Cherokee. Lights and battery packs and reflectors on fold-up stands and cables and a box of lenses and a satchel full of film.

"Queen Anne Hill, you say?"

"According to Louie Chen."

"That's the high-rent district." Thor's big hands flexed. "Why didn't he tell me? I'm his dad, after all."

I said nothing.

"Are they sure? About the dope, I mean."

"They did an autopsy, Mr. Nielsen. The blood doesn't lie. And he was number nine in a string of murders."

"They're saying Rollie made the stuff?"

"Yes."

Cindy came out with the pizza. Thor glanced at it as she set it down, then looked away. "Damn," he said. He stood up, walked to the railing, and stared out to sea.

"Mr. Nielsen? Are you okay?"

"Sure. Sure I am." He stood there, arms folded across his chest.

Cindy handed me a slice of pizza on a paper plate. I let it sit. With a shrug, Cindy sank her teeth in. She chewed. She sipped her Pepsi. It was darker now in the west, a line of orange atop a Pacific cloud bank. With a sigh, Thor Nielsen turned back to face us. "That pizza smells pretty good."

"Want some?"

"Might as well." He sat down, watched while Cindy cut him a slice of pizza. He bit off the end of a pizza wedge. "What's this ice stuff you were talking about?"

"It's a new drug. I don't know much about it."

"I do," Cindy said.

"You do?"

"Um. We learned about it in school. A sheriff's deputy showed some slides and a video, about what it does to you. And then our chemistry teacher explained how easy it was to make."

"School has changed since I was a kid."

"Sorry, I didn't mean to—"

"No. I'm interested. Go on."

She looked at me. I nodded. "Well," she began. "Ice is the street name for a derivative product of methamphetamine hydrochloride. The formula is pretty simple, CH sub two and CHCH sub three."

She looked at Thor to see how he was taking it. "The manufacturing process is called cooking. You make it in a crude lab with maybe a couple thousand dollars' worth of special glassware and a heat source and stuff. They used to start with phenylacetone, but the regulators restricted that, so the cookers—those are the people who make the ice—started using ephedrine, which is the base ingredient used in cough-control medicines sold over the counter." Another pause, her cheeks bright with color. "It's more expensive than coke, but a coke high lasts only thirty minutes while the ice high can last thirty hours. An ice addict feels like Superman."

"Phenol-what?"

"Phenylacetone. We saw some. It doesn't look like much."

"How come?"

"I expected it to foam over, you know, like in a mad scientist video."

"You heard about this from a deputy?"

"Um. They have this program. It's called D.A.R.E. It stands for—"

Thor Nielsen blew his nose. He was crying now, shaking his head. Still blowing, he excused himself and went inside. Cindy looked at me.

"Uh-oh," she said.

"He'll be okay."

"I guess I got carried away, huh?"

"You did great."

"Thanks, Matt."

I tried some pizza. It wasn't bad. Cindy worked on her second slice. I heard movement inside the house and Thor Nielsen came out. His eyes were red from crying. "I'm real grateful for the info."

"I didn't mean to go on like that," she said.

"It's okay. It's . . . okay."

There was no light conversation for a while because Thor kept talking, throwing questions into the air. He didn't want answers. He just wanted to talk. Why the place on Queen Anne? Why the unlisted number? How many trips to California? Why hadn't he stayed closer to Rollie? Was there a curse on the Nielsens? His voice got thick as darkness fell along the beach.

6

IN THE GREENISH GLAZE FROM THE ARC LIGHTS, THOR
Nielsen's face was pale and sickly. He had stopped talking,
shut down in midsentence.

"Look down there," Cindy said. "A fashion shoot."

Down below on the Quad, a model with thin arms and a
milkmaid chest was coiled like a python around a willing
lamppost while the photographer circled her, camera close
to his face, firing away. She wore a lime-green dress, the
skirt slit to her hipbone. Her legs were bare and naked-
looking. The high heels were lime-colored to match the
dress. A crowd had gathered to watch—the same two marines, some college joes wearing UC Irvine sweaters, a gag-
gle of tourists. At the edge of the crowd, their backs to the
beach, were three skateboarders. The guy with the Dodger
cap in his yellow sweatshirt and two of his pals.

A Newport Beach patrol unit came around the corner,
moving like a white cat, two uniforms inside. The driver
looked up at my place, a man looking but not looking. Was
I under surveillance?

Cindy went inside. As we talked Thor Nielsen pounded

the heel of his hand on the arm of the director's chair and tried to reach some tough conclusions. "It fits, doesn't it, Murdock, my boy being a chemist and all, easy as pie to cook that stuff. Damned if it doesn't fit. And two addresses? If he was into real estate, why the hell didn't he tell me? I know something about real estate. Damn!"

I didn't say anything. He went on talking. I watched the show on the Quad, strobes singing as the model gyrated, held the pose, gyrated, held again. A van came around the corner. The driver wore yellow shooting glasses. His hair was pulled back behind his neck in a ponytail. The van was a Chevy, dark green, with double doors at the rear and a sliding door on the passenger side. It stopped in front of the B&B and the driver said something to Dodger Cap, who nodded. One of the skateboarders, a hefty kid in baggy shorts, shouldered his skateboard and climbed into the van.

There was no sign of the NBPD patrol unit.

A voice called up from down below. "Cindy? Cindeerella?"

"Hey, Phyl." I walked to the railing. "Come on up."

Phyl Murphy wore a black sweatshirt with long sleeves and a logo in front that said THE GRATEFUL DEAD ARE UNNNNN-GRATEFUL. Her jeans had the requisite rips in the knees, and a melon slice out of the right buttock, under the pocket seam. Streetlights gave the purple hair a greenish tinge. She looked bedraggled, zonked, out of it. Kids on drugs are tough to handle. You know they're using. You talk to them, they don't listen.

"Hi, Phyl. Welcome."

"Hello."

"This is Mr. Nielsen."

"Hello."

"Have a seat, young lady. There's pizza if you're hungry."

"No, thanks. Haven't got much time."

Cindy came out the door with a Pepsi. Phyl drank it like a thirsty lumberjack, head tilted back, her throat working, her nose sucking air. Holding tight to the can, she looked at me. "Cindy said you had some photos."

I handed her the photos of Rollie Nielsen. No expression as she flipped through them, but a sudden tightness around the eyes when she set them down with a snap on the wooden table. She stared past me at something in the general vicinity of San Francisco, Seattle, or Nome, Alaska. She glugged more Pepsi, then went through the photos again. She knew him.

"I think maybe," she said.

"You saw him?"

She nodded. "Could have. He wore shades."

"Would you mind telling us again?"

"Am I in trouble?"

"I don't think so."

"I mean, if he was a—" She stopped before she said drug dealer. "The cops would love to get their hands on this."

"No cops, Phyl. I promise."

She went through the photos one more time. She set them down, stared at the Pepsi. A shiver rippled through her. I remembered being fifteen. Always whirling, on tilt or about to be, always scratching for a toehold on slippery life.

Phyl was here because Cindy had worked on her. Phyl was in over her head. She didn't have much to gain by helping us. Maybe she knew that when she crimped the Pepsi can and stood up. "I gotta go," she said.

"Phyl," Cindy said. "Phyl, Phyl—"

Alone now, resolute, Phyl headed for the stairs. Thor's face was steeped in sadness. Beyond Phyl, on the Quad, I saw the Chevy van easing into a parking slot. The rear door of the van faced my building. Phyl started down the stairs. Down below, the model had unbuttoned the top of her dress to show the camera she wore no brassiere. Because of the show, no one noticed the van. The air hung still and murky over the Quad. Behind the sheeted clouds, the moon was a dim yellow glow.

"Phyl?"

"See you later, Mr. M."

I was about to order her back, slam her with adult authority, when the rear door of the van flew open and a guy with an Uzi raked the stairway, creating a scatter of wood chips skittering up at Phyl Murphy. I grabbed her arm but the bullets had already ripped into her. Blood spots appeared on the white logo. Her eyes went wide with shock. Her body convulsed. By the time I got her up on the deck, she was fading. I was moving fast, cursing, no time to check. Thor was hurt, blood running down his left arm. Cindy was hurt. How did they target us? I thought of Bernie Dodds.

Bullet holes in my deck, screams from down below, shots, shouts, the roar of internal combustion engines. Thor dragged Cindy inside. I was right behind him with Phyl. Glass on the deck, bullets slashing the air. To the east, at the edge of Balboa Boulevard, I saw Dodger Cap reloading from the flat roof of Beach Realty. He'd exchanged his skateboard for an automatic weapon. Against the bright yellow sweatshirt, the gun looked dark and deadly.

Blood dark on Cindy's T-shirt. She moaned. "Uh-uh."

In the brief lull I grabbed the Arnica bottle, tossed it to Thor. "For shock!" I yelled. "Give some to Cindy."

"Okay." He indicated Phyl. "She gonna make it?"

"I don't think so."

"Damn." Thor's eyes blazed. "Lend me a gun, Murdock."

I tossed him the key to my gun case. While he found us some weapons I phoned 911. Yelled my address. Yelled for help, cops, paramedics, anyone. "They were just here!" I yelled. "A patrol unit! They were here a minute ago!" The voice, dull as a robot, was asking dumb questions. I hung up.

"Cindy?"

"Hurts," she said. "Oh wow Matt it hurts golly shit!"

Blood oozed from a wound in her back, below the rib cage. Her face was pale beneath her tan and her eyes kept rolling up inside her head. Pain and shock. The slow ooze of blood meant the bullet had not hit a big vessel. She needed medical attention. Cindy gave me a weak smile. Thor Nielsen grunted with appreciation as he loaded the magazine of my Winchester pump. He asked what I wanted. I chose the Colt Diamondback and two speed-loaders. Thor hunkered down to guard the front door. "You got a plan?"

Bullets ripped a swath across the deck and into the wood door frame. Both windows were out. Light from the street-lamps winked in the glass shards on the floor. My palms were bleeding. And my left knee. "We'll wait for help."

Thor peered out. "That prick on the balcony to the right, he's moving out."

"Let him go. Let them all go."

"Where's Phyl?" Cindy said.

"Resting," I said.

"Is she—"

I shook my head.

"Did you get them?"

"No."

"It's Bernie, Matt. Bernie Dodds. He must have—" Her eyes closed, opened. "Go after them." She made a motion with her head. "Go."

"An eye for an eye, Murdock," Thor said.

I exhaled. I looked down at Cindy as the smile faded. I crawled to the doorway where I checked my weapon: eighteen rounds, six in the chamber, twelve in two speed-loaders.

I crawled through the bedroom to the storeroom. Stuffy in here as I stood up to unlock the window. My rope ladder is mounted on a swingaway roller wheel, handy for escape in case of fire if you can't use the front steps. I locked the wheel into position and let the rope ladder drop. I was on my way down before it hit bottom. Hands shaking now, trouble getting the key to unlock my pickup door. More trouble starting the Ford. Backing out, I clipped the corner of the building. I slammed into first and rolled around the corner toward the Quad on two wheels. All I could hear was the revving of my engine.

No shooters on the balcony of Beach Realty. The van's doors were open and as I turned left toward the parking lot, I saw a ramp running from the lip of the rear door to the gray asphalt. The hefty kid in green was in the act of wheeling up the ramp into the van. From behind a palm tree, the guy with the Dodger cap covered him. The tourists had scattered and the marines, hunkered down, were carrying someone to the safety of the public johns. There was no sign of the Jeep Cherokee. Camera equipment lay scattered across the sidewalk.

The shotgun went off and I looked up to my deck to see the barrel of the Winchester. A wisp of smoke floated from the muzzle and the muzzle was withdrawn, out of sight. Thor was reloading. Dodger Cap fired a quick burst at my deck before he zigzagged his way up the ramp and inside the van. With a *whump,* the doors closed. Thor's shotgun went off again, and the rear window of the van disintegrated into shards.

As the van pulled away I saw the third skateboarder. He lay on his back with one leg pulled up under him. Blood covered his torso and his automatic weapon lay three feet

away from his outstretched fingers. His skateboard had
been dumped over. The wheels were not moving.

Score one for Thor Nielsen.

The parking lot on the Quad is a maze where lanes twist,
bend back on themselves. The city fathers built it that way
so they could squeeze more cars in. I was inside the entrance to the maze, headed the wrong way, while the van
with the bad guys roared toward the exit. I threw the Ford
into reverse and was almost out of the maze when the Jeep
Cherokee swung in behind me.

The model was driving and the photographer was leaning
out the window on the passenger side, grinding away at the
action with a video instacam. Blood on film makes for
photo prizes and fame among the paparazzi. The model
braked. I kept on going, slammed into the Jeep with the
rear of my pickup, lost some precious seconds. The photographer yelled at me. I skirted around him, slicing off green
metallic Jeep paint with my front bumper. With the pickup
rocking, I roared up Balboa after the van.

The van was fifty yards ahead. My speedometer hit sixty,
sixty-five, seventy. My Ford's a 1973, 420 horses under the
hood. The van was heavy and didn't move like it was
souped up, so I caught it just before it swung onto the
Coast Highway, heading northwest toward Huntington
Beach. A tidy shopping center here, and behind it off to the
right along the channel the pricey homes of Balboa Coves.

I rammed the van from the rear, sent it skidding sideways
into a string of parked cars. Sound of metal crunching as I
mashed the rear door shut. No sign of the driver. I was out
of the Ford, holding the Diamondback with two hands as I
approached, civilians stopping to stare. A fat man in Ber-
muda shorts crossed my line of vision. A woman in a summer frock grabbed his arm and pulled him down behind a
purple Mazda. I was on the left side of the van when I

heard a shout and an Uzi firing. At the same time Dodger Cap darted across the street. His destination was a knot of civilians he could use for cover. I yelled for him to stop. He shot at me with his Uzi, but the bullets went too high. I led him like a duck in the air and squeezed the trigger. I thought I'd missed, damn, and then he toppled in slow motion, lifting off the skateboard and hanging in the air for a long moment like a sky diver and then settling to the asphalt with a crunch. The skateboard rolled to the curb and stopped.

I ran to him. People were shouting. A woman screamed. Somewhere behind me, I heard a baby crying. Adrenaline zipped through me, I felt fire along my spine. As I held the muzzle of the Colt to the neck of the guy in the cap, I thought of Cindy, hurt, the blood oozing.

"Who hired you?" I'd forgotten their names. "Who?"

"Ahhh, *pinche pendejo cabrón puta puta puta!*" His throat was slick with greasy sweat and he smelled bad.

"They're getting away!" someone said. "Hey, you? Mister?"

I did not look up. I could not stop them from getting away. I had one of them. He coughed, fear rose up in his eyes, and his belly expanded under the yellow sweatshirt as he sucked in air.

"Who hired you, *amigo*? What's your name? *¿Cómo se llama?*"

"Julio," he said. *"¿Donde está el médico?"*

"On the way. Who hired you? Bernie? Joel? Who?"

Julio shuddered. Not much blood oozing. He grabbed my wrist, made a strangled sound. Then he grunted and his rib cage sank, flutter of air from his mouth and nostrils, no pulse.

I stood up, copper taste on my tongue.

I left him there and ran to the highway. Cars whizzed by,

but there was no sign of the driver of the van or the hefty kid in green. Feeling tired now, feeling whipped, I walked back to the van. A knot of people had gathered around Julio. A man wearing a golfer's cap stood with his foot on the Uzi. Inside the van I found two revolvers and six clips of ammo for the Uzi automatic weapon.

I was behind the wheel of my Ford, the Colt tucked into my belt, when the first squad car wheeled up to the scene. Three of Newport Beach's finest leaped out, guns held steady.

"No one moves, okay! No one effing moves!"

7

HUMID INSIDE THE POLICE CRUISER, HUMID AS A steambath. I sat on the left, on the street side, with a view of my deck. The window of the cruiser was open an inch, not enough space for ventilation.

A thick wire mesh separated the rear seat, where the perps were stashed, from the front, where the law sat. The upholstery was ripped open on the seat and there were scuff marks on the seatback. Sweat trickled down my rib cage, widening the dark splotch on the blue work shirt. My hands were bagged in brown paper and cuffed behind my back, making it impossible to find a comfortable position. The cuffs had been ratcheted down too tight.

Outside the cruiser, a young cop with thick arms and broad athlete's shoulders stood with his back to me. His equipment belt, loaded with fifteen pounds of police gear, was the most visible part of him as he gave his full attention to a trio of beach beauties being escorted by a female officer toward the yellow police barrier. The trio wore Day-Glo spandex and had come, along with a couple hundred gawkers, to sniff the blood.

I didn't know what time it was. Phyl Murphy was dead. Cindy and Thor had been taken in the same ambulance to St. Boniface Hospital. Wally St. Moritz and Leo Castelli, my pals, were locked in earnest conversation with Lieutenant L. R. Archer of the Newport Beach PD. They were citizens and taxpayers. The mayor ate breakfast at Leo's. Wally had friends on the City Council. Let the machinery work.

I was tired and sore and angry. My guns had been confiscated and a team of technicians, forensics guys, had been in my place for at least an hour. Julio was dead. His last name was Mendez. I'd overheard a cop saying Julio was a member of Los Boleros, a gang operating out of Santa Ana. I was sorry he was dead. If he'd been alive, maybe he could have talked, connected us to Bernie Dodds, and then to Joel with the Isuzu, and then to Mr. Big.

Out along the beach, a Newport Beach SWAT team had deployed, caps on backward, weapons at the ready, as they swept the area.

A SWAT officer stepped down from the pier to the sidewalk near the public toilets, about sixty feet in front of us. He was holding a bullhorn, addressing some teenagers on skateboards. In the parking area, a forensics man was shooting photographs of the area where the van had been. There was no sign of the Jeep Cherokee.

I closed my eyes, tried to relax. Knuckles rapped on the window and I opened my eyes to see the round face of Detective Nick Giordano. Freshly shaved, his face looked blue and metallic. Yellow eyes studied me, smug humor there, young guy strutting. Giordano's suit was natty, with that tailored look. He had a thick neck and a bodybuilder's way of moving, swinging his shoulders like they were hooked to a wrecking ball. He opened the door and grabbed my shirt and hauled me out. I smelled cologne, heavy stuff, sickish, and garlic on his breath.

"You're in my way," he said.

"Can I go now?"

"Ha ha," he said.

From across the Quad came the voice of Lieutenant Archer. "Take off the cuffs, Detective."

"The fuck." Giordano muttered to himself as he unlocked the cuffs.

I started to leave but he braced me, stood close, face six inches from mine, giving me the garlic. Rubbing my wrists, I leaned against the patrol car. A list of things to do gathered on the pinup board inside my head. Go to hospital. See Cindy. See Thor. Call Zeke Amado, get him going on repairs. Call insurance guy, get him going. He'll probably slot this as an Act of God, and therefore not eligible for reimbursement. Check with Webby Smith, get him going on the gang, what was it called, Los . . .

"Where the fuck do you get off, shooting up the neighborhood? Who the fuck you think you are, General Fucking Westmoreland?"

"They shot first, Detective. Four shooters with Uzis. They killed a kid. While waiting for you boys in Newport khaki, we shot back."

"I don't like you." Giordano's face was aflame with anger. "You're a cowboy and cowboys are dangerous. This is my case. You get in my way once and I'll have your ticket pulled. You get in my way twice and I'll throw your ass in the slammer and eat the key."

"You through?"

His hands clenched. They were fat hands. "Get lost," he said.

I tried a parting shot. It was dumb. I tried it anyway. "Here's a tip, Detective. Check out a kid named Bernie

Dodds, lives in Irvine, hangs out with the boyfriend of Phyllis Murphy, recently deceased. Get the connection? When she was killed, Miss Murphy was about to ID a playground pusher who's in tight with Bernie who"—I stopped. Enough. I was ranting. I didn't trust him—"and if you'll get me pencil and paper I'll draw the dots."

"Dots? What dots?"

"Dots for you to connect to make a line that leads you to the killer."

"Don't push." His eyes flashed hate.

I turned my back on him and walked over to where Wally and Leo stood with Lieutenant Archer. The Lieutenant was a born bureaucrat. His dream was to become captain, then chief, then mayor. Tom Bradley had done that, up in L.A. In an age of crime, cops are knights in blue armor.

The Lieutenant wore a thousand-dollar suit, Italian shoes, and the requisite gold Rolex. He shook hands with me. I was a taxpayer, a property owner, a voter. "On the Q.T.," said the Lieutenant, "this was an invasion that left a blot on the city's shield. What the city fathers want is peace and security. Can't sell surf and sun with bullets flying and we're grateful to citizens like Mr. Murdock here who can—" His beeper beeped, calling him away, and I stood with Wally and Leo.

Outside, the yellow police crime-scene ribbons, the TV trucks waited, panting.

"I phoned Zeke for you." Wally handed me a clean shirt. "He'll be over in the morning with new window glass. I left a message on the machine of the insurance agent."

"Thanks for the shirt. Where's my Ford?"

"Giorgio's lot on Balboa." Leo handed me the keys. "Thought it would be safer there."

"Thanks." I turned to Wally. "Drive me to St. Boniface, okay?"

"For medical attention, I trust."

"I need to see Cindy. Check on Thor Nielsen."

"Your client was high on adrenaline," Wally said. "Kept asking about you."

I folded the bloody shirt. "What about Cindy?"

"Still unconscious, Matthew."

"Get me over there, okay?"

"All right."

Leo said he'd post his cook upstairs to guard my property. His cook was named Frederick. Frederick was from Jamaica. He weighed 220 pounds. On his days off, he lifted weights up in Venice, at Muscle Beach.

"Thanks, Leo."

"Thanks yourself. For driving off the barbarians."

"They were just kids," I said.

Ten o'clock on Thursday as Wally and I entered the lobby of St. Boniface Hospital. My eyeballs ached. My head pounded. The hospital hush—the silence of death and disease—made me queasy.

At the desk, I let Wally dig for information. One mention of Thor Nielsen's name and the desk man called the cop in charge. The cop was Mac Ryan, a grizzled thirty-year man from the Newport Beach station. Mac remembered me as the instructor from a police academy refresher course in small arms. We shook hands. I introduced Wally. Mac gave the go-ahead to the desk man.

Cindy was in Recovery, the desk man said, following emergency surgery. The slug had missed her vital organs. Her prognosis was good. Thor was on Four, in the Tower.

In the elevator, going up to Four, Mac Ryan ruminated about what had happened. "This is off the record, but the department's bracing for an invasion. It's bad now, the recession and all, but it's gonna get worse. Those kids in

Santa Ana, the gang guys, are L.A.-trained. They come from nothing, half of them born south of the border, and they see our beach as the good life. If they can't steal it, they blast it with an Uzi. Between me and you, Murdock, you performed a public service tonight. Two invaders down, a zillion to go."

The elevator doors opened like a zipper and we walked down the hall. A cop sat outside Thor Nielsen's room, reading a paperback. Mac Ryan left us at the door with a handshake. We went in. The room was standard hospital, two beds, one window, pea-green walls, one TV. Thor was propped up in bed, watching the screen. His right arm was in a sling. When he saw us, he clicked off the picture with his remote. "Murdock, glad to see you. I was worried."

"Thanks. How are you doing?"

"Two slugs. Both of them went through. How's little Cindy?"

"She's in Recovery. How's the pain?"

"When it hurts too bad, I punch that buzzer and a nurse dumps some liquid stuff into that gizmo there." He pointed to a pouch, clear plastic, that hung from a metal strut. A clear tube ran from a rubber nipple on the bottom of the pouch to a needle taped to the inside of Thor's arm. "Any idea who shot us and why?"

"The kid you shot was named Vallardo. Mine was named Julio Mendez. They belonged to a gang called Los Boleros."

"*Bolero* means dance," Wally said. "Or the music that accompanies the dance. Or a kind of shorty jacket worn by the dancers."

"Death dancers," Thor said, shifting to get comfortable. "That friend of Cindy's, she didn't make it, did she?"

"No."

"Damn shame, seemed like a nice girl."

"The drugs got her, Thor, pulled her down."

"She knew something, didn't she? About my boy."

"It sure felt like it, Thor."

"You got any ideas?"

"The link is Bernie Dodds," I said. "After I rattled his cage today he alerted Joel who alerted someone higher up —our local Mr. Big—who hired those gang types."

"Los Boleros is a new gang in the area," Wally said. "New gangs have much to prove. For them, this was a sterling opportunity to demonstrate their manly prowess."

"And make some bucks," I said.

"A crass motive," Wally said, "when compared to manhood ritual."

"Joel," Thor said. "He's the dope dealer, right?"

"According to Cindy he is."

"Hard to believe all this. A man doesn't know his own son any better than that. It's real hard to believe, even in California." A tear ran down his cheek. He pawed at it with his good hand. He took in a deep breath and sighed. "So, what's the next move?"

I looked at Wally. "Bernie Dodds," I said.

The silence built in the room. "Murdock?"

"Yes?"

"I got a hunch about Seattle."

"What hunch?"

"Rollie's from there. This dope business started up there. The cops are hot to get into his place. That should tell us something."

"The case is here, Thor. He was killed here. Mr. Big hangs out here."

"How do you know that?"

"He's out there," I said. "I can feel him."

Thor opened his mouth to say something. He grunted. The effort made him cough, a raspy hacking sound. When he finished, his voice had no strength. "How about if I ordered you to go up there?"

"I run the case. If you want someone else on it, say the word."

"Nah. I'm just being testy. It's those dead kids, this damned arm, my boy, the whole works. Do whatever you have to. And forgive an old fart for butting his head on a wall, okay?" He coughed again. "Guess I'm tireder than I thought, fellas."

"We were just going," Wally said.

"See you tomorrow," I said.

"Yeah," Thor said. "By then I should feel better."

When we left the room, he was staring at the blank TV screen.

8

IN THE RECOVERY AREA, A NURSE ALLOWED US TO look at Cindy through a plate-glass window. Only a moment, she said. Cindy was pale in her narrow bed, dark hollows under her eyes, her face contorted in painkiller sleep. The bedsheet, a harsh gray-blue, was up around her neck so you couldn't see the damage done by the bullet.

"Christ," I said.

"She'll survive," Wally said.

"How the hell do you know?"

"She's a Duke," he said. "They have excellent blood."

Mac Ryan came toward us, his face heavy. "Got a minute, Murdock?"

"Sure."

"The Murphy kid, we can't locate her mother. You know any other relatives?"

"They're divorced. I think Mr. Murphy's moved to Portland."

"Can you give us an ID? There's some paperwork that they want at the station."

"Now?"

"Won't take a minute. Come on."

We followed him into the elevator. The doors closed. He pressed the button for the basement. In the basement was the Cold Room. "Too bad about these kids. They've got everything, good homes, good clothes, money. They keep coming in here on slabs, more this year than I can remember."

"Not a good year for kids."

"Not a good year, period."

The door opened on Level B. We followed Mac Ryan toward a sliding glass door that led to the Cold Room. In front of the door was a desk. An attendant sat behind the desk, reading *People* magazine. He wore high tops and a smock, knee length, surgical green. He stood when he saw Mac Ryan.

"Number five, Jimmy."

"Number five, right this way, folks."

Chilly in the Cold Room on the bottom floor of St. Boniface Hospital on a hill above Newport Beach. They kept bodies here for a day or two before transferring them to a funeral home for burial or to the county facility for autopsy. Six drawers on the left, six on the right, an even dozen drawers. Handles on the drawers, for pulling them out so the living could view the dead. Jimmy pulled out number five. The body was covered with a sheet. He watched us, watched our faces as he pulled back the sheet. Her purple hair was matted with dried blood and there were bullet holes across her chest. Her face was death pale, the eyes closed.

"That's her," I said. "That's Phyllis Murphy."

Jimmy slid the drawer back. With a look at me, Wally left the room. Mac Ryan waited until Jimmy left the room, then he held out a plastic sandwich bag.

"Ice," he said. "Found it in her purse, half an ounce, along with a half-smoked pipe."

"Christ," I said.

"How was she at your place? How'd she seem?"

"Edgy, young, looked at you out of the corners of her eyes."

"Was she high?"

"I don't think so."

"Kids like this, you wonder where the parents are at."

We walked outside. Wally sat on a steel bench, clenching the metal edge, chin on his chest. "That poor tyke," he said. "That poor little tyke."

A bell bonged and the elevator door opened and a uniformed cop stepped out, followed by Janice Murphy. She was a brunette, bouncy, late thirties, with a short haircut and eyes set close together. Tonight she wore a pleated Mexican skirt and a peasant blouse that displayed tan shoulders. Makeup on her face, blue eyeshadow. Her eyes looked terrified.

"Mr. Murdock! What's going on? What's happened?"

I looked at the cop. He shook his head and stared at the floor. With these things, there's no easy way.

"Better go with the officer, Mrs. Murphy."

"This way, ma'am. Please."

Jimmy slid the door open and they trooped into the Cold Room. It didn't take long. Janice Murphy came out crying, blowing her nose, wiping her eyes with a white handkerchief. "Why is she there? Why is Phyllis in that room? You said Cindy was here?"

"Upstairs, Mrs. Murphy. In Recovery."

"Is she . . . will she—"

"She's got a good chance."

"Were they together?" Her eyes locked on to mine. "Was Phyl with Cindy?"

"They were at my place."

Dull nod from Janice Murphy. "A gang shooting, the police said. I don't believe it. How? A gang shooting in the heart of Newport Beach when everyone knows the gangs hang out in Santa Ana. What happened, Mr. Murdock? Was this one of your . . . cases?"

"Ma'am," said Mac Ryan.

"Leave me alone." Janice Murphy stepped close. There was liquor on her breath, and the lingering smell of pot smoke. "Your place? What were they doing there? I knew this would happen. I knew it. I warned little Miss Cindy. Stay away, I told her. I thought Phyllis got the message. I was sure of it. What in God's name were they doing at your place?"

"Trying to help."

"Trying to help? Trying to help! Help who? Since when did you need help? You know what we hear at our house? We hear Matt This and Matt That. We hear Matt Matt Matt." Her nose was running so she stopped for a blow. "It's your fault, all of it. I don't forgive you. I have friends. I know people in this town, important people. Violence follows you, mister. I hate that. You won't ever work here again."

A nurse appeared in the doorway. Her name tag said N. JARVIS. She led Janice Murphy away. "Come along now. Come along."

The elevator door closed. Mac Ryan touched my arm. "Hang tough," he said. "She's in shock and full of grief. She'll calm down."

"She's right. If they hadn't been at my—"

"They die anyway, Murdock. They ride the knife edge and they fucking die and there's not a damn thing any of us can do!"

"Maybe," I said.

"Let's go, Matthew."

We rode the elevator up, away from the Cold Room. It was a bad place to end your days. We shook hands with Mac Ryan. My hands felt clumsy, frozen. In moments like these, it was better to be a cop. Cops had a process to fall back on. Cops had police procedure. I remembered procedure from my days as a cop. In the event of a killing, gather the dead. Transport them to a cold place. Inform the next of kin. File a report.

Procedure offered comfort. I had no procedure. But I did have Bernie Dodds.

My Ford was parked where Leo had promised, in Giorgio's lot in front of the Beach Bar where Balboa angles into Coast Highway. I asked Wally to stay at my place until I took care of some business. He argued with me. Don't go, he said. This time the cops were serious.

"I'll be okay," I said.

He drove off and I leaned against my Ford. I had no energy for this. Anger buzzed through my head as I walked into Giorgio's. My eyes burned as I ordered coffee. I carried the coffee into a hallway that smelled of beer belches. In the mirror in the men's room, my face looked a hundred years old. I rinsed my face, took a deep breath. The beard needed a trim. There was a phone on the wall between the rest rooms. I phoned information and dialed Dodds, Bernard L., in Irvine. A woman answered. Music in the background, easy listening played too loud against a wall of spiked laughter and the dull drone of party conversation. The woman spoke slowly, her words on a slant, like she was under the influence of some controlled substance.

"Mrs. Dodds?"

"Speaking. But to whom am I speaking?"

"This is Sergeant Jordan, of the Irvine police. Is your son at home?"

"What?"

"This is the police. Is your son at home?"

"God. No." The voice sharpened as it came awake. "Is there a problem, Officer?"

"No problem, ma'am. A friend of his has been hurt in an automobile accident. The friend listed your son as his emergency number. We'd like to get in touch, is all. Is your son a type A?"

"Blood, you mean?"

"Yes, ma'am. We need blood."

"Oh God," she said. "When you called, I thought—"

"Is there somewhere he might be found, ma'am? I could send a unit over there?"

She covered the phone and yelled at someone. When she came back on, she said, "Try the hamburger place."

"Yes, ma'am. Would that be Carl's?"

"No," she said. "Geronimo's. What did you say your name was again?"

"Jordan," I said. "Sergeant Jordan."

"But I thought you said—"

"Let me give you my badge number, ma'am." I gave her a fake number and hung up. Irvine information had a Geronimo's Burger Palace at the corner of Irvine Center Drive and Culver. I phoned Geronimo's. Their hours were eight to midnight. It was 11:02 when I drove across the Lido Bridge.

Two patrol units from the Newport Beach PD passed me, heading toward the beach. Rolling east on the Newport Freeway, I kept checking the rearview mirror for whirling blue lights, Giordano's bird dogs. I was still shaky from the attack on my place. Adrenaline rushes swept my mind out to sea. I was up one minute, down the next, like a kid riding a merry-go-round.

To steady my head, I lined up the events of the case: Rollie Nielsen, a chemist, makes ice—maybe in Seattle, maybe in the Mojave—and then sells it to Joel. On Saturday, Rollie recruits Phyl as his substitute mule. To one up Cindy, Phyl brags, flashes the money. Cindy tells me. Cindy sees Thor's photos and wants to play junior detective. I roust Bernie, who alerts Joel. My place gets shot up. Phyl dies.

Questions hovered. Can Joel make a decision to bring in shooters? And what were the shooters on that gave them the crazy courage to risk so much? And who was Joel's boss? Who was Mr. Big?

Bernie Dodds knew. Or he knew who knew.

My mind rode a painted horse, up and down, up and down, around and around in a tight circle. I took a deep breath. Time for a charge. Time to ride in, guns blazing. Maybe Thor Nielsen was right. Maybe I should hop a plane to Seattle, start over from that end.

The 405 freeway was five lanes across southbound and five more heading north and all ten of them were in business as I took the Culver off-ramp and headed inland along the concrete corridor. Woodbridge Village was on my right, lurking behind a berm. Six lanes here on Culver, all six in business. Irvine is a city where the sidewalks roll up at 9:05 P.M. and the streets hum through the night. Rubber, asphalt, headlights, smog. This is southern California, land of the fast lane. We never stop.

At the strip center—anchor tenants, a string of shops two blocks long—everything was shut down for the night except for Geronimo's Burger Palace.

On the asphalt, forty cars were circled like wagons in a western movie. A girl on roller skates did figure eights in between the cars. She wore skintight warm-ups, hot pink, and a T-shirt that said GERONIMO'S. Her job was delivering food and drink on a gleaming tray. I parked the Ford at the edge of the circle and signaled to the skater.

In the center of the circled cars, three kids were break-dancing to a tune played on a ghetto blaster. The music was loud and ugly. Two of the kids were black, one was Anglo. The skater was at my window.

"We're closing," she said. "Twenny minnuts."

I slipped her a five. "You seen my man Bernie around?"

"Bernie who?"

"Bernie Dodds, who else?"

"Who wants him?" She tucked the five into the elastic of her warm-ups.

I gave her another five. "I'm his uncle from Phoenix. Where is he?"

"You a cop?"

"No. This is business."

She rolled her eyes. "Business. Like frigging zow."

"Well?"

She scanned the parking lot. "He was here. Just a minute ago."

"In his red Trans Am?"

"Yeah. Right. You want something?"

"A beer," I said.

"No license," she said. "Not with all these teeners."

Pot smoke hung thick on the air, but the waitress failed to see the irony. I ordered a diet Pepsi and she wheeled away, her cheeks pumping, and I eased the pickup around back of the buildings on the retail strip and came out on the other curve of the wagon circle. Still no sign of Bernie Dodds. I waited. Maybe he wasn't here.

Across the parking lot, the skater emerged from Geronimo's. Platter of burgers in one hand, tray of drinks in the other. She scanned the parking lot, saw my pickup, and started over.

In the wagon circle of cars, doors slammed and engines revved as Irvine's youth prepared to move out. Where could you escape to after a hot night at Geronimo's? A minivan backed up and I saw the Trans Am, low-slung and sexy as a lizard, with Bernie Dodds in the act of opening the driver's door. He wore gray tonight, gray jeans, gray jacket, dingy gray shirt.

The air was filled with the rumble of internal combustion engines and I thought of my own youth. We had more horsepower back then, more gas to burn up hunting for who we were. I was jerked out of my nostalgic teen memory by a patrol unit of the Irvine PD, rolling up onto the asphalt. There were two cops inside, baby-sitters here to watch the exodus at closing time.

Bad timing for me.

No way I could hammer on Bernie Dodds here, not with cops around. The Trans Am backed up, braked. A girl in basic teen black broke from a knot of kids and ran over to open Bernie's passenger door. She climbed in. Blue exhaust billowed as Bernie and his date rolled toward the exit. I followed. The Irvine patrol unit was behind me, headed the other way. My hands were tight on the wheel. Behind me, in the rearview, I saw the waitress on roller skates. My diet Pepsi was on her tray. Her fist was raised and her mouth was open as she yelled after me.

The Trans Am zoomed south on Culver, with me three cars behind. He took the freeway. I took the freeway. He zoomed up to sixty-five, then seventy, and I tromped on the gas and pulled even with him. Instant fear on his face when he spotted me, a good sign of guilt. He kicked ahead of me and I was catching up when I saw blue lights whirling in my rearview.

It was a patrol unit from the city of Irvine, only one cop this time. Black uniform, neat mustache, a guy in his early thirties, polite, deferential, calling me sir.

He checked my driver's license. Was I armed, sir? No, I was not armed. Thin smile as he asked me to follow him, please. I followed him back to the beach, to the parking lot at Fashion Island, Newport's snazzy shopping center. We sat there, not talking, in our separate vehicles. I had a feeling I was in the grip of professional courtesy. The time was after midnight.

9

I KNEW I WAS RIGHT ABOUT THE PROFESSIONAL COUR-
tesy when an unmarked car rolled up. The door opened
and out stepped Detective Giordano, beefy as a prison bull.
He showed his badge to the Irvine cop, who drove away.
Giordano grinned at me and I smelled cooked onions, stale
grease, cigarettes. His eyes glittered in the green neon.

"Out of the car. Assume the position."

I was a cop once. Some of my best friends are cops. I
understand cops. It's not smart to talk back to a cop. Smart
mouthing is stupid because cops are on edge. They get
trained to stay cool, but sometimes the work punches
through the veneer of training and they lose their cool. As a
civilian, it was my role to listen. I had smarted off once
tonight. Twice would be real dumb. I tensed when Giordano patted me down, running thick hands up my legs to
search for a weapon.

"Okay, wiseass, over to the unit."

I let him hold my arm while we walked to the unit. His
fingers were strong. He sat me in back, behind the wire
mesh, while he sat in front. I watched him pour a cup of

coffee from a thermos. I thought of bed. My windows were shattered. I had not taken the time to assess the damage. At least they hadn't burned my house down.

"Thought I told you to lay off," Giordano said.

I said nothing.

"So the first thing you do is try to muscle that kid, what's his name, Bernie. You call his house, his mama calls the Irvine PD, checking you out. I'd already alerted them. An Irvine unit spots your vehicle, now you're here. Wise up, pal. Join the twentieth century. You probably don't know we're in an information age here. We are wired in."

I said nothing. Red lips working, he sipped from the plastic cup. The coffee's rancid smell turned my stomach.

"You're dumb, Murdock. You're old and you're slow and you're dumb. A guy like you, he should look for a different line of work. You're too old to be a bouncer. Night watchman, maybe? Pimp? You could run young stuff. Like that Duke kid, hey?"

Stomach grinding, I stared at him through the wire mesh. "How you doing on finding out who killed the Murphy girl?"

"We'd be doing better if you hadn't wasted that Julio. He was our best lead and now he's on the fast escalator to Bolero Hell. You screwed up my case, playing cowboy."

I said nothing. After another five minutes of lecture, the Information Age, Cowboys, Civilians, the Hard Life of the Cop, he hauled me out of the car and leaned me against the driver's door and hit me in the stomach. One medium punch and I doubled over, bringing a big chuckle from Giordano. He hit me again. He was out of shape. We both wheezed from his effort. He was hitting me when a car pulled into the parking lot, headlights on high beam. He stood there, fat fists clenching, a tubby guy from back East trying to find himself on the beach in California. He hawked up a gob of spit and fired it at me, *splut* on my sleeve. He warned me again, one more goof and I'd lose my license, he said, and I heard his car door slam and the grinding of his starter, and then he drove away.

I levered myself to my knees. I heard voices, laughter in the distance. No Good Samaritan hurried to help. I made it to my pickup. I drove back to my place. A stranger waited for me, sitting on the stairs. It was Agent Loomis, our CIA bartender.

"Murdock?"

"Go away."

"Agent Loomis here. I heard about the shooting. A bad scene. I'm sorry, truly."

"You sound like you're really broken up about it."

He stood up. In the streetlights, his green bartender's shirt looked eerie. "Our man has left the area. Thought you should be alerted."

"What?"

"Our hitter, the alleged European professional. He's gone."

"How do you know?"

"There's been a hit."

"Where?"

"Palo Alto. That makes number ten."

"Same MO on the hit?" I said.

"Yes. A twenty-two behind the ear followed by a call to the local authorities."

"Why are you telling me?"

He handed me an envelope. "We had a deal, remember?"

"Yeah." I didn't trust this guy. He was corporate. He was smooth. He wore $60 haircuts.

"Now I'd like some time with your eyewitness."

"My eyewitness"—I pushed past him—"is dead."

"But I thought the little—"

"Her name was Phyllis Murphy. Those pricks killed her."
I dropped the envelope on the stairs. "Now get the fuck
away!"

I was close to slugging him. If he followed me up, I
would. Maybe he knew that. Maybe he knew that, because
he did not follow me up.

My motion detector was broken, shot to hell, so the spot-
light did not come on. Wally St. Moritz was asleep on the
sofa. On the floor beside the sofa a baseball bat. Good
old Wally. I covered him with a spare blanket. No need to
lock the doors, because the windows were blown out.
Someone had swept up the broken glass. Two more soup
mugs had been broken. Only three left. There were bullet
holes in the door of my fridge. I opened the door and found
a Bud Light. The bullets had not gone through the door. I
popped the top on the Bud and walked to the entertainment center, where I punched the power button on the
stereo and nothing happened. I drank a swallow of Bud
Light, strolled to the bedroom. I took Arnica.

Three beers later I was snoozing. I dreamed I was in a
ring with Detective Giordano. He was clumsy. I was quick,
murderous Murdock, fists flying. Blood sprang from his
greasy nose, daubing the white canvas with red as I
pounded him silly.

The ringing of the phone woke me. It was Louie Chen,
calling from Seattle. "Sorry to call so late, Mr. Murdock,
but I think I've unearthed a clue."

I rubbed my eyes. "What?"

"A lead," he said. "A possible clue."

"Jesus. What time is it?"

"Quite late. I apologize."

A yawn grabbed me, cracked my face. Louie Chen was in
Seattle. Maybe the air was better there. Rollie Nielsen's

dad had hired me to find out who killed his boy. A day on the job and the score was three more dead, two wounded, and half a million in property damage. "Can this wait?"

"I have some photos that seem interesting."

"What photos?"

"From Rollie's condominium, on Queen Anne. I drove over there after our talk—did I tell you about the camera?"

"What camera?"

"It's in the entry, an automatic device. When someone walks in, it takes his photo. Or hers."

"Hidden camera?"

"Yes. Top of the line."

"Okay, shoot."

"There is a woman who comes to water Rollie's plants. I have her on film."

"Terrific. And now I've got to get some sleep."

"There are also some tapes."

"Tapes?"

"Videotapes."

"From the same place?"

"From the bedroom."

"What's on them?"

"I haven't had time to view them."

"Tapes," I said.

"Half a dozen," he said. "I assumed you would want to know."

I yawned. My mind felt like the interior of a vacuum cleaner bag, filled with fuzzballs. The computer would not compute. "Could I call you back tomorrow, Mr. Chen?"

"Of course."

We hung up. I tried to sleep. Images floated at me, faces. Cindy, Dodger Cap, Giordano, Agent Loomis, Phyl Murphy, Thor, a blond hit man with a skeletal smile.

I tried to compute the new information. The hit man had

left our area. Killing number ten in Palo Alto. Photo of a female, entering Rollie's pad. Videotapes from the bedroom.

Semi-sleep is worse than no sleep. I woke with a drumming headache to smell smoke thick on the air. In the east, toward the Sierras, you could see the pale orange glow of a brushfire. I started the coffee, my own blend of Kenya Blue, Colombian, and Viennese. Wally was still asleep. Outside my house, nudged up against the yellow crime-scene ribbons, was a blue-and-white patrol unit. A shield on the driver's door said NEWPORT BEACH POLICE DEPARTMENT. The cops had me under surveillance. The word was out: Watch Murdock, wait for him to slip, haul him in. No way I could detect with cops bird-dogging me. No way to get to Bernie Dodds.

I phoned the airport. Alaska had a seat on a flight that left at 8:01. I booked the flight and phoned Louis Chen to tell him I was flying to Seattle. He said he'd meet me at the airport. Wally woke up and I told him where I was going. Look at some pictures, I said. Look at some videotapes.

"And get out of town," Wally said.

"That too."

"A capital idea. Wait until the bloodhounds tire, then you return."

Wally agreed to stick around until Zeke Amado showed up with tools and new window glass.

In his Saab Turbo, Wally drove me to John Wayne Airport, where construction crews had been at work for three years, rebuilding. In front of the terminal, TV cameras rolled and pretty ladies in orange blazers waved political placards as a handsome blond man held a press conference. The placards said: VOTE NO ON DRUGS, SEND SHELBY TO D.C. The photo on the placard showed the handsome blond man smiling a toothy smile.

"Shelby Carruthers," I said. "One of your tennis friends."

"He plays at Le Club," Wally said. "He also plays squash, racquetball, handball, baccarat. Loves to win. He is not counted among my friends."

"I like the way he bribed the Coastal Commission so he could sell off that last strip of Laguna Beach to make the money to put him into politics."

"But there's no proof," Wally said. "Just hearsay."

"Fat cat goes to Washington," I said.

"*Buen viaje,* Matthew. Have a good trip."

"Take care of Cindy for me."

"Of course."

My bird dog, the Newport Beach cop, watched me flash my boarding pass at the departure gate. A pretty girl in shorts and an orange blazer grinned at Wally as she tried to pin on a VOTE FOR SHELBY button. Wally rolled his eyes as he raised his hand in salute. I waved back. I yawned. So long, California. So long, bird dog. Maybe I could sleep on the plane.

10

A

AT SEA-TAC AIRPORT—SO NAMED BECAUSE IT serves both Seattle and Tacoma—I deplaned to find Louis Chen waiting to guide me around Rollie Nielsen's city.

Louis Chen was a surprise. From his voice on the phone I'd expected a scholarly fellow, wizened, scrawny, wearing thick glasses.

Instead, the guy who shook my hand was over six feet and whipcord lean, a jock with a shy smile and a steady gaze. Almond eyes, earring in the left ear, black hair worn long enough in back for a four-inch ponytail. Louis Chen wore a gray shirt open at the neck and black pants and tennis shoes that were white on gray, with an orange insert that said AIR SOLE.

"Mr. Murdock. Welcome to Seattle."

"Thanks."

"How was your flight?"

"Good. Better than I'd hoped."

"Do you like flying?"

"Not much. You?"

"I find it exhilarating."

A sign said DOWN FOR BAGGAGE CLAIM. Louis Chen moved well, gliding with a fluid ease that made me feel old. Tall people loomed around us, fair-skinned Scandinavians with eyes the deep ice-blue of fjords. Outside, through the windows as we waited for the baggage to arrive, I studied the Seattle sky, three shades of gray, with dark clouds scudding, blown by a westerly wind.

"That shooting last evening. It made the national news."

"You're kidding."

"No. A stringer from Los Angeles put it together for *Good Morning America*. There wasn't much hard data, I'm afraid. Just your name and an old photo and footage of broken glass. Names of the injured are being withheld."

"A girl died, Mr. Chen. She was fifteen."

"I'm sorry."

"Rollie's dad was shot. He'll be okay."

"I'm glad to hear that. Can we assume a connection?"

"Somebody did."

I kept watching him. Maybe he was in it with Rollie. Maybe not. We stood at the baggage claim in silence, waiting for the conveyor to start pumping out luggage. "The cops think Rollie was dealing drugs, Mr. Chen."

No reaction. No flinch. No reflex jerk of muscle.

"Do you see your luggage, Mr. Murdock?"

"Not yet. It's a red backpack from Eddie Bauer."

"This is his headquarters, you know. The home of the flagship store."

"I know."

"Is that it?" He pointed through the bodies toward the circular conveyor.

"Looks like it."

"Wait here, please."

Louis Chen dove through the crowd toward the conveyor. A woman turned to watch him. She was blond and intense, with frizzy hair framing a sharp, chiseled face. She wore a pink jacket and a matching skirt. Beyond her, a student type in green camouflage pants lifted his luggage off the conveyor belt. Beyond the student a man was studying me. Medium height, medium build, wearing a gray trenchcoat over a dark gray suit and half hiding behind a pillar. Louis Chen plucked my backpack up like it was balloon-light. He looked at the man in the trenchcoat, who was grabbing a suitcase, leather, with flashy buckles.

Louis Chen came back with my backpack. "Ready to go? My van's parked on six."

"Friend of yours?" I indicated the man with a jerk of my head.

"Who?"

"The guy in the gray raincoat."

He turned to look. "He watched me too."

"Ever see him before?"

"No. Never. This way, Mr. Murdock." He shouldered my backpack and led the way into the parking structure.

His vehicle was a van, white shell with green lettering that spelled out the name of his business—Perimeter Control Home Security—and a phone number with a 206 area code. The letters were painted on metal panels attached to the skin of the vehicle with Phillips-head screws. Interesting. He tossed my luggage in back. I saw a neat interior, wires smartly coiled and hanging from hooks, electronic gear on metal shelves.

"So, Mr. Chen, how come you had my name to give to Thor Nielsen?"

"Your name is in my computer, Mr. Murdock."

"You're kidding."

"Not at all. It's the way I keep up."

"Keep up with what?"

"The security business. We're growing to keep abreast of

crime. I started my files to stay ahead of the competition. Aside from the systems—sales, installation, service—I have a special interest in surveillance equipment and personal security, which spills over into bodyguards, which spills over into private investigators. To find you, I keyed in Investigators, Private, Southern California." Serious face, hands steady on the wheel.

"How do you get the information?"

"Oh, quite a lot comes over the modem. In addition, I subscribe to industry periodicals—this business spawns a new journal every month—and a clipping service for newspapers and magazine items."

"This I have to see."

"Of course. Do you use a computer in your business?"

"No."

"You really should, Mr. Murdock. I find it an indispensable tool."

Indispensable. Quintessential. Exhilarating. Louis Chen was a guy who liked big words. Back to reality. I unfolded the AAA map I'd borrowed from Wally. The U-District where Rollie Nielsen lived was north of the university, which was north of the Lake Washington Ship Canal and a body of water called Portage Bay. Half of the map was blue. Blue meant water. Water meant different transportation. I noted bridges between Seattle and Bellevue. I noted ferry terminals. Water, water, everywhere.

A quick stop at a toll booth and then we swept out along a gray curved road toward a highway sign that said INTERSTATE 5, NORTH TO SEATTLE. The speedometer read 62 miles per hour.

"This baby moves, Mr. Chen."

"I installed a turbo booster." He smiled with pleasure. "A legitimate business expense."

"The speed limit's forty-five. You're not worried about cops?"

He pointed to a fuzz-buster mounted on the dash. "This picks up radar within a radius of a mile and a half. When it beeps, I slow down."

"Nice gizmo," I said. "What does it cost?"

"It retails for around six. I got it for around three."

"Six hundred dollars?"

He nodded. "That is correct."

I sat back in my chair and watched the world zoom by and thought about money. Maybe it wasn't too late for me to get into the home security game. We took the on-ramp onto Interstate 5. More traffic here, heading north.

"You haven't asked any questions."

"About what?"

"About Rollie and the drugs."

"I wasn't sure you wished to inform me."

"The cops think he was an ice cooker."

"Ah," he said.

"You don't seem surprised."

"No. Not really."

"How come?"

"Rollie was . . . flush. His condo—you'll see what I mean soon—had to cost four hundred thousand. He paid me in cash for the security system. There was no balking at price. We used to be friends. This summer he seemed so . . . smug, overbearing, with every expression underlaid with a sly wink. He—" He broke off to look sideways at me. "That's why you're here, isn't it? You suspect that Rollie and I were—"

He didn't finish and I didn't say anything and we sat there with the ghost of Rollie Nielsen perched between us. Good work, Murdock. Real smooth.

The traffic thickened as we drove north. Louis Chen was

a good driver. He knew where his space ended, where someone else's space began. "Mr. Murdock?"

"Yes."

"I was able to locate Rollie's professor at the U-Dub. I made an appointment for tomorrow."

"Great. What's his name?"

"It's a she, I'm afraid. Professor S. O. Lindstrom. She was reluctant, I prevailed."

"Good work, Mr. Chen."

"And if you look down to your left, you'll see an envelope. In it are the photos I mentioned."

I opened the envelope to find two photos of a woman. In one she wore jeans and a parka. In the other, she wore a cape and dark slacks. She had long hair, dark in the photos. Neither shot showed her face as she bent to water the plants. You couldn't tell much about the apartment from the photos. In one photo, afternoon light bloomed through the view window. In the other, the window was curtained. Maybe she was Rollie's maid. Rollie was killed last Saturday. Today was Friday. Five days in between, two photos.

"Nice work, Mr. Chen."

"Thank you."

"How does the camera work?"

"It's an electronic device. A trip switch fires the camera as the body entering breaks a laser beam. There's a time delay of two seconds. The camera resets when the door is opened again."

"Why can't you hear it clicking?"

"Music plays," Louis Chen said. "Ever hear of Mantovani?"

"Not for a long time."

"Rollie had a bizarre sense of humor. Mantovani comes on as the door is opened, so it drowns out the shutter clicks."

"Did you install that too?"

"Yes."

"So according to the system, the lady made two visits?"

"Yes."

"Any idea when?"

"The soil was moist yesterday. It would seem probable that she was there only hours before."

"So she's got a key."

"Yes. And knowledge of the alarm cutoff."

"How did you get in, by the way?"

"Rollie had neglected to change the entry code on the keypad."

"No other visitors on the camera?"

"Not that I could ascertain."

"So there's one key loose in the area."

"That is my assumption."

He nodded. I nodded back. Not so tense now as Louis Chen identified a big sprawling complex to the left as Boeing Field. We churned up a hill, bridges bulking above us, and then we came around a long C-curve and I saw the Seattle skyline, buildings thrusting up from concrete to announce the downtown. Blackberries grew wild along the embankment. In this gray place, under this gray Seattle sky, I felt alien, off my turf.

Rollie Nielsen's U-District place was a huge three-story home converted into a rooming house at the north end of Fraternity Row near the campus. The street with big-trunked trees turning red and yellow in honor of autumn. Coeds moved along the sidewalk, red-cheeked and lovely, kicking up leaves. Looking south from here, you could see the campus of the University of Washington. Like Thor Nielsen, Louis Chen called it the U-Dub.

We circled the block a couple of times. No cops in sight,

so Louis Chen parked behind the building and we walked up the stairs to the second floor. Rollie's unit, according to Thor Nielsen, was number 2A. There was no name in the nameplate holder beside the door. I knocked. No answer. I squatted down, sweat popping out on my forehead as I broke my first law in the city of Seattle, and inserted the probes of the German lockpicker. It's electronic, battery driven, with a readout like a fuzz-buster, lots of lights when you're hot, black dial when you're not.

Clicking sounds, a soft whirring as the tiny computer assessed the lock mechanism. A green light came on. I pressed a button. There was a solid click. Presto, the lock was open.

"Impressive," said Louis Chen.

"It's great when it works."

"I read about it in a surveillance industry journal. It's quite expensive."

I swung the door open, looked into a bedroom converted into a kitchen–living room: a fridge, a hot plate, a laundry sink full of dishes. The room was L-shaped. The alcove was a closet. A small-screen TV sat on a cheap stand. The VCR was ancient, the tape deck battered. The most expensive piece of gear was a Campagnolo racing bike that hung from hooks in the ceiling. The only sound was the buzz of an electric clock, chrome-plated, on the wall next to the TV. No trip wires across the doorway. No booby trap behind the door. No smell of chemicals being cooked, but the strong odor of food rotting, on its way out.

"I understand," Louis Chen said.

"Understand what?"

"The police. They suspect the ice lab might be here."

"Right."

He gave me a look. "I'll check for an alarm."

"Be careful, okay?"

"Of course."

I checked out Rollie's cassettes: Kingston Trio and Joan Baez next to The Police, Bon Jovi, Criminal Nation, and Hammerbox. No Mantovani here. In the alcove was a student bookshelf made of bricks and lumber, paperbacks on the top two rows, hardbacks to the floor.

The hardbacks were chemistry and biology, fat textbooks crammed with technical lore. A vertical unit on the textbook shelf held pamphlets from Greenpeace, Big Green, and Eco Evergreen. There were books on saving the environment: rain forests, pollution, acid rain, recycling. Among the paperbacks was a copy of *A Tale of Two Cities*. Remembering Gaspard, I tucked the book into my jacket pocket.

Next to the environmental pamphlets I found post office receipts dating back to May. The destination address was Greenwood Station, a P.O. box in Seattle. I folded the receipts and tucked them inside the Dickens paperback.

At the end of the apartment, the narrow living room made a turn into a tight little kitchen where a door opened out onto a small balcony. Chaise longue here, a rack holding an empty bottle of Coppertone, three spent Heineken bottles, and a short stack of magazines. The magazine on top was a professional police magazine. The lead story was called "Fighting Ice: Drug for the Year 2000."

Mildew smell in the bathroom. On the wall were centerfolds of three *Playboy* Playmates, two blondes, one brunette.

"No sign of any alarm," Louis Chen said from the doorway.

"How much you think the electronic gear is worth?"

"Two thousand, perhaps less. In today's market, the stereo is an antique. Likewise for the television. Quite different from his Queen Anne affluence."

"Two houses," I said. "Two sets of gear."

"But no ice lab."

The bedroom contained one double bed, a dresser, a narrow desk, photos, and one piece of art on the wall. The art was a painting of a street scene, gray streets and gray buildings, and in a plate-glass window a slash of red for the setting sun. The signature was St. Cl——.

A framed photo on the dresser showed Thor Nielsen, a blond woman, and two kids. The boy, eleven years or so, had a face like Rollie Nielsen in his college photo. The girl had long blond pigtails.

On the wall above the dresser, pinned by a red pushpin, was a Polaroid of a woman in dancer's tights. The camera had caught her at the ballet rail, right heel resting on the rail as she bent at the waist, arms reaching forward. In the black leotard, her body looked curvy, lush. Her face was hidden by her outstretched arms.

I pocketed the Polaroid.

In the corner by the window was a desk. On top of the desk was a Macintosh computer. Louis Chen turned it on, a cute *beep beep beep* as it warmed itself up. A little hand pointed to a question mark and kept on pointing.

"What have you got, love letters?"

"Formulas. I'm not the chemist Rollie was, but it looks like organic, with those triple bonds."

I looked at the screen. "All I know about chemistry is that the right formula in the hands of the right brewmeister makes beer."

"Perhaps I should make some printouts."

"Suit yourself."

A buzz as the printer started, then the sound of it, zipping across the page. I went through the bedroom drawers. No address book, no business cards. A cheap camera. I had two drawers to go when I heard car doors slamming in the street outside. Through the window I saw two patrol units, white with blue trim, of the Seattle PD. Backup units, waiting for the officer in charge.

"Cops," I said. "Turn that thing off."

He flipped the switch and the screen went dark. He ripped off the computer roll, folded it. As we left the apartment, I noticed he carried a stack of computer discs. Locking the door, I remembered the camera. Too late. No time to go back. Louis Chen's eyes were jumpy and his chest was heaving. When you're trapped, the impulse is to run like hell. Take the stairs four at a time. But that's dumb. I am a professional. I forced myself to take deep breaths.

"Count your breaths," I said. "Walk slow."

"I am extremely nervous," he said. "Extremely."

My heart hammered against my rib cage as we made our descent. Outside, through the cheapo chintz curtain stretched across the front-door window, I could see the uniforms, shirts of royal blue, navy blue pants, as the officers stood in the street adjusting their belts, guns, walkie-talkies. By the time they reached the front door, we were in Louis Chen's vehicle, easing east on 50th Street. He made two loops and we were heading west again. He drove under the freeway. I took a deep breath.

"Mr. Murdock, I congratulate you on your timing."

"Cutting it close, you mean?"

"Precisely that, yes."

We drove along. I decided to come clean. "I didn't mean to cut it that close, Mr. Chen."

"Really?" He looked disappointed.

"Really."

"It was better than any film," he said. "It was . . . stimulating."

"I can't believe Thor gave them the address."

"Perhaps they traced Rollie through the university police. They are quite thorough."

"Good thought." I checked my map of Seattle. "Where's Rollie's penthouse from here?"

"Queen Anne Hill." He pointed to a spot on the map near Seattle Center. "Not far."

11

ON THE DRIVE TO QUEEN ANNE HILL, LOUIS CHEN showed me the security beeper he'd sold Rollie Nielsen. It was the size of a pack of Marlboros, with a little red light that came on when an intruder broke the security beam.

"Has a solid feel," I said.

"Top of the line," he said.

"Where was it?"

"On Rollie's coffee table."

"How long have you had it?"

"Since yesterday, when I found the photos."

"The little girl with the pigtails, that was Rollie's sister?"

"Yes."

"Did you know her?"

"No. She died when he was in high school."

"And the mother?"

"Rollie's mother was sick when I first met Rollie. She stayed in bed quite a lot. The doctors couldn't agree on a diagnosis. The only reason he went to graduate school was to learn enough so he could discover a cure to save her."

"Looks like he got sidetracked."

Rollie Nielsen's condo on Queen Anne Hill was light-years away from his gradpad walkup on Fraternity Row. The building was called the Queen's Arms, a reference, no doubt, to Queen Anne, for whom the hill was named. It was a ten-story structure in the pricey section of a pricey neighborhood, a pinnacle on a choice hilltop with views to the south and west. The elevator was smooth. Louis Chen punched in the combination for the front door. Music came on as we entered, Mantovani, to blanket the click of the camera. He marched to a control panel to punch in the code to disarm the alarm.

"One camera's there." He pointed to a recessed fixture in the ceiling. "Another one across the room. This turns them off." He flipped the endmost switch on the panel of light switches. "The installation tested my powers of invention."

"Nice gadget."

From the corner of the penthouse living room, you could see downtown Seattle and beyond that majestic Mount Rainier. To the west was Puget Sound. Beyond the Sound rose the Olympic Mountains, their jagged tops dusted with powdered-sugar snow.

The walls of the penthouse were stark white. The floor was a chessboard for giants, black squares and white squares, three feet across. The living room had a balcony with access through French doors. The furniture was white, highlighted by pillows. All the pillows were bloodred. The electronic gear was indeed First Cabin. Nakamichi CD, Bang & Olufsen stereo, a wall-sized Sony TV with three VCRs. The music duplicated the stuff from the U-District, but here there was more heavy metal, more acid rock. In a locked cabinet beneath the TV I found three-dozen videotapes with names like *Debbie Does Aruba, Miss Darling's Darlings,* and *Fleshdance 2000.*

In a drawer of the slick ebony entertainment center I found maps of Seattle, Greater Seattle, Orange County, Newport Beach, San Diego, San Diego Area, and cities around San Francisco and the Bay Area. In another drawer I found a stack of business cards bound by a rubber band. Half a dozen were cards from real estate brokers. On the back of one card was a note, written in blue ballpoint: *Mr. Nielsen. Have buyer at $450,000. 30-day escrow. Please call!* I pocketed the stack.

The kitchen was white with black appliances—stove, fridge, dishwasher, microwave. Beer in the fridge, a half bottle of Tanqueray gin, ice cubes, and some frozen TV dinners. The toaster and electric can opener and coffee maker were red. The decor was eerie: black, white, red. He showed me the security system, trippers and infrared gizmos and timers and an arming box that belonged on the bridge of the starship *Enterprise*.

"The video footage," I said. "He shot that in the bedroom?"

"Yes. It's this way."

Rollie's bedroom was Bachelor Pad Decadent. King-size bed with black silk sheets. A vibrating chaise. A hot tub covered with platinum quilted fabric to hold in the heat. On the ceiling above the bed was a huge mirror. The painting on the wall depicted a fantasy scene, a space serpent, scaly, with pea-green eyes, coiled around the naked body of a beauteous blonde.

"This is a test, Mr. Murdock. If you were a lusty young bachelor, rich, reveling in your manhood, where would you mount your video camcorders?"

"Two of them, right?"

"Yes."

"Okay, I'm betting the overhead mirror is two-way. One camera there."

He nodded, but said nothing.

I moved to the wall to the right of the bed. I pulled aside the painting. Behind it was a hole in the wall. In the hole you could see the round snout of the video camcorder.

"It took me quite a bit longer," Louis Chen said.

"Yeah. But because of you, I knew what to look for."

"That's very gracious of you."

"The videotapes you mentioned, were they X-rated?"

"Yes. Rollie and a number of women."

I showed him the photo of the woman in leotards. "Look at this while I check out the closet."

"Very well."

Rollie's closet, a big walk-in, contained a dozen suits with labels like Brooks Brothers, Klopfensteins, Hart Schaffner & Marx. There were jock clothes, boxes of new tennies, baseball shoes with cleats, three new pairs of Air Soles still in their boxes. Inside a garment bag at the back of the closet I found play clothes: teddies, bustiers, garter belts, crotchless panties, filmy brassieres.

Rollie had money. Rollie spent money. I left the closet. Louis Chen stood at the window, looking out. "She looks familiar," he said. "Most of the women on the tapes wore masks. Where did you get this?"

"Took it off the wall above the dresser in the U-District."

"Perhaps when you view the tapes."

"Yeah," I said. "Is there an answer machine?"

"Yes."

"Let's get the tape. Might be something on it."

I got the tape. We left the condo. Going down in the elevator, Louis Chen asked me a question: "Doesn't it bother you?"

"What's that?"

"Invading someone's home, going through someone's possessions. It made me feel somewhat like a thief."

"I don't take money or jewels. I take stuff that might help me with the case. If I have the chance, I'll return the stuff."

"The file says you were a policeman."

"I was. For about a year. Why?"

"You have an air of thoroughness when you search a place. As if you were following your nose. As if you knew exactly what you were after."

I smiled. The elevator came to a stop. We walked out into the crisp October air. Off to the west, the wind had sliced a hole in the gray, letting through a swatch of blue sky. "It may look that way," I said. "But I'm just poking around."

"This is fascinating," said Louis Chen. "I have much to learn."

It rained on us as we drove toward Louie Chen's office. I was lost again. Gray buildings here, gray sky, dark gray asphalt on the streets and against the gray a brilliant splash of color as the sun came out, washing the afternoon with magic. It was early afternoon in Seattle. I was nowhere with the case.

"Any investigatory conclusions, Mr. Murdock?"

"Just the obvious stuff."

"Please? I'm quite curious."

"The condo's a playpen, a bachelor fantasy come true. Silk sheets to impress the ladies. A foothold in a hot real estate market. The area maps could connect us to Rollie's sales turf." I showed him the broker's card with $450,000 penciled in.

"So Rollie was selling out and moving to California?"

"It's a good guess."

"Fascinating." Louis Chen turned a corner. We were heading up the hill. "May I try my hand at deducing?"

"Fire away."

"The rooms on Fraternity Row are a facade, a mask. There, Rollie posed as a graduate student to deceive his father. The photos were there, the chemistry texts."

"The smells."

He stopped for a red light. "Am I still a suspect, Mr. Murdock?"

I grinned. "Less and less, Mr. Chen."

"Is there something I can do to help the process along?"

"A beer would do wonders."

"Ah." He grinned at me. "I'm most curious to know about the paperback book that protrudes from your coat pocket."

I pulled out the copy of *A Tale of Two Cities*. I briefed Louis Chen on Gaspard and my Turf War scenario, coke dealers versus ice cookers. "Let's say you're a Medellín master of coke. You spend ten years carving out a piece of the drug market. You bribe customs people, judges, politicians. Then along comes a gang of ex-cons and college boys and they're selling a hot new drug called ice, cutting into your sales. It's cooked in America, so they don't have to fool with customs agents. What would you do?"

"Fight for my territory, I suppose."

"Me too."

"I'm also curious. How does Gaspard fit in?"

"It doesn't." I closed the book.

"But you're hopeful, correct?"

"Eternally, Mr. Chen."

The front of Louis Chen's building faced Phinney Avenue. Next door was an upscale Mexican restaurant, the Santa Fe Cafe. My stomach rumbled, reminding me how long it had been since breakfast. The building to the south was Phinney Ridge Heating and Cooling.

A girl working behind the plate-glass window of the

Santa Fe Cafe waved at Louis Chen and he waved back. She was blond and rosy-cheeked and healthy-looking.

"That's Estelle."

"I think she likes you."

"You do?" The guy was blushing.

The exterior of his building was gray clapboard with white trim. A sign on the front door said: PERIMETER CONTROL HOME SECURITY. His office was downstairs, his digs upstairs. He unlocked his front door and stepped aside so I could go in first. Neat reception area, like the inside of his van. Gray carpet here, contemporary furniture that looked comfortable.

He tossed my backpack onto the sofa and led me into his office. Neat here, too. Two computers, a Mac and a Leading Edge. Three chairs for clients, a big gray desk for the boss, a wooden filing cabinet, gleaming oak, right out of the past. He turned on a computer. It beeped to say it was ready. He clicked a couple of keys and a screen came up with my name on it. *Matt Murdock, Private Investigator. Newport Beach, California.* There were cross-references to my time with Uncle Sam and the LAPD. And a list of newspaper sources, mostly the *L.A. Times* and the *Orange County Tribune.*

"So if I wanted more information in depth," Louis Chen said, "I could access that by modem."

"How many private eyes do you follow?"

"At the moment, forty-seven."

"Just because there are links to the security business?"

He blushed. He had a poet's face, sensitive, on the edge of being delicate, and when he blushed he lost ten years and turned into a kid again. "I have a confession, Mr. Murdock."

"Shoot."

"My big dream is to become a sleuth. A private eye."

"You're kidding."

"I'm dead serious. It's the only reason I'd ever burgle private property. Look at my bookshelves."

I looked. In alphabetical order on the shelves I saw a huge collection of detective fiction, names like Chandler, Christie, Hammett, Macdonald, Marsh, Sayers. An entire shelf was devoted to back issues of a magazine called *Black Mask.*

"Take my advice, Mr. Chen. Stay with home security."

"Everyone says that. Especially my parents."

"Oh?"

He nodded. "My mother wants me to be an artist. My father thinks I should follow in his footsteps and become a scholar of Chinese literature. Would you like to see the videotapes? They are this way."

He opened a door that said SYSTEMS, PRIVATE, and we were in a world of electronic gear. Buzzers, whistles, sirens, chimes, alarms, lights. His economy system cost $500, installed. His Executive Alert started at $5,000 and went right up, depending on the number and variety of bells, whistles, and remote beepers.

"You do all your installations?"

"Not anymore. Most of my time's spent selling and troubleshooting in the aftermarket. I have this network of techies who need the work."

"You sound pretty busy."

"A sign of our times, the backlog is awesome."

"Can you afford to take Friday off?"

"Mr. Murdock, I would not have missed this. Not a single minute. I am, as they say, all ears."

He punched a button to activate the VCR and a picture swam into view on the screen, a woman in a garter belt, high heels, a see-through bra, a mask, and a transparent raincoat. She was curvy, with straight black hair and olive skin, and she was dancing, shoulders shaking and dark hair flying. A man in a mask lay in bed, watching. There was no sound.

"I identified seven females," Louis Chen said. "Six brunettes and one blonde."

"Are they all masked?"

"Yes. One other thing. The footage on the blond female seemed not to be shot at the condo."

"How tough is it to pull some prints off the tape?"

"Simple enough, since I have that equipment."

The woman had joined the man on the bed. I yawned. I was not in the mood for home-video porn. "I should get a motel, Mr. Chen."

His face narrowed in a frown. "I assumed you would stay here, as my guest. Your room is all ready."

"I like to be on my own."

"Mr. Murdock, I insist."

I looked at him. He was a young guy on the way up, serious, hungry to be a private eye. If you worship private eyes, you're hard up for heroes. "Are you sure?"

"Positive."

"Okay. But no more of this Mr. Murdock stuff. My name's Matt."

"Call me Louie."

"Okay. Louie."

He stood up. "I could use some exercise after all the indoor work. How about you?"

"Looks like rain," I said. "Maybe I could have a beer instead, analyze those tapes while you exercise."

Louie Chen laughed. He tossed me a Husky sweatshirt and pointed me up the stairs. I felt soggy. Too many loose ends on this case and the real problem was south of here in California. When I came down, dressed for running, he handed me a spare house key.

We were pals.

12

I T WAS LATE AFTERNOON, THE GRAY NORTHWEST TWI-
light pressing down like moth wings, as Louie Chen parked
the van in the QFC lot. QFC means Quality Food Center.
Next door was a 76 station. Across the street was a sign that
said TOPLESS GIRLS, NOON TO MIDNIGHT. "Welcome to peaceful
Ballard," he said.

"It's cold, Louie. I can see my breath on the air."

"Come on." Louie looked loose, like a jock in peak con-
dition.

We ran west along 85th Street, getting honked at by
young blond ladies in large GM cars, Buicks and Chevys
and Oldsmobiles, and Louie Chen waved at them and they
honked some more and then zoomed off in clouds of black
exhaust, large-bottomed vehicles filling the street. At the
end of 85th, he led me down a long flight of stone stairs and
into a rain forest that dripped with silver Seattle mist, and
then through a park where the leaves were wild, scarlet and
canary fighting deep autumn brown.

We crossed an asphalt road that snaked its way down the
same hill in switchbacks, and into a tunnel that ran beneath

a railroad track and we came out of the tunnel onto a beach, Golden Gardens was the name, and we turned left and ran along the beach past a boat-launching area where men in yellow slickers stood around smoking and chewing the fat. This was Shilshole, Louie Chen said, a dock with a spectacular view, sharp-peaked mountains, the swooping sea gulls, a woman on a boat wearing a Husky sweatshirt, a man watching her through binoculars from the deck of a sailboat called *Viking XVII*.

I was tired but we ran on, curving past waterfront eateries, Charlie's and Anthony's Home Port and Ray's and the Azteca, and the road curving, boats on the water to our right, a sleek yacht just getting under way and a powerboat gunning past.

On the return trip, just to test me, Louie Chen picked up the pace. By the time we reached his van I was hurting.

"How far was that?"

"Five miles." He started up. "I trimmed the distance today."

"Thanks."

Back at his place, he gave me first shower while he went to his darkroom. My heart rate returned to normal. The blood sang through my veins. I was no longer sleepy. My room had a view of the Cascade Mountains. For a midafternoon snack we ordered pizza from Domino's. Turned out we liked the same toppings: Italian sausage, pepperoni, green pepper, mushrooms, anchovies, extra sauce, extra cheese. Louie Chen ate four pieces. I ate two. For gritty entertainment, we watched Rollie's videotapes, dancing and stripteases leading to some sweaty coupling on the bed. With the brunettes, Rollie was on top, macho man in the missionary position. With the blonde, he shifted gears while she spanked him, popped his rump with a baby bullwhip.

The blonde wore a black leather shirt with cuff links that glittered. Grainy images on this video, which had been shot at the U-Dub pad.

Outside, the gray had given way to a spectacular sunset. This Rainier beer was not bad. For the first time since my arrival, I felt a tiny kinship with Seattle. In the back of my mind, I still wondered about Louie Chen and the man at Sea-Tac.

The tapes were done. I was on my third Rainier and feeling no pain and Louie Chen, waving his second Rainier in the air, was telling me about his career plans: to sell the security business for a fat profit, use the money to open his detective agency. I told him he was crazy. He was arguing the merits of the Louis B. Chen Detective Agency when Rollie's security beeper sounded.

"Come on!"

"Right behind you."

It was ten minutes from Louie Chen's office to Rollie Nielsen's penthouse on Queen Anne Hill. Tilting on the corners, blasting past traffic signals and stop signs, we made the trip in seven minutes. Clutching his walkie-talkie, he parked around the corner and hurried into the building while I did an inventory of the cars on the street. Volvo, 740, gray. Volvo, 244, white. Honda Civic, white. Honda Accord, gray flannel. Pickup, Ford, Idaho plates. Olds, early eighties, brown, dent in left rear fender. Ford Fairlane, Oregon plates.

A cold wind hit the back of my neck and I shivered. I was wearing my Levi jacket, okay for California, but thin for Seattle. Should have brought my down vest. I headed back for the van.

It was warmer out of the wind. I rubbed my hands together, blew on my fingers. October weather in Seattle was

February weather in California. The walkie-talkie crackled and I pressed the Talk button. "Murdock here."

"Louie here. The subject is exiting now. Do you copy?"

"That's a roger. Who is it?"

"The plant lady," he said. "Female Caucasian, dark hair, wearing a parka, jeans, boots. She's tall and, well, beautiful."

"Good work."

Ten seconds later he came around the corner, running for the van. He tossed me his walkie-talkie and leaped up behind the wheel. With a grin at me, he said: "She is quite attractive."

"Is that the same as beautiful?"

He nodded as he started up. To our right I saw a figure in a parka climbing into the Oldsmobile with the dent. Washington license tag H-121-30.

The Oldsmobile pulled out and we followed. She drove down the hill, made a left, then a right. Louie Chen described the area as Lower Queen Anne. Mountain view here, but no water. Up ahead, the Olds showed a left blinker and turned into a driveway that led to a covered parking area. The building was a three-story brick. The address was 805. While he waited, I hustled through the drizzle into the parking structure to find the Olds parked in slot 307. If the parking slots correlated with the units, each floor had ten apartments. Across the parking garage, a red sign said ELEVATOR. I rode the elevator to the first floor, where I checked the mailboxes. Number 307 was St. Cloud. No first name, no initial. Just the two words, St. Cloud.

St. Cl——, like the initials on that painting in Rollie's U-District apartment. Signature of the artist.

We sat outside the building of Mademoiselle St. Cloud until ten o'clock. Louie Chen dozed. I did not. I could never sleep on a surveillance. Her apartment looked down on the street. Twice I saw her move across the window. Louie Chen had a pal in the Seattle DMV office. Now that we had her license number, we could find out her full name, her phone, her height, weight, birth date. At 10:01 I said I'd had enough and Louie drove back to Phinney Ridge. He dropped me off at his place, and then, jazzed by the thrill of the hunt, he headed back to keep watch.

The rain fell heavier as I jogged to his front door. If October was this cold, what would December be? Or January?

I used the spare key. Nice and warm in here. In the kitchen, I found beer and wine but no whiskey. I poured myself a glass of Washington State red, Seattle's answer to Mondavi of California. Not bad. In the bathroom, I stripped down. I stayed in the shower until there was no more hot water. I dried off and put on a T-shirt and clean jeans and a pair of Louie Chen's warm boot socks and crawled into bed.

While the bed warmed, I pulled out the stack of business cards I'd found at Rollie Nielsen's condo. It was a half-inch thick. The card with the $450,000 number belonged to Magda Arntson, Windermere Realty. The next one was George Fuchs, Evergreen Realty. Then Coldwell Banker, then ERA, then Seattle bankers, then California real estate brokers, two in Newport Beach, one in Laguna. I did not recognize the names. The last six cards were duplicates: Chick Dickens, Insurance Adjuster, with a P.O. box in Loma Linda and a phone number with a 714 area code.

Loma Linda was out by Redlands and San Berdoo. Another Chick Dickens was the author of *A Tale of Two Cities*. Brother to Gaspard? I wrapped the rubber band around the cards and turned off the light.

Someone was shaking my arm. It was Louie Chen. He was excited, wide grin, eyes dancing a jig. He'd been watching the lady from Rollie's penthouse. He was bursting. He wanted to talk.

"Talk? What about?"

"The case, Matt. How it's developing. I've got some notions I need to test out."

"What notions?"

"St. Cloud is French, right?"

"It's a racetrack in France. A town in Minnesota."

"How's this?" He snapped his fingers. "Minnesota thoroughbred."

I rubbed my face. "What time is it?"

"It's early." He checked his watch and paced around. "Four-forty." His energy zapped the room. "Is surveillance always this stimulating? The possibilities, I mean."

"Always," I said.

"Did you see her walk?"

"No."

"It's sultry. It's purposeful. It's . . ."

"Do I see Louie in love?"

"What?" Silly grin on his face. "What do you mean?"

I pulled the covers up to my chin. I closed my eyes. He paced, talking, his voice fading as I drifted off. When I woke up, pale blue light filtered through the windows. I climbed out of bed. Louie Chen was not in the bed in his bedroom. He was sprawled on the sofa in the living room, smiling as he slept.

I started the coffee. It was done when I came out of the bedroom, dressed for the day. Louie Chen bounced awake, checking his watch, talking about our mystery lady while he brushed his teeth. Then we divided our PI duties. I would check with Rollie's chemistry prof at the university. Louie would keep watch on his newest heartthrob, Mademoiselle St. Cloud.

Strengthened by coffee and a Danish from Larsen's Bakery, a local outfit, I took a cab to the U-Dub.

13

PROFESSOR S. O. LINDSTROM WAS BLOND, LATE thirties, with hazel eyes and a nervous look behind the blue-tinted glasses. She wore a white lab coat over a tweed skirt. The medium heels made her eyes level with mine.

The corridors echoed with an empty sound as we walked along. It was Saturday. Smell of chemicals here, something always cooking on the Bunsen burner. I handed her Louie Chen's card, explained that I was his associate. The professor did not smile. She led me into her office, a cubicle the size of my bathroom back in Newport Beach. She indicated a chair and checked her wristwatch. Her wrists were lean, the skin pale. Nothing on the desktop except a coffee mug used as a pencil holder. Clean lady. She crossed her legs and lit a cigarette.

"As I told your associate over the phone, Mr., ah, Murdock, I've already spoken to the police about this."

"Not about this, Professor." I tossed a stack of photos onto the desk. I waited while she went through them, no expression on her face. When she finished, she stacked them up, edges aligned, then looked at me. Deep crease in her forehead, eyes narrowed to slits.

"What is it you want? Money?"

"Not money. Tell me about Rollie Nielsen."

"What do you want to know?"

"What kind of guy he was. What he was working on. How you got to know him. Anyone you know who had it in for him."

"His project wasn't a methamphetamine derivative with the street name of ice, if that's what you mean." She waved at the door, the corridor beyond. "The lab's not here."

"How did you meet?"

"I'm on his thesis committee. I have to pass on what he does for his doctorate."

"Was he finished with course work?"

"Last summer. All he had left was his dissertation."

"What was his project?"

"Personal research. His mother died of something rare, a variation on Lou Gehrig's disease. Rollie—I mean Roland —was searching for the miracle cure."

"How far along was he?"

She stabbed out her cigarette, got up from the chair, and walked to the window, where she stood looking out, her arms folded across her chest. "What are you going to do with those photos?"

"Tell me what you know and they're yours."

"The negatives?"

"Included."

"How does this man, Mr. Chen, fit in?"

"He was a college roommate of Rollie's."

"Where is he?"

"Working."

"All right." She turned to stare at me. "We were intimate, Roland and myself. We are adults. No crime was committed. I'm shocked by the photos. I had no idea he was . . . taping us. I find, however, on further reflection, that it was not totally unexpected. He had a dark side, I suppose you'd say, that's what attracted me to him. All those out-of-town trips . . . I knew there were other women. The fact that there were so many rather"—she paused to hunt for the precise word—"rather unnerves me. At the same time, it makes the situation, *my* situation, quite ludicrous. I feel foolish. I feel used. His lustiness attracted me, touched a chord, as they say. I'm sick he's dead. The police wouldn't say how he died." Her eyes looked the question.

With my index finger I pointed to the spot behind my left ear. "Some twenty-two slugs, Professor, one right here."

Her face did not change. Her eyelids flickered, drawing shutters across her mood. "How awful." It took her a minute to regroup. "Where did he die?"

"California. In a motel on the beach."

"The tan," she said. "That's where you're from. California."

"You should be a detective, Professor."

"All scientists are detectives, Mr. Murdock."

"What can you tell me about ice?"

"I've read about it. I haven't actually made any. What would you like to know?"

"How tough is it to cook? What kind of equipment would you need? How big a place?"

She ran a hand along the side of her cheek. She took a deep breath. "The process is quite simple. You'd need beakers and a heat source, some rudimentary safety devices. I understand that labs have been established in bedrooms, basements, motel rooms, mobile homes."

"Rollie Nielsen was a chemist. That should make it easier, right?"

Her smile was cool and professional. "Like falling off a log, as they say. Roland's strength was his willingness to explore, to hold the tried-and-true methods up to the light. There is a very good chance—and I did not tell this to the police—that he could have developed a new process. Faster. Safer. More streamlined." She tucked the photos into a desk drawer. She closed the drawer. "Would there be anything else?"

"Did you give the cops Rollie's address? The place near the university?"

"Yes."

"Did you know he had a second place? A condo on Queen Anne?"

"No." Her face registered bleak surprise.

I stood up. The interview was over. "Thank you, Professor."

She spoke as I put my hand on the doorknob. "Mr. Murdock?"

"Yes?"

"When you find the person who killed him, I hope you deal with him harshly."

I nodded. I said nothing. I went out, leaving her alone. I found my way back down the corridor.

Outside, with the rain drifting down, I thought I saw her watching me from a third-floor window. Blond lady, white lab coat, Ph.D., books and articles and slick leather shirt and a baby bullwhip and an appetite, buried under that cool Nordic exterior, for wild wild lust.

Shivering in the wet, I hiked west to University Ave. to call a cab to take me to our Saturday surveillance outpost on Lower Queen Anne.

Louie Chen and I spent Saturday afternoon with Mademoiselle St. Cloud. We sat outside her apartment house in

Louie Chen's van in the low-rent district of Lower Queen Anne Hill. We were waiting to hear from his buddy at the Seattle DMV for an identity to go with the license plate on the Olds. Raindrops slid down the windshield. The sky was Seattle gray. He'd removed the PERIMETER CONTROL panels and replaced them with panels painted the same color as his van.

"Louie," I said. "You've got a criminal mind."

"Why?"

"Those panels, plain white. A very sharp idea."

His grin widened. He was getting to know me. "Part of the detective's protective coloration. My next purchase is a German lockpick like yours." There was a pause. "You think I'm being foolish, don't you?"

"About what?"

"Wanting to open my own detective agency."

"There's more money in the home security game."

"But this is hot, Matt. It's real. It's interesting, it's consuming, it's so—"

"Is there more coffee?"

He poured me a half cup from his thermos. He'd brought along some files from the cabinet in his office. He had files on my opposite numbers, private eyes in L.A., Phoenix, Austin, Houston, New Orleans, Miami, New York, Boston, Chicago, Cleveland. He had a PI file and a case file and a villain file and a victim file.

I was impressed with Louie Chen's memory. He knew names, court dates, villains and victims, terms of sentencing of my cases. He knew stuff about me that I'd forgotten. I yawned and stretched. Too much coffee, too many memories crowding in. Blazer. Cindy. Jane. Meg. Roxanne. Kathy. Time for a pit stop.

I don't like working surveillance. You drink too much coffee and then you have to pee. An old cop at Hollenbeck in L.A. taught me the first rule of successful surveillance: finding a toilet. There was one at a gas station two blocks away. I went first. When I came back, jogging up the hill in the gray afternoon, I saw exhaust pumping from Louie Chen's tailpipe. Beyond the van I could see the Oldsmobile of Mademoiselle St. Cloud heading down the hill.

"Hurry, Matt. Hurry!"

While we tailed her Louie Chen devised a plan of approach that made him the knight in shining armor: "We follow the subject until the right moment arises. I envision a downtown street, not too crowded. Playing the bad guy, you harass her. I shall come charging in, Zorro to the rescue. We shall do some shoving. Do you know how to fall?"

"I know how to fall."

"Karate?"

"A little."

"Excellent. Good. Following our improvised altercation you'll limp away while I calm the subject with a Starbuck's latte. Things will move along, latte to lunch, lunch to dinner. I'll keep you informed, of course, as to progress."

"How will you find out about her connection to Rollie?"

"I haven't come to that yet."

"Let me know, okay?"

"You're not happy with my plan?"

"When you break your cover, the lady will not be happy."

"I've thought of that. Give me a minute."

"Okay."

"Look," Louie said. "Ms. St. Cloud is my age, a member of my generation. Instinct tells me things will work out."

"Good luck, Louie."

"So is it okay?"

"I do the masher routine. You rescue her. She swoons. I got it."

"Are you sure you can fall convincingly?"

"Trust me, Louie. I know how to fall."

We were headed downtown, where the streets ran at funny angles and I tried to pay attention to the names. Westlake. Stewart. Olive Way. Pine. Fifth. Pike. Union. Pylons down the center of a one-way street, Louie Chen still talking, and the shadow of a monorail sliding along overhead. I felt like a rat in a maze. We followed her up a hill to a parking garage, SATURDAY, ALL DAY, $4.

Louie Chen dropped me off and I walked past a fountain into the lobby and spotted the elevator and the stairs. Benihana restaurant on one side, a drugstore newsstand on the other. I heard footsteps on the stairs and stepped out of sight. She passed me. She wore the parka from the photos, boots and jeans. Under one arm she carried an artist's portfolio. Louie Chen was right: She had a good walk, an easy way of moving. In the boots, she was tall, five-nine, maybe five-ten. Her dark hair hung down her back in a thick French braid.

Good walk, neat lady.

She turned west out of the building and I followed her down the hill. Louie Chen caught up to us and drove on by, looking worried. We crossed some busy streets—Second Avenue, First Avenue—that ran parallel to the gray water. Big signs beckoned me to Pike Place Market. The lady did not go there. She went instead to a warehouse overlooking some railroad tracks. A sign in letters three feet high said this was the Art Institute. She went in.

On the walkie-talkie, Louie Chen directed me up the street and I joined him in the van. He was talking on the cellular phone, making notes as he nodded. He finished talking, thanked the caller, and hung up.

"Are you wondering how I knew where to find you?"

"Okay. How did you find me?"

"The portfolio. It led me by deduction to the Art Institute."

"You think she's an artist?"

"I always knew it. From the beginning."

I indicated his notes. "Who was on the phone?"

"My friend at the DMV." He read from his notebook. "Her name's H. L. St. Cloud. There's no clue what those initials stand for. Residence listed at that address on Queen Anne. Her age—calculated from the birth date—is thirty-three. I'm surprised, since she looks younger. I'll be thirty next month. Hmm. Where was I?"

"Vital statistics."

"Her height is five-ten, her weight one thirty-four. She's required to wear corrective lenses when driving. Parking tickets, six so far this year, and she's got one speeding violation, fifty-two mph. Mine was not the first inquiry on her."

"Who else wants to know?"

"The Seattle police."

"When?"

"Late last evening."

"Did you get a name on the inquiring officer?"

"I overlooked that. Want me to call back?"

"Wouldn't hurt."

His face sagged. "I have a lot to learn, don't I?"

"You're doing great, Louie. Hang in there."

14

THE AFTERNOON SLIPPED AWAY. LOUIE WENT FOR hamburgers and came back with fish and chips. Changed his mind, he said. He told me about the first woman in his life, a blonde named Myra. She was married, early thirties. Louie was fifteen, working as a sack boy at the QFC, and Myra smiled at him and he fell in love in the rain in the parking lot with his arms full of groceries. Talking about her turned his voice rough with memory.

I filled him in on the loose ends from southern California: Bernie, Joel, Phyl, Los Boleros, Detective Giordano, Agent Loomis, the alleged European hit man. A black Buick drove by. Something clicked in my head. Had it been by before?

At 3:30 Louie left me in the van and went inside the Art Institute. He was gone fifteen minutes. He came back with a report. Mademoiselle St. Cloud was the instructor in a life drawing class. The model was nude. "How do you feel about art, Murdock?"

"I'm partial to nudes."

"Me too." He was blushing. "I thought I'd be the Chinese Michelangelo when I was a kid. I drew all the time, sketches and diagrams and stick figures. I took art in college. There was this blonde named Krista Jorgensen who set up her easel next to mine. Krista could draw with her eyes closed. I decided, watching her, that I was cut out for something else."

"At least you went to college."

"You didn't?"

"I was a high school dropout."

"I should have done that."

"Done what?"

"Should have dropped out, joined the army, seen the world."

The black Buick slid by again, Washington plates, tinted windows. "That's four times," I said.

"You joined the army four times?"

"No. Four times for that black Buick."

"What black Buick?" He adjusted his rearview mirror. "Where? I see it. I missed it." He slapped his thigh. "Oh boy."

"It'll be around again."

"I'm impressed," Louie said.

"How come?"

"You sit there. You look like you're half asleep. But boy do you see stuff, the world around you, I mean. It shows me how much I've got to learn about the business."

I opened the door. "Time for my pit stop. You take over."

"Got it." Louie handed me my walkie-talkie. "I'll log that Buick."

"Great."

Hollow sound of my footsteps as I walked down the corridors of the Art Institute. Dark in here, dim with the weight of centuries of painters, Rembrandt and company.

Did oil paints emit the same pungent smell in the Italian Renaissance as they did in Seattle in the nineties?

I found the men's room and felt better. I walked down a hallway lined with lockers, memories of school. Names on the lockers—Berryman, Borneman, Brown—suggested the alphabet. St. Cloud's locker was around the corner, in the staff section.

I was drinking at the water fountain when I heard voices coming down the hall. I stepped into a studio where a lone painter worked, brushstrokes making blue and yellow slashes on a canvas that was super black, and I watched the hallway through paint-spattered glass. Artists, nodding and chatting, surrounding St. Cloud, who wore a smock over a black jersey. Two guys, four gals, all six with the hollow-eyed look you get from eyeballing the world through your own private prism. Writers had it. Musicians. Painters and sculptors.

I gave St. Cloud time to pass before stepping out into the corridor. I saw her down the hall, snapping the padlock on her locker. I stepped back into the recessed doorway of the studio just as she turned to look my way. I could feel her mind reach out, feel it searching the space around her, probing for me with deep radar. Dressed for the street now, she walked away from me. I pressed the Talk button on my walkie-talkie. "This is Murdock."

"Louis Chen here. Go ahead."

"She's leaving by the side door."

"Uh-oh, that's a one-way street."

"What's the plan?"

"The plan is . . . you stay with her while I make a U-turn."

"Roger."

"And stay in radio contact, all right?"

"Over and out."

I waited until she had crossed the street and I followed. She walked a couple of blocks and turned into a doorway that said METRO. I followed. Steps led down. I punched the Talk button on the walkie-talkie and called Louie Chen. "I'm in a tunnel. I see buses."

"It's the underground, Matt. I've got nowhere to park. Has she spotted you?"

"I don't think so."

"Good. I'm on the Buick."

"Where is it?"

"Still circling the Art Institute."

Together, Mademoiselle St. Cloud and I rode a bus powered by electricity through a tunnel to a stop that said NORDSTROM'S. I knew Nordstrom's from Orange County, an upscale department store, too rich for my pocketbook. While she bought underwear, I called Louie Chen, but couldn't raise him on the walkie-talkie. Lost among racks of women's clothes, I felt eyes on my neck, someone watching, but when I turned there was no one.

We left Nordstrom's. We walked north on Fifth Avenue, past yuppies and street people to the street corner across from Eddie Bauer, with the rain slanting at us, silver drops against the gray flannel buildings of downtown Seattle. We walked up the hill and I watched her cross to the building that housed the parking garage. I buzzed Louie on the walkie-talkie. "Louie, where are you?"

"At a traffic signal on Western, Matt. I've lost the Buick. Where are you?"

"Heading into the parking building. How soon can you get here?"

"Traffic's getting heavy. Make it three minutes."

I went through the door and down the stairs. No sign of the Olds on the first floor. I took the stairs two at a time, swung open the heavy steel door, and saw St. Cloud in trouble. A man had her backed up against the Olds, pressing into her with his pelvis, a big hand clutching her throat. He wore pale trousers and a baggy tweed coat.

The trunk of her Olds was open, and both rear doors. I was already moving toward her when the black Buick, tires squealing, came around the corner to brake with a squeak behind her Olds. Two guys jumped out. The driver wore a red jockey jacket. On the back of the jacket was the number 42, painted in iridescent white. The other man wore a blue suit and a snap-brim hat. I stepped behind a concrete support beam and took my belt out of its loops. I wished for my arsenal, twelve hundred miles to the south in California. The belt wrapped around my hand, feeling naked and vulnerable, I ran for the Olds.

The man in the snap-brim hat grabbed St. Cloud and she hit him in the gut with her elbow, doubling him over. The man in the tweed got her arm in a hammerlock, jerked her by the hair. I didn't yell as I ran. Louie Chen's strategy for romance, such careful planning, was down the tubes.

The man in the tweed coat heard me, turned away from his prey, growled to his pal, who hauled out a gun. I flicked out with the belt, the heavy buckle snapping his face, making him jerk back, surprise in his eyes as the gun went off, the echo loud in this confined space.

"Yow!" He clawed at his face with one hand, and then someone swung on me as I powered a right into soft belly flesh. The gun clattered on concrete.

Out of the corner of my eye I saw St. Cloud kick her assailant, driving the point of her toe into his knee area, knocking him sideways. Pain in my left ear, pushing me to my knees. I rammed my knuckles at someone's crotch, heard a grunt of pain.

Dull glint of yellow light on metal: the man in the hat, holding a knife. "Come on, sucker," he said. "Come on."

I took a deep breath. I'm no knife artist. One bad move against a real knife fighter and you get your guts dumped on the floor. The knife sliced at me in a yellow arc. I pivoted, dodged, felt the blade cut me, left side, somewhere in back. I hate losing blood. I hate getting cut. I hit him with a tackle, driving him into the side of a car, and heard something go pop. He went to his knees, toppled over.

St. Cloud shouted. "Watch out, he's got—"

I turned to see the man in the jockey jacket aiming the pistol at me. St. Cloud was on one knee, shaking her head. I had no place to hide, no place to run. Behind Jockey Jacket, deep in the recessed dark, I saw movement. Then a sound, like compressed air spitting out, *splfft,* and Jockey Jacket spun around, then sank to his knees.

Someone shooting, from the shadows, with a silencer.

I looked that way, saw only gray-brown darkness. St. Cloud grabbed the gun, crawled to the man in the tweed, and stuck the gun into his ear. No movement from him. St. Cloud looked over at me. A strand of hair hung down across her forehead. Her eyes were angry, not scared.

"You're hurt," she said. "You're bleeding."

I felt blood leaking out of me, behind my back, under the shoulder blade, and for a long moment I felt death descend like a curtain, and then the pain came, bringing tears to my eyes.

"Shit," I said.

"Do you want a hospital?"

"No. No hospital."

"What then?"

"Get me someplace so I can check it out."

"The police will—"

"No police."

She nodded okay. "What about . . . them?"

"Can you drive?"

"Yes."

Before I could say anything more there was the sound of a car motor whining and then headlights flashed on the curved walls and Louie Chen's white van swung around the corner. He braked, jumped out, his eyes wide as he took in the scene. "Murdock, what?"

Biting my words, I told him what to do. The man in the jockey jacket was dead, shot from the shadows, so Louie Chen got his arms and St. Cloud got his feet and they loaded him into the trunk of the Buick. The man in the tweed, breathing but still unconscious, got placed neatly behind the wheel. We relieved them of their identification. Jockey Jacket's name was Barney Quinn. Tweed Coat was Earl J. Flick.

They dumped the third man into Louie Chen's van. While I watched, my head whirling, Louie wired the guy's wrists with Romex and St. Cloud ran a rag across the surfaces of the Buick to clean the prints off.

"My place?" Louie said.

"Anyplace."

Feeling woozy from the knife wound, I climbed into the passenger seat of the Oldsmobile and we followed Louie Chen out. The spiral ascent made me want to throw up. I bent forward to put my forehead on my knees. Each time I get hurt, I think the wound will kill me. One day, it will.

And then we were out of that place, the headlights bright on the curved worm walls of the parking garage and I was sick to my stomach, thinking of the gun, the knife, the odds because all three goons were younger, and of Arnica in my jacket pocket that I was trying to reach with my good hand so full of blood.

15

"**W**HAT IS IT?" SHE SAID.

"Huh?"

"What are you reaching for?"

"Arnica. It's a—"

She turned to stare at me. We were stopped at a traffic signal in downtown Seattle on a level patch a couple of blocks from the parking garage. I couldn't find the walkie-talkie. Must have dropped it in the melee. Raindrops on the hood of the Olds gleamed bloodred from the stoplight.

"Some of my best friends are homeopaths. Where is it?"

"Coat pocket, lefthand side."

She dug into my pocket and I bit my lip against the widening flash of pain as she brushed the wound. "Sorry." She came out with the Arnica. No fuss from St. Cloud as she opened the bottle and tapped six white pellets into the cap and told me to tilt back while she dumped them under my tongue. The lady knew homeopathy.

The signal turned from red to green and she capped the bottle and we were rolling again, following Louie Chen's white van out of Seattle's downtown.

"That man, the one in the red jacket. Is he really dead?"

"No pulse, no breath. He's dead all right."

"What on earth happened?"

"He was killed with a silencer, someone shooting from the shadows."

"But who would—"

"Thought you might know."

"What?"

"Maybe you have a protector."

"Very funny." She braked for the stoplight. The sudden stop sent pain through my wound. My head swam. "You followed me. I saw you in Nordstrom's, lurking. Give me one reason why I shouldn't drop you in front of the police station."

"Rollie Nielsen," I said.

"Rollie?" She stared a hole through me. "What about him?"

"He's dead. Murdered."

"You're joking. This is some kind of—" She shook her head. "Where did he die?"

"Southern California. In a ritzy motel. Is this the first you heard about it?"

"What are you, some kind of policeman?"

"I'm a private cop. My name's Murdock. Rollie's dad hired me."

"His dad? What for?"

"The cops were dragging their feet. Mr. Nielsen wanted action."

"Why are you here?"

"The trail led this way."

"And you followed me because you think I'm involved?"

"We picked you up at Rollie's condo. You were all we had . . . until today."

"And now you have?"

"Three goons."

"One of whom is dead."

"Yeah. But the one we captured might talk."

"I don't believe this. I don't believe this is happening."

She brushed a stray hair away from her face. Behind us a car honked. The light had turned green. She started with a jerk, drove a couple of blocks.

"So you're a detective then? What they call a private eye?"

"Yes."

She smiled, baring fine white teeth. "I do have to admit you showed some good timing back there. Some very excellent timing. Who's your friend in the white van? You didn't introduce us."

"His name's Louie Chen. He was a college pal of Rollie's. He wired the Queen Anne place for burglars."

"You're not kidding, are you?" Her voice was edgy with raw emotion. "Rollie's really dead?"

"I'm not kidding."

"So his father hired you and you're here in Seattle nosing around."

"That's right."

"And you don't want to get yourself checked at a hospital. That alone sounds suspicious." She cut her eyes at me. She was a fine-looking woman, strong, resolute, earthy. We rolled along between the tall buildings.

"The hospital will call the cops," I said. "The cops will ask questions. After a while they'll get around to Rollie Nielsen. They'll keep us cooling our heels for a day, maybe two, while they check stories."

"Keep you, maybe. Not me."

"Look at it this way, lady. Three goons means local muscle. Local muscle suggests connections, which suggests a local Mr. Big. Now you ask yourself: Who thinks you know about Rollie Nielsen? Who wants to talk to you real bad?"

A shiver ran through her. She said nothing.

"So," I said. "Tell me how well you knew Rollie."

"Rollie and I were . . . friends. But only just."

"You had a key to his place. You knew the code on his alarm system."

"I watered his plants. I collected the mail." She changed the subject. "How's that shoulder, mister?"

"Burns like hell."

"Does your friend know homeopathy?"

"No."

St. Cloud made a decision. She put on her right-turn blinker and pulled over to the curb so Louie Chen could come alongside. Change of plans, she said. We were going to her place, where she had some homeopathic stuff for my wound. I didn't care. I was tired, battered by thugs. I had been saved by some stranger in the shadows. I wanted to lie down, rest, close my eyes, stop thinking. The lady was a puzzle. She knew karate. She kept her cool. I was in her hands. Louie Chen did not protest about the change of plans. We drove up the hill and he swung in behind.

"You know my name," I said. "I don't know yours."

She shifted down for the climb. "My last name's St. Cloud. It's French Canadian. My initials are . . . H. L."

"What do they stand for, the initials?"

"The *H* stands for Hana. It's pronounced Hah-nah. The *L* stands for Lakota. Kids in school made fun of me, calling me Hey-nah and Tonto Stupid and other less creative variations, so I made them call me H. L."

"Made them how?"

She showed me a fist. "I was a scrappy kid."

"Lakota, that's Indian, right?"

"It's a Sioux language. My grandmother's maiden name

was Mary Hana Lakota. My father, he was French Canadian, decided it would test me to go through life with a name that sounded Indian."

"You look Indian."

She smiled at that, a secret smile, and in the streetlight I saw teeth and a tightening of her chin and throat. There was a rip in her parka, along the shoulder seam on the right. A strand of dark hair hung down along her cheek. I was aware of her legs, the strong thighs firm and round inside the faded jeans, and I wondered, as she made a left onto her street, how she would look with the hair let down, riding on a white horse, naked, through the streets of a medieval town.

Dream on, Murdock.

"You say what you mean, don't you, Murdock?"

"Saves time."

"In answer to your implied question, I'm one-quarter Indian, mostly Sioux, with probably some Chippewa and Algonquin from my father's wide-reaching roots. He was a liar and a storyteller who tailored truth to fit his mood. Here we are, home again."

Inside now, out of the rain, she parked in carport number 307 between a Dodge minivan and a Jeep Cherokee topped with ski racks. We climbed out. She directed Louie Chen to a visitor slot and she laid down some law about our prisoner.

"I don't want him in my house. He can stay until we get Mr. Murdock bandaged. Then he's out of here. Understand?"

"We got it."

In tight silence, the four of us rode the elevator up to three. She said nothing in the elevator. She looked at me, measuring me like a tailor measuring a customer for a suit of clothes, and then her cheeks got red and she looked at the floor and then at the door as it opened. Louie Chen pretended not to notice.

She led the way out and down the hall, shoulders back, little quivery shimmy in her hips. The pain in my back throbbed in time with a pain over my left eye, but I still got pleasure from watching her walk.

A soft click as she opened the door to number 307 and we entered an artist's lair, Oriental rug, handmade coffee table, gobs of pillows, a couple of director's chairs, a sofa that reminded me of home. Against the wall was a vintage stereo connected to a turntable. The shelves were filled with long-play records. Record covers were stacked on the wall beside the entertainment center. She was thirty-three, a generation away from me. I wondered what kind of music she liked.

This was a big room, multipurpose, with three covered easels standing like sentinels, guarding the window. North light. The kitchen area was laid out like my kitchen back in Newport Beach. Cooking island with a built-in range. Hers was newer than mine, with a chrome exhaust blower. Above the island, pots and pans hung from an arty rack, copper hardware, black rivets, black iron hooks. The fridge was old, a GE the same vintage as mine. On the cabinet next to the sink, in a prominent spot, was an Olympic vegetable juicer. It had been recently used and now lay in pieces, drying out.

"Sit here."

I sat in a director's chair under a recessed spot that beamed down from the ceiling over the kitchen sink. The canvas was red, but not faded. While Louie Chen secured the prisoner in a storeroom off the kitchen, Hana St. Cloud helped me off with the Levi jacket and the borrowed vest and she cut away most of the shirt and then sponged the area with a wet warm cloth. The blood had dried. I grunted

as she pulled the strips of cloth away. She gave me more
Arnica. I nodded as she poured me a shot of brandy. The
brandy felt good going down, warm, bracing. Heat in my
throat, the smell of her, less hurt from the wound.

Louie Chen came back holding a wallet.

When my shirt was off, she cleaned the wound. Pain
darted at me, small pins, then arrows with blunt points.
Pain gouged me on the left-hand side.

"Feels as deep as the Rio Grande Gorge," I said.

"It's three inches long," she said. "But not deep. Not like
these others. My God."

I felt cool fingers on my back as she touched one old
wound, then another, and another.

"How awful," she said.

"Trophies of war," I said.

"Where?"

"Vietnam. Serving the Queen."

"That awful place."

She left me there. Louie Chen was brewing herb tea. I
sipped the brandy. I looked at Louie Chen. He shrugged,
shoulders up, eyebrows arching, palms turned up. "Does it
hurt?"

"It hurts."

"Isn't she something?"

"She's something, all right."

"I'm jealous, man. I'm sorry, but I am." His face was a
grimace of pain. "Just wanted you to know, okay?"

"Okay."

"She's . . . well, she's—"

Louie didn't finish his speech of admiration because
Hana St. Cloud came back, carrying a wicker basket piled
high with gauze and bandages. A strand of hair had fallen
across her forehead. Around her neck was a thin gold
chain, her only jewelry, which caught the light when she

moved. The wicker basket contained tape and gauze and homeopathic ointments. Thuja. Arnica. Ledum. Aesculus. Hypericum. While I read the labels, she consulted a book.

"Arnica," she said, snapping the book closed. "It worked on the inside. Should work outside."

"You're the doctor, Doctor."

She applied the ointment with her fingers and pasted on three butterfly bandages to help close the wound. The tape made me wince. I was aware of the heat from her body, the weight of her breasts inside the black jersey as she bent over me, and her cool fingers. Her face was dark and exciting. Her hair was jet-black, thick with a healthy fullness. I liked watching her. She did not seem nervous with three strange men in her house. She had not seemed nervous in the parking garage. Her karate skills were better than mine. I was impressed. I wondered who her men friends were. Louie Chen was sitting on the sofa, checking through the wallet.

She found me a shirt, a man's size large. It had paint spots on it, and traces of her earth mother smell. She helped me on with the shirt.

"All right," she said.

"All right what?"

"I'm grateful you showed up, both of you, but I want that man out of my house."

"That was the deal, Louie. Let's vamoose."

"His name's Stearns," Louie said. "Here's his wallet."

Louie tossed me the wallet. I was slow grabbing for it, so it bounced off my chest and dropped onto the floor. Plastic cards spilled out. Hana St. Cloud stooped to gather up the stuff.

"Borklund?" she said.

"Right," Louie said from the doorway.

"What's a Borklund?" I said.

"Borklund Industries," Hana said. "They're big in-surance, timber, transportation."

"Borklund Shipping," Louie said. "Lots of export and import. Mr. Borklund, his first name is Bjorn, is Seattle's own King of Crime."

Hana St. Cloud showed me a card. "This man Stearns works for Borklund Security."

My head had stopped whirling. I felt strong enough to look at the contents of the wallet. Our goon in the business suit was J. K. Stearns. His driver's license said he lived on First Avenue, in unit F2. He had $700 in hundreds in his wallet and another $440 in fifties and twenties. He carried Amex, MasterCard, Visa, Diner's Club, Discover, Sears, Hertz, AT&T, and American Airlines. There were no photos in his wallet. Three business cards in his coat pocket, one from a police sergeant at the Seattle PD named Roanoke. There were two cards, gray with white lettering, that said BORKLUND SECURITY. They looked like keycards.

"What do you know about Mr. Bjorn Borklund?"

"Old and tough," Louie said. "He must be seventy. He runs the dirty parts of King County, the underworld be-neath the gorgeous green."

"I still want him out of here. That was our deal."

"Fetch the prisoner, Louie."

St. Cloud stared at me. "Are you all right?"

"I'm great," I said. "Just great. Thank you for the—"

The whirlies hit me as I stood up. I grabbed for the edge of the cooking island as the floor swirled up to meet me. The last thing I saw was St. Cloud, dark face, almond eyes, full mouth.

And then I was gone.

16

I CAME AWAKE ON A BED, MY MOUTH DRY, MY FACE slick with sweat. The knife gash had stopped hurting. A trapezoid of light flowed from the closet onto boots, Birkenstocks, hiking socks, running shoes, shorts, leg warmers, shirts dabbed with paint spots, a wraparound skirt, a silky crimson blouse. From the other room I heard voices.

St. Cloud's stuff cluttered the top of the dresser. Combs and photos in frames and a bookshelf beside the bed. One shelf was devoted to the creative process. Another held books on mind control and hypnosis.

The phone was cherry-red to pick up color from the landscapes and still-life studies on the walls. Mounted on three easels were three self-portraits. One showed St. Cloud standing at the easel, painting herself, wearing the crimson blouse, the wraparound skirt, and spike heels. One showed her in jeans and the parka, looking back over her shoulder on a city street, probably done from a photograph. The third was a nude.

She sat on a high wooden stool, her hair falling down past her shoulders. Mahogany flesh, dark curves, subtle shadows. No tan lines, no traces of the bikini stripes of civilization. Her bare toes were curled around the rungs of the stool. Both arms were bent at the elbow and held out straight like wings so her hands could hold a death's-head mask over her face. The mask was triangular, with narrow slits for eyes and sharp bone-white teeth. It did not look human. Staring into that mask, bleached white by a hot desert sun, I had the sense she was laughing at me. The portrait was signed Lakota.

Through a door that led to a studio, I saw stacks of canvases and boxes of paints. I sat up. The whirlies had passed. I headed for the bathroom.

The bathroom, surprise, was neat and orderly. Towels hung straight. A hairbrush and comb aligned side by side and then a hair dryer. In a rack next to the commode was a sample of her reading material. *Mother Jones* magazine, *Seattle Weekly, Environment,* and an old *Newsweek.* The lead story in *Newsweek* was Tienanmen Square. Long time back, that story.

I used the facilities. I flushed. I untucked the shirt for a peek at my bandage. A nice neat job, slight tinge of blood soaking through the gauze, but Murdock was on the mend. In the bathroom was her smell, fragrant, like fresh earth turned over.

When I returned to the main room, Hana St. Cloud sat on the sofa with her feet curled under her, sketching. Louie Chen sat beside her, studying a floor diagram. There were coffee mugs on the table, and a plate of sandwiches. The coffee smelled wonderful.

"Hey," Louie said. "Sleeping Beauty awakes."

"How are you feeling?" asked St. Cloud.

I tried grinning. My face did not crack. "Better. How long was I out?"

"A couple of hours. Would you like some coffee?"

"Love some." I sat down in a director's chair. "Where's our man from Borklund Security?"

"Resting," Louie said. "After the interrogation."

"Interrogation?" I said.

St. Cloud spoke from the stove. "He told us everything, Mr. Murdock. We played good cop, bad cop and he sang. Like a—"

"Canary." Louie finished it for her.

Two kids, grinning the same grin. While I'd been out, Louie and Ms. Hana St. Cloud had gotten cozy. She handed me the coffee and I took a sip. Nice brew. I nodded at them. The mug was white, with a blue stripe around the rim. "Who was the bad cop?"

"I was," St. Cloud said. "Louie straddled a chair backward, holding a gun on him, while I pounded him with a rubber truncheon."

"She's tough," Louie said. "She'd make a great cop."

More smirks passed between them, shutting me out. "Very funny, guys. Tell me about the diagrams."

Louie showed me a diagram. "This is Big Daddy's gangland hideaway. It's on Whidbey Island. They were supposed to take Hana there after they grabbed her."

"Today?"

"Tonight," Louie said. "Even as we speak."

I checked my watch. The time was after nine. "Did he locate the house for you?"

"Here." Louie pointed to an *X* on a highway map of the Puget Sound area. "It's on the western edge, a beach place."

"How do you get out there, to this island? What's it called again?"

"Whidbey Island. There's a ferry. It leaves the mainland from Mukilteo. Takes about twenty minutes."

"How late do the ferries run?"

"Didn't I tell you?" St. Cloud said.

"You told me," Louie said.

"Told you what?" I said.

"Hana said you'd want to go out there so you could hassle Big Daddy. I said you'd be too tired."

"You want to roust him," St. Cloud said. "Like you rousted the garage gang."

"Roust?" I sipped my coffee.

"A term of the PI trade," Louie said.

Roust, I thought. Truncheon. "Anything else?"

Louie Chen's face lit up: "The way they found Hana was interesting, Matt. It seems that Big Daddy has a contact inside the police department, a mole I guess you'd call him. When the cops went through Rollie's place yesterday, they found film in a camera. Hana was on the film. They ran her photo through a scanner at the DMV—it's a new process that prints pictures in hundreds of computer dots clustered to form an image, like photos in *The Wall Street Journal*— and that gave the mole her name and address, which he relayed to Big Daddy, who sent Stearns and his goons to grab her."

"Any idea what they want with you?" I asked St. Cloud.

"Just a guess. Once they found out I knew Rollie they thought I knew something else."

"The Stearns guy is just muscle," Louie said. "He follows orders."

I drained the coffee cup. "Anything else?"

Louie held up a keycard. "This plastic card opens the doors of the house on Whidbey Island. There are three guard dogs. There's a man who lives in a caretaker's house on the beach. And since this is Saturday, you will find Big Daddy entertaining one or more scarlet ladies."

Impressive. I had to admit it.

"Okay. Now tell me how you got him to talk."

More grins. They were sure enjoying it.

"Hypnosis," said St. Cloud.

"Hypnosis?"

"Autosuggestion. He was an easy subject."

I remembered the books on hypnosis in the bedroom.

"You should have seen it, Matt. Hana swung this crystal. The guy sits there watching her, then his eyes follow the crystal, back and forth, back and forth. Then they close. Then his head drops forward, like this, chin on chest. Then he tells us, his voice sounding drugged, about the house where he grew up and pretty soon he's telling us everything."

"Where was he born, just out of curiosity?"

"Spokane," St. Cloud said. "In the fifties."

"Spokane." I looked from St. Cloud to Louie. Hypnosis. Photo scanners. Clustered computer dots. Two grinning kids from Seattle who made me feel old. I held out my hand, palm up. "The keycard, Louie."

He pulled his hand back. "No way. I'm coming along."

"On the Big Daddy roust," St. Cloud said.

I glared at her. "Hand it over, Louie."

"No. This is part of my OJT as a private eye."

I exhaled. I was a loner and loners work alone. On the other hand, I was a stranger in town and Louie Chen knew the territory. Also: He had the expertise to shut down an alarm system, which a fat cat like Big Daddy would have. I favored him with a short nod. "Okay. Fetch the prisoner and let's get moving."

Louie left the room.

"What will you do once you get there?" St. Cloud asked.

"I'm not sure."

"You're not much of a planner, are you?"

"Don't have enough information yet."

"You mean you just blunder along, getting knifed and shot at, until something turns up or you die?"

"Ha ha," I said.

She stood up. I watched her. I liked watching her. She moved to the window and stood there, her arms crossed, her back to me. I took a bite of sandwich. She spoke without turning around.

"I was just thinking, Mr. Murdock."

"Oh?"

"It might be easier to get there, out to Whidbey I mean, if you had a boat."

"I don't think Louie has a boat."

"Rollie had one." She turned to face me. "He let me use it."

"How tough is it to operate?"

"Easy enough. Especially if I came along."

"Not a chance, Ms. St. Cloud. No deal."

"I'm volunteering. My responsibility."

"No."

"Why not?"

"You know why not. Those are tough guys. They don't care who they hurt. There might be shooting."

"I can handle myself. Remember the parking garage?"

"I remember."

"No you don't. I helped you up off the floor, mister. I brought you here to my house. I bandaged your wound. When you passed out, I helped Louie carry you into the bedroom."

"So?"

"So you're hurt. You've had a shock. You're human. So don't get all macho on me, all right?"

"I'm not being macho. It's just that I know damn well—"

She came across the room and stood staring down at me. Way back inside her black eyes I saw bonfires blazing, dancers dancing to ceremonial drums. Her smile was fierce, made more defiant by the upward cant of her chin. Her lips were lush, sexy, tempting. We locked eyeballs. "I had my first fight when I was seven when a stupid little boy called me Tonto. I bloodied his nose. I fought my way through grade school, boys mostly, but some girls when they were big enough. In junior high I fought when some snotnose put his hands on me. My granddad taught me how to box. I know karate. Last summer I defended myself when a mugger tried to—"

Louie entered with Stearns. His suit was rumpled. A blanket was wrapped around his shoulders. He looked whipped, dark circles under his eyes, a runny nose.

St. Cloud made a huffy sound and stalked into her bedroom. I could hear her rustling around in there. Louie sat Stearns down on the floor, legs in the yoga position. St. Cloud came back carrying a cardboard box. Inside the box was an army-issue .45, an automatic. There was a holster but no gunbelt, and two boxes of shells by Remington.

"Nice piece," I said.

"It belonged to my granddad."

I racked the slide to make sure the piece was unloaded, and then I held the blade of a kitchen knife in the breech, angling it until it shot a reflected light beam up the barrel. "Needs cleaning."

"He taught me how to shoot."

"Have you ever shot anyone?"

"No." She took a deep breath. "It was me they came after, remember?"

"I remember, Ms. St. Cloud. You have any gun oil?"

"No. I owe them one."

"How about some machine oil then?"

"I think so. Yes."

"Got a coat hanger?"

"Yes."

"And some pliers?"

"In the kitchen in a drawer. Louie," she said. "Say something."

"I think she should go, Matt."

"No way."

"She can run Rollie's boat."

"You guys really worked on this, didn't you? Really planned it out."

"You were asleep, Matt. We just tossed some ideas around."

Behind me, I could hear her opening drawers, slamming cabinet doors. "How about those pliers, Ms. St. Cloud?"

"Here." She handed me pliers. "And stop calling me Ms. St. Cloud. My name is Hana."

"All right. Hana."

"And I'm going, right?"

"Sure. Come along. Call your friends. Let's have a parade."

"Men!" she said, and huffed into the bedroom again.

There was no bona fide barrel cleaner, so I improvised with paint thinner. I cut a length of coat hanger. I stuck a clean swab of paint rag onto the end of the coat hanger and dipped it into the paint thinner. I ran the wetted swab into the barrel, being careful not to scratch the riflings. Two slow pumps before I pulled it out, bringing dirt and grime and a wet fuzzball.

Hana St. Cloud came back with the machine oil. Her hair was pulled back away from her face, accenting the almond shape of her eyes. She had changed into lace-up hunting boots and boot socks with red tops. She carried a down vest and a sweater.

I oiled the .45. I handed it to her, but she shook her head. "It's yours, for the night."

"You should take better care."

"It's been waiting for someone who cares."

Louie Chen spoke from the sofa. "We've got that other piece, from the guy in the parking garage. And we should stop off at my place and pick up some Kevlar vests."

"What about me?" Stearns said.

"Keep your lip buttoned and I'll cut you loose."

"When?"

"When I'm ready."

We marched Stearns down the hallway to the elevator. We took the elevator down to the parking garage. There was no sign of Big Daddy's goons as we climbed into Louie's van. The time was after ten as we headed across Queen Anne Hill to Phinney Ridge.

"What we need," I said, "is a soft spot. A Big Daddy bruise to press on. What do we know about this guy?"

"I knew a girl who became his mistress," Hana said. "Her name was Darlene. We had classes together at the university. She caught his eye at a party and he wooed her with money and gifts. She ended up with an apartment on the water and a fancy Corvette."

"When was this?"

"Ten years ago. No, twelve."

"So he likes the ladies," I said.

"Lots of them, it's rumored."

"Did Louie tell you Rollie was cooking ice?"

"Yes."

"So maybe Big Daddy figures, since you have a key to Rollie's condo, that you also have a second key."

"To the ice lab," Louie said. "It makes sense."

"What kind of place would it be?" Hana said.

"All you need is four walls and a heat source," I said. "His prof over at the U said cooking ice would be no problem for a chemist like Rollie. The equipment is cheap, maybe two thousand dollars. The cops were hot to search Rollie's room near the university because they figured the lab might be there. The prof also said Rollie could have developed a new process for cooking ice."

"Maybe that's what they're after," Hana said.

I wrote it down. *New Process.*

"Rollie had the soul of an entrepreneur," Hana said.

"Maybe that's what's in those formulas," Louie said.

"What formulas?" Hana said.

"Louie pulled some formulas off Rollie's computer."

"What did they look like?"

"It looked like organic," Louie said. "Chemistry was never my bag."

"This is sounding more logical," Hana said. "I'm excited. And I know people who could help us."

"We could check it out with Rollie's prof," Louie said. "Matt's seen her but I haven't. I feel out of the loop."

"There's something else I wanted to ask about," Hana said.

"What?"

"While you were sleeping, Louie told me Rollie's murder was just one in a string. Is that true?"

"According to my contact with the CIA." I went through the serial killer theory of Agent Loomis. When I finished, Hana gave me her smirky look.

"I've never known anyone who was buddy-buddy with the CIA, Mr. Murdock. I have to say I'm wildly impressed."

"The name's Matt," I said.

"I'm still impressed."

"The pay is lousy," I said. "And I smell something gamy about the CIA guy."

"What's his name again?"

"Agent Loomis. His first name's Gerald. He's in his thirties, a guy on the way up."

"How did you find him?"

"They found me."

"How?"

"From a computer at Langley, linked to a computer at the Pentagon, where my service records are on file for eternity." I tapped the pencil on the pad. "Let's get back to the formula. What if Rollie had cooked up something that Big Daddy wanted? What would it be?"

"A formula for combating disease," Louie Chen said.

"Good. What disease?"

"Cancer," Hana said. "Parkinson's. The common cold. Or flu. Rollie needed money. Big Daddy saw a way to make zillions."

"Remember that his mom was sick," Louie said. "And he was trying to cure her."

I wrote it down: *Chemical Cure For????*

"I don't see Rollie as that idealistic," Hana said. "He was cooking ice. The scenario I like is the speeded-up cooking process. More ice, cooked faster. More powerful ice."

"Good." I wrote down *Process,* and then dollar signs.

"Speedo Ice," Louie Chen said, turning right onto his street. "That sounds like Rollie."

"Let's play What If," I said.

"Okay."

"So what if Big Daddy and Rollie had a deal?"

"To buy the formula?" Hana said. "I like it."

"Yes. And what if Rollie has a second buyer in California?"

"Competitive bids," Louie said.

"Greedy, greedy," Hana said. "Poor Rollie."

We kept the what ifs going until Louie stopped at a QFC market, where we bought hamburger meat and three boxes of Sleep-Eze for the dogs. From there we drove to Louie's place. We left Stearns in the van while we went inside. Louie hunted up three Kevlar vests, his pistol, and some duct tape. Hana brewed coffee and tea. I doctored the hamburger meat.

17

THE BOAT, A FORTY-FIVE-FOOTER WITH AN EN-closed cabin, was moored to the dock at Shilshole. The time was close to midnight, the temperature in the low forties. Hana unlocked the door to the enclosed cabin. Blankets were stacked in one corner. The name of the boat was *Ice Princess*.

We stowed Stearns on a bunk in the main cabin, his wrists and ankles secured with fourteen-gauge Romex. He didn't like it. But I didn't want him alerting Big Daddy.

Louie Chen poured tea. Hana started the engine and gave me instructions on what to do to get us loose from land. The motor throbbed, a powerful sound. Blue exhaust puffed from the rear of the boat, merged with the fog. I'd been part owner of a boat once, a yacht anchored on Bay Street in Newport Beach. Water makes me edgy, all that wet space. I was born in El Paso and I know the desert.

The cold seeped into my bones as we eased away from the dock. I had on two shirts, a borrowed sweatshirt, and my Levi jacket with the knife slash. Louie Chen wore gray and kept prowling.

Hana's socks had red wool tops. She wore a man's shirt, wool. Over that a sweater and a down vest. The tea warmed me. Steady at the wheel, Hana did not seem to mind the cold.

"You're not doing this just for money," Hana said.

"No."

"What is it? What drives you to take these risks?"

"Thursday afternoon down in sunny California I was poking around in the case. Must have touched a nerve because Thursday night my place was shot up by a gang of local hoods trying to act like men. A friend of mine, a kid, got caught in the crossfire. She'll live, but she was hurt bad. Another kid died. Thor Nielsen was wounded. I want the bums who did it."

"And you think they're here?"

"The trail ran out down there. Plus, the local cops were rousting me. There's something here. I can smell it. Maybe it's Big Daddy Borklund. Maybe it's someone else." I gave her a long look. She smiled, peered through the windshield. The boat plowed along. My legs felt rubbery.

"What was your friend's name?"

"Cindy Duke."

"A kid, you said."

"She's fifteen. I met her a while back. I was hurt and she helped me out on a case. Then last year I helped her out of a tight spot."

"She sounds like someone very special."

"She is."

A pause before she spoke. "They actually shot bullets at your home?"

"Yeah. Real bullets. Broke windows, cups, glasses. Ruined my stereo."

"California," she said. "Ugh."

We stood there, not talking, while the engines throbbed

beneath our feet. She watched the black water, the black sky. I watched her.

"So tell me about you and old Rollie."

"What do you want to know?"

"Where you met. How long you knew him."

"We met in late spring, so I knew him six months or so. We met at an environmental rally staged by the Eco Greeners, our local version of Big Green. A friend introduced us. Rollie called the next day, invited me out. I'd already made up my mind he was not for me—too eager, too boyish, too macho predictable—and then he called me again, for a party on this boat, so I said okay. I love boats. Water is my weakness."

"How was the party?"

"Not bad. There were two other couples. One of the women was a call girl, very high class. Rollie made his pass, a very obvious one. I refused him." There was a long pause. "I want to get something clear, Matt. About Rollie and me."

"There's no need."

"I want to." Level gaze as she looked at me. No joking around here, this was serious stuff.

"Okay. Shoot."

"Rollie was . . . attracted to me. He was a randy guy. He wanted a physical relationship. It was sad. Here was a guy, bright, educated, a hard worker. But for me he had zero sex appeal and that made him whimper and whine. He did have access to drugs—a girl I know dated him just so he could supply her—but drugs are not my narcotic. Rollie was a chemist. It's not illogical to think he was making this ice stuff, maybe even selling it. But it's his life, right? I'm an artist. I like brushes, oils, watercolors, the feel of canvas. Art is my drug. What Rollie does, that's his business. I watered his plants because he let me use this boat."

"Use it for what?"

"For getting away. I love the water. Out here, I stop thinking like Monkey Mind and get in touch with myself."

"Monkey Mind?"

"Um. I heard it from a Zennie. Monkey Mind is that animal who chatters from a tree inside your head. I start to paint, she says you're dumb, Hana. You can't paint. Stop painting, Hana."

"Monkey Mind," I said. "Mine chatters away when I get stymied solving a case."

There was no talking for a while. Then she touched my arm, a gesture of friendship. I liked that, liked having her touch me. I had an urge right then to take her in my arms. Now was not the time. I asked more questions.

"So Rollie gave you the keys."

"He hoped it would make us closer, a careful boat bribe. Rollie was clever about that. He'd find out what you needed and feed it to you in small doses, try to get you hooked. Quite the manipulator."

"What did you think about his trips out of town?"

"I thought he had a woman down there, a California beach dolly. A blonde with big boobs and long legs and a perfect Playmate ass." She cut her eyes at me. "He invited me down a couple of times. When I refused, he got that hurt look in his eyes and stopped asking. From time to time, he'd call to rhapsodize about the sun and surf. To me, he just sounded like a lost little kid."

"What about that snazzy bachelor condo?"

"The money for it, you mean?"

"Yeah."

"He said he'd sold a formula to a major drug company. Bongo bucks, he said."

"What kind of formula?"

"Cough control."

I stood leaning against the bulkhead, not saying anything. I felt jealous. I had no right to feel that way. We had only just met. I didn't know her. I felt it anyway, jealousy, wild and raw and green, cutting through.

"Well, Mr. Murdock?"

"Well what?"

"Well, why don't you say something?"

"Okay," I said. "Here's something. It pisses me off."

"What pisses you off?" Sudden smile, white teeth in the boatlight glow, shadows dancing on her dark face.

"You." I said, growling. "With him. With anyone."

"Well well." Wider smile now. "Well well well."

The outer door slid open and Louie Chen came in, blown by a wet wind. His hair was slicked back from the rain. He wiped his face with a towel, looked at Hana and me. "Did I walk in on something?"

"I was just telling Mr. Murdock here about my relationship with Rollie."

"Uh-oh, sounds private. Maybe I should go."

"Please stay. I want you to know too."

"Okay."

I sat in a director's chair and said nothing while they compared their views of Rollie Nielsen. He'd managed to fool everyone—his dad, his friends, maybe even his customers—but he hadn't fooled a bullet.

"The guy keeps surprising me," Louie Chen said. "I mean, we lived together for two and a half years. I visited his farm, lots of times. I knew his folks, thought I knew him pretty well. And then he does this dope stuff."

"He fooled me, too," Hana said. "He let me know enough to make me think I knew him. Just enough."

"Dibs and dabs," Louie Chen said. "Did you trust him?"

"No. But I thought I knew him."

"We were both wrong."

"Yes."

After a bit, they moved from analyzing Rollie Nielsen to people they knew in common, Seattle's thirtysomething set, Starbuck's coffee, Ivar's, favorite bookstores. They shifted from that to larger topics: rain forests, the plight of the homeless, dangers to the biosphere, Greenpeace and Eco Greeners, saving the world.

It got too abstract for me so I went to check on Stearns. He sneezed on me, so I left him alone and stood on the deck. Lights off to the right, no moon. Inside the cabin, I could see Hana and Louie Chen talking. They had lots in common. They were young, bright, concerned. I liked Hana, liked her power, her pull.

It was after midnight when we pulled into an inlet, a narrow slice in the shore. Dark here, dark and cold with the wind whipping across the waters of Puget Sound, curling down from Canada and the North Pole. Hana wasn't shivering. Louie Chen, his jacket still unzipped, acted like it was the Fourth of July and ninety-two degrees in the shade. I was cold. So was old Stearns. I gave him another blanket.

"Where is it?"

"Up the beach, a half mile, maybe a quarter."

"One screwup from you, Stearns, and I'll dump you in the surf."

"Take me back with you, okay?"

"If you behave."

We left the boat as the moon poked through the cloud cover. In the shelter of some island pines, Louie Chen handed us each a Kevlar vest, part of his Future Shock collection, he said. I helped them check their weapons. Louie Chen had his .32 Smith & Wesson. Hana had the pistol from the man in the jockey jacket. I had the army-issue .45, the only weapon with much kick, and a hiker's walking stick. In his backpack, Louie Chen carried the walkie-talkies and the duct tape. In her backpack, Hana carried the doctored meat.

We hiked a quarter mile into the wind, north along the shore, the water on our left. Out on the sound, you could see lights from a big ship chugging north. Small shape on the hill to our right, a house with a tiny light burning. A fence blocked our way, strands of wire too tight to shinny through, so I made a hole with wire cutters from the boat.

Another hundred yards along the wet sand and Stearns pointed to a house on the ridge. It jutted out from the cliffs, a three-story job with sharply angled roofs and decks sticking out like lower lips. On the top floor, a light burned.

In front of us, maybe twenty yards in the occasional moonlight, was a firepit and some benches made of driftwood. A set of 4x4 support posts held up a corrugated plastic roof. Beyond the firepit was a smaller house, a guest cottage.

"Music," Hana whispered.

I heard nothing. "Where?"

"From the caretaker's house. There."

"You sure?" Louie Chen said.

She knelt down to place her hand flat on the beach. "Feel that," she said. "Sounds like acid rock."

My hand touched wet sand. It was cold. My heart pumped, but I could not feel the throb of music.

"Let me check it out."

"Why can't we bypass?" Louie asked. "If we're quiet, he might never know we were here."

"If there's a guard, we can't risk him coming up behind us. We don't know how many people are in the main house."

"How about this dog food then?"

"On the stairs," I said.

Louie trotted off with the doctored hamburger meat.

Hana gave my arm a squeeze and I headed for the guest cottage. I felt the music as I stepped onto the catwalk, jungle music with a heavy bass throb in a relentless, moronic rhythm.

On the wall beside the front door was a rack containing three pairs of shoes. One pair of beach flip-flops. One pair of boots. Next to the boots was a pair of Adidas runners, new, the same size as the boots and wide as a water ski. Footgear for a giant.

I listened at the door, my heart going, remembering the flutters preceding combat. I tried the handle and the door opened. Dark in here, the music louder, pumping out from a door across the room, angry voices wailing about sin and Satan, to the tune of steel guitars and a battalion of drums and raucous cymbals.

Heavy metal or acid rock, it was all crap.

18

LOCKED IN THE JAW-WRENCHING THROB OF THE MU-
sic, I played the flash around the walls. I was in a combination kitchen and living room that ran the length of the front
of the house. To my right was the sink and a littered
drainboard. Empty pizza boxes, liquor bottles, a silver keg
of beer, ashtrays filled with gunk. The smell of stale sweat
mingled with the unmistakable odor of marijuana. Light
came from the oversize fridge, a black GE big enough to
cool down a tiger shark. The door had been left standing
open by the party-hounds. Next to the fridge was a matching freezer, black mirror door, silver handles.

No one here, so I moved to the next room, eased the
door open. On the TV screen several naked persons
squirmed, writhing against each other like snakes. The
throbbing music came from the latest state-of-the-art com-
pact disc player, an assembly of stacked electronic gear next
to the TV. Electric blue lights bounced happily along a
band, growing larger as the volume soared, then receding
back to neon normal. The tune was unrecognizable jungle

junk—*screep, thumpa whump DA, screep DA, thumpa whump*—designed to jazz your love button when it wearied.

The far end of the room was in deep shadow, but I saw motion in the gloom. You couldn't hear much because of the music. A figure was there, doing push-ups in time to the music and the blue neon beacon. Squinting, I made out a large man with a hairless head.

I eased back against the wall, trying to figure how to take him with the least effort, and just then the bozo jumped up, a mountain of a man. In his right hand he held his push-up partner, a limp pinkish-hued female without any clothes. He yelled. And then he threw his lady at me.

She flew through the air at my face. I dodged and she hit the wall with a muffled *whoof,* arms and legs pumping slowly like waterlogged balloons. She wasn't a lady at all, but one of those seagoing rubber dolls taken along by Japanese sailors on long voyages. In the skewed half-light from the TV screen, she looked like a bottle blonde.

The bozo charged. I hit him square on the side of the neck with the muzzle of the .45, but his momentum carried us past the rubber lady, into the litter, and all the way into the kitchen. He wore an orange T-shirt that said JULIUS, and that was all. His head rammed into my stomach, knocking the breath out of me. I tonked him again with the .45. He was made of cast iron. He shoved me into the fridge, cracking my back against the shelves. I heard glass shatter behind me as I hit him twice in the nose. Blood spurted from his face as he swept the .45 away with one large paw. His hands went around my throat and I stomped on his bare toe. He grunted, gave me a look at his ugly teeth, and dug both thumbs into my Adam's apple. Water ran from my eyes. He brought a knee up, aiming for my crotch. I twisted aside, felt his knee numb my thigh and hip, jabbed him in the throat with my elbow, and felt his hold loosen. I poked him twice more in the throat with my karate knuckles and then once behind the ear, in a special spot that brings a cloak of darkness to the brain.

He tackled me as he went down and we were grappling on the floor when a figure appeared out of the gloom. One quick chopping motion and the big guy went limp.

"Are you okay?" Louie Chen's voice.

"Whew," I said. "Thanks, Louie."

Hana came through the door with Stearns. She helped Louie roll the bozo off me. I sat with my back to the wall, breathing hard, while they tied him up with duct tape. I felt winded and old. Damn.

"Why didn't you call out?" Hana said.

"No time."

"Why didn't you shoot?" Louie Chen said.

"Too noisy." I sucked in air.

"What shall we do with Stearns?"

"Tape him to the bathroom plumbing."

"Neat idea," Louie said. "I love this OJT."

We waited for a quarter of an hour and then Louie went out for a recon. He came back grinning. "Two of them are asleep, snoring away."

"How many did he say there were?"

"Three," Hana said. "I remember."

"What now?"

"We go."

We left the guest cottage and headed up the stairs past the sleeping dogs. Steps curved along the cliff. Out of the wind, it was not so cold. When we were halfway up I heard a growl, and then the skittering of claws on wood, and a shape loomed at us, huge in the moonlight. I tossed the meat at him. He took it on the snout and kept coming, launching off the stairs at eye level and coming right at me, teeth bared, a growl rumbling in his throat. I hit him with

Louie's walking stick, knocking him aside. Claws scrabbled
on the damp rocks and he charged again. I dodged. He
sank his teeth into my sleeve. Behind me, Hana let out a
muffled screech. I had the .45 out. I was ready to shoot him
when Louie Chen saved me. Out of the corner of my eye I
saw him whirling to deliver a karate kick into the dog's
head, near the ear. The dog sagged, let go my sleeve, and
crumpled.

I was puffing.

"I'm shaking," Hana said.

"Thanks, Louie."

"You okay, partner?"

"A hundred years older."

"Want to rest?"

"No."

We moved on up the stairs to the lower level of the big
house. A small deck led to a glass door. Behind the glass
door I saw plants in pots sitting on shelves. A greenhouse.
My hands were shaky, so it took a while to slide the keycard
in. The lock clicked open. Louie Chen went in first, Hana
next, and me bringing up the rear. Warm in this hothouse.
A glass roof slanted down at thirty degrees. Some rose-
bushes, other flowers whose names I did not know. Louie
disarmed the alarm.

We moved into the house, not talking. Music boomed
down the stairs, a military march, lots of brass and a big
bass drum. Laundry room to the right. Next to that a
workout room equipped with a Total Gym, a stationary
bike, and a NordicTrack. Next to the workout room a spa, a
sauna, and a Jacuzzi with a blue plastic cover to hold in the
heat. A bedroom at the end of the corridor. The bed was
not made. On the bed was a suitcase, open to show
women's clothes, stockings, underwear. A second suitcase

rested on a luggage rack. Strong smell of perfume on the air, sweetish, sicky.

"Visitors," Louie Chen said.

Hana picked up a black teddy, sheer, filmy, and tiny.

"Preteen," Hana said. "That filthy man."

Guns out, we climbed the stairs into a living room with a cathedral ceiling. View deck along another glass wall, with a kitchen and dining room to the left. Two walls of books here, paintings that looked expensive. Above us was a balcony with a wrought-iron railing. The music was louder now.

"Tunes for halftime," Hana said. "John Philip Sousa."

"You are amazing," Louie Chen said.

"Liberal arts education," she said. "Plus I was a twirler in high school."

"Shh, you guys."

The downstairs was deserted.

We climbed the wide stairway, which branched at the top. Purple carpet here, one door to the left, two to the right. More Sousa rumbled from recessed speakers high in the ceiling. On the floor diagram, all three doors led to bedrooms. Big Daddy, as the master of the house, occupied the super suite to the left. According to the diagram, the two rooms on the right were for guests, call girls, visiting crime kingpins, whoever.

Hana flipped the balcony switch to Off. A faint glow of light from below shadowed our path.

The first room we checked was empty, no one home. I pointed down the hall. "You guys take Big Daddy. I'll check in here."

I waited until they had their ears to the door, gun muzzles up, flashlights on high beam. I clicked my flashlight button once and they went in, and then I was inside my room, the .45 solid in my hand, windows in front of me, a big arc light on a pole guarding the front of the house, bulk of the bed to my right, big dresser above me, big easy chair farther along.

And the sounds of hunching coming from the bed.

I flipped the button on my flashlight. The bed swam into focus, two sets of eyes, a flash of skin, a gasp as a small person scurried backward, out of the circle of light.

By then I was at the side of the bed, my gun muzzle pressed into the neck of the man. He was a chunky guy, bald, with a hairy chest and bad teeth.

"Who the fuck are you?"

"Royal Canadian Mounted Police." I turned on the light. "Roll out of bed, onto your belly."

When he was flat on the carpet, I checked the drawer of the bedside table. One Beretta, loaded. One lid of marijuana. No more guns under the pillow or under the mattress. Out of the corner of my eye I saw movement, someone crawling for the door. I caught her in my flashlight beam. It was a kid, a girl with thin legs wearing a see-through teddy, like the kind Rollie Hansen kept in the garment bag back at the Queen Anne condo. She stopped when the light hit her. She sat with her back against the wall, using her hands to shield her eyes from the light.

"Are you okay?" I asked the little girl.

Her only reaction was a shiver that shook her frail shoulders.

"What's your name?" I asked the guy on the floor.

"Dill. What's yours?"

"Up on your knees, Dill. Hands behind your head, fingers laced."

"Why?"

"March."

"Where?"

"Across the balcony. To the other bedroom."

"Shit," he said. "I'm buck naked."

"Tough," I said.

"Let me put something on."

"It's safer this way."

We stopped at the doorway and I saw the little girl was an Asian. Her lipstick was smeared, her dark hair tousled. Her eyes looked drugged. I asked what her name was. She didn't answer. Then Hana was at the door, with another little girl. This one was a redhead. She wore a fur coat, high heels, and dangly emerald earrings. Her eyes, the tilt of her head, told me she was the con artist, the leader.

"Oh, Matt," Hana said. "Isn't this pitiful? They're just children."

"It's sick, all right."

"Are you all right?"

"Yeah. Where's Louie?"

"He's in there, with Big Daddy."

"Secured?"

"Louie taped his wrists and one ankle."

"You take charge here, okay?" I indicated the girls.

"All right. Where are you going?"

"To find a bruise to press on." I prodded Dill with the .45. "Move it," I said.

He waddled ahead of me, his bare cheeks shaking.

From the other room, music still played, horns blaring away in a rousing march for halftime.

19

BIG DADDY BORKLUND SAT ON THE FLOOR, HIS legs covered with a blanket, his wrists taped together, his right ankle taped to the bed frame. He was healthy and tanned. Lean face, shock of gray hair hanging down across his forehead. He looked me over with yellow eyes that were cold and rheumy, like frosted sherbet that had stayed too long in the deep-freeze.

Louie Chen sat in a chair facing Big Daddy. He smiled when he saw me. The pistol was tucked in his belt.

On the TV screen a jock ran around a track. I punched the Off button and the picture faded. I turned the volume down on the marching band. I handed Dill over to Louie, who secured his wrists before marching him downstairs.

"Who the hell you think you are, busting in here?"

I decided to fake it. "I'm the guy who can lead you to the formula."

"What formula?"

"Nielsen's formula."

He blinked. "You knew Nielsen?"

"I know people who know Nielsen."

"If you've got it, why not call? I'm ready to deal."

"You sent your goons after the lady." I nodded at the bathroom door. "They got rough. One's dead. One's hurt. Two more are tied up in your guardhouse on the beach."

"Who the hell are you?"

"Like I said, I know Nielsen."

It was a big bedroom, Persian rugs, parquet floor, some fine art on the walls. Electrical equipment in a wall unit to the right. A king-size TV, sweet little speakers, green winking lights and a shortwave radio and all the wires neatly tucked away. Shelves above the bed extended to the wall. No books in the room, just videotapes and a glass cabinet containing statuettes of nude ladies, four to six inches tall, sleek and exquisite.

"Why'd you kill Nielsen?"

"Didn't."

Still hunting for that soft spot, I picked up an ivory figurine of a lady wearing a sarong, a jug of water balanced on her head. I dropped the figurine. She shattered on the parquet floor. The yellow eyes did not blink.

"You trailed him down to Newport Beach and blew him away."

"I didn't know Nielsen. Up until yesterday he was a voice on the telephone. One time he's the Iceman. The next time he's God. I can't say I was in love with his attitude, but what motive did I have, for Christ's sake?"

"Your goons blew it. You still didn't have the formula, so you went after the lady."

"Horse puckey."

I picked up a second statue. This one was ebony, a woman with keen breasts jutting, almond eyes, the face of a dark angel. I hated to drop her. She made a faint splatter when she fell. No flinch from Big Daddy.

Still no soft spot, no bruise to press on.

The videos.

His collection was a history of sport. Football, basketball, baseball, soccer, rugby, ice hockey, boxing, martial arts, tennis, volleyball, mountain climbing, Olympics back to the twenties. One tape said *Nurmi, Amsterdam, 1928.* Another said *Rose Bowl, GT vs. CA, 1929.*

"GT stands for Georgia Tech?" I said.

"You get the gold star."

Another said *Schmeling, 1929–1930.* It was a priceless collection. It took effort to locate the film. It took money. It took technological expertise to transfer it to video format without ruining it. I checked the tape in the VHS player. The label said *BB: Olympic Training, 1939.*

"Who's BB?"

"Up yours." His voice caught.

I moved to the fireplace, poked around until I found some hot coals. I added paper and kindling. I pumped some bellows to redden the coals. When I had a good blaze going, I moved to the videocassettes and selected half a dozen, which I carried back to the fireplace.

"You prick," Big Daddy said.

I tossed in a Schmeling.

Big Daddy lunged at me. The gray duct tape brought him up short. "Those films are—"

I tossed in two Rose Bowls, 1932 and 1933.

More curses. I grinned, tossed in an Edmund Hillary, the guy who climbed Mount Everest.

"You lousy stinking prick, I don't even know this guy and—"

"That smell," Hana said from the doorway. "What are you burning?"

"Big Daddy's collection," I said. "A priceless video history of the sporting life."

"Okay, okay," Big Daddy said. "You made your point. Let's talk about the formula."

"There are three of us," I said. "I like things equal. Three hundred thousand and we lead you to the formula."

"One hundred and you deliver the formula to me, along with replacements for those tapes."

Hana moved to the case where the videotapes were stored, stood there with her hands on her hips, thinking. She tossed me a tape. Olympics, Berlin, 1936. I relayed it onto the flames. She tossed me a second tape, a third. Stink of melting plastic, scorched tape.

"What fun," Hana said.

"You crazy bitch! Stop it!"

"Three hundred grand."

"Two hundred," he growled. "Not a penny more."

I activated the machine and punched the Play button and there on the screen, grainy footage turned sepia by time, was the young runner, lean and rawboned. He wore baggy shorts and a BVD tank top and spike shoes. I turned up the volume on the military music again, Sousa, *oom paaa pa pa pa, pa pa paaa.* Big Daddy's jock past: a bruise to press on.

"Why," Hana said. "It's Mr. Borklund."

"You could sure run," I said to Big Daddy.

"I was fast, all right."

"When was this?" I said.

"I was in training," Big Daddy said. "For the 1940 Olympics."

"Those were never played, were they?"

"The damned war got in the way. Hitler and Churchill."

"You were a beautiful young man," Hana said, pressing the Eject button.

This time Hana did not throw me the videotape. Instead, she walked across the room to the fireplace. Big Daddy waited, yellow eyes narrowed as she held his footage close to the flames.

"Okay!" he yelled. "Three hundred grand! Okay!"

We'd found his soft spot. We could break statues of naked ladies. We could burn footage of sports figures down through time. But when we threatened to torch his precious jock past, Big Daddy agreed to our price, $300,000, for Rollie's formula. He'd pay one third now, two thirds when we turned it over.

Just one problem: We didn't have the formula.

Didn't know what it was. What it did.

I snipped the duct tape that tied Big Daddy's ankle to the bed. I walked with him downstairs to his study, where he opened a safe to get the $100,000. I walked him back upstairs, where I taped him to the bed again. Before leaving his fat-cat island retreat, I cut the telephone cables and did some major damage to his electrical system.

We left Dill and the bozo and Big Daddy on the island, but we took the girls and Stearns. The Asian girl still hadn't said anything, but the redhead chattered away. They were employees of a lady in Vancouver who ran a call girl service that specialized in teenyboppers. The lady's name was Mama Yen. The price tag for a night with one teenybopper was $1,000. Two teenyboppers for a weekend cost $3,000 and the client coughed up for expenses.

Only a fat cat can afford the best.

Stearns sneezed as we strapped him into a bunk in the main cabin. It would take a major detergent to wash this dirt out of the bedsheets.

Louie Chen stayed below to brew some tea. The teenyboppers sat on a bunk in the second cabin, the Asian silent, the redhead chattering away. Her subject was rock stars. I went up to the quarterdeck. Hana stood at the wheel, legs spread wide.

"How's everything down there?"

"Cooling down."

"You're quite a salesman, Mr. Murdock."

"How so?"

"Either I'm dreaming or I just watched you con a major crime figure out of a major sum of cash with the promise of a formula you don't have."

"You do hypnosis. I con dirty old men out of big bucks."

"What if he sends more nasty people to get back at us?"

"We'll give him another bloody nose."

"We do make a good team." Her voice was furry.

"Yes. We do."

"How did you think of burning his videotapes?"

"He's a jock. His soft spot is his jock past. The last time he felt squeaky clean was when he trained for the Olympics."

"But you don't think he killed Rollie?"

"Not now I don't."

"But you're still mad. I can feel you seething."

"More like a low boil," I said.

"You're mad because of her, right? Because of fifteen-year-old Cindy in the hospital back in California?"

"Because of Cindy," I said. "Because of you. Because of anyone they go after."

"It's what you do, isn't it? You do this to balance the scales?"

"Blunder around, you said."

"I was angry. I was miffed at you."

"Not anymore?"

"No." Her voice was soft now, inviting. "Not anymore. I like what you do. You go with the flow. You're a careful observer. You don't hurt people for fun. I like it that you saved me this afternoon. Actually, it was yesterday, wasn't it?"

"Seems like a long time ago," I said. "Eons."

A silence. Then she said: "How long were you in Vietnam?"

"Five years in the sixties. They carried me out in a medevac during the Tet offensive."

"Wounded?"

"Yes."

"Where?"

"Upper thigh." I pointed to the spot, four inches from my crotch, where I'd taken a major hit from the enemy.

Hana shivered and looked away. There was no talking for a moment. She put a hand on my hand. I felt heat. She took a step toward me, until we were close enough to rub noses, and then she leaned over and brushed my cheek with soft lips. "You're a nice man, Matt Murdock."

"I'm a tired man, Hana St. Cloud."

"Too tired to come home with me?"

"Not that tired." I took a deep breath. "Are you sure?"

"I'm sure. I've been sure since I patched up your poor back."

"What about Louie?"

"Louie is not invited."

Pause while I listened to my heart beating.

"Who'll tell him?"

"He knows."

"He's a romantic. He might throw a fit."

"Give the guy credit. He knows."

We released Stearns on the street near a taxi stand. His future did not look bright.

The girls were next. We drove to a house in Ballard. Hana ran to the door and rang the bell. A yellow light came on and I saw Hana talking to a woman in a bathrobe. We left the girls with her.

"Who is she?" I said.

"Her name's Suzanne. She takes care of runaways."

"Part of your network?"

"This is my town. I know the nooks."

"Nice nooks."

"I feel like the A Team," Louie said.

"Home, Louie," Hana said, kissing him on the cheek.

It was Sunday morning, still no light in the east, as we drove across the city toward Queen Anne Hill and I remembered other dark mornings, rolling out of bed at 4:00 A.M. to deliver papers in El Paso, when the Sergeant worked at Fort Bliss, and after that in Fayetteville, North Carolina, when he transferred to Bragg, and after that in Killeen, Texas, when he worked at Fort Hood. I remembered the morning air, cold in winter, cool in summer, no people, no sound except the radio as I folded papers in tight squares and then when the papers were folded and ready for sailing I'd ease the idle screw higher on my 1939 Chevrolet—a green two door with dual carbs, overhead cams, and a rebuilt V-8 420-horse engine—and I'd lock the steering wheel and stand on the running board with the Chevy moving at a sedate four mph down the silent streets, sidearming those squares of news home to the customers. Zap, into the screen. Pow, onto the porch.

I had never been so free.

"What are you thinking?" Hana said.

"Dawn," I said. "It always comes."

"Comes up like thunder," Louie said. "Out of China."

" 'acrost the Bay,' " I said. "Kipling. The soldier's poet."

Hana squeezed my arm. "This man. He makes deals with

crooks. He saves people. He reads poetry. What else is there?"

Louie Chen looked at me. He gulped. He looked away. There was no more talking on the way to Hana's. It was a long ten minutes before he let us out near her elevator.

"See you guys later," Louie said.

"We'll call," Hana said, and climbed out.

"Louie, I—"

He bopped me on the shoulder. His smile was strained around the edges. "Hey, man," he said. "Hey."

Puff of blue exhaust as Louie drove off, one toot from his horn. Hana took my hand.

"Come upstairs."

She stood close to me in the elevator. She said nothing as she leaned into me, her fingers tight on mine. There was no need for words. Inside her place she locked the door and came into my arms for a hug. Her hair smelled of salt spray. Her body was warm against mine.

"So, Mr. Murdock. Just how tired are you?"

"Less and less and less."

"Is it too early for a drink?"

"It's never too early for a drink."

"Brandy for warmth?"

"Brandy sounds good."

With a firm grip, thumb on my belt buckle, she towed me to the kitchen cupboard where she kept the booze. "Glasses are there," she said.

I opened the cupboard and grabbed two glasses. She poured and we clinked glasses and drank. With the first sip, Big Daddy faded, his yellow eyes, the videotapes in the fire, the teeth of those guard dogs.

"How is that knife wound?"

"Burns some."

She set her glass down. She unzipped my vest and pulled

my shirttails out and told me to turn around so she could check my wound. Her fingers were cool on my skin.

"That bandage needs changing."

"Okay."

I sat on the stool with my shirt off, sipping brandy while she changed the bandage. Snip of scissors, the sound of tape being ripped. Adhesive tape used to smell like rubber. Now it smells like plastic. The burning stopped.

"Better?"

"Better. Thanks."

She handed me my shirt and she walked over to the stereo. When she squatted down, the jeans pulled tight across her bottom and thighs. The music started, an oldie, "Slow Boat to China."

"Hey," I said, humming along.

"My granddad," she said. "He taught me to dance. This was one of his favorites." She stood there, waiting, tapping her foot. I got the message.

"May I have this dance?"

"Yes."

We danced to the music, boots off, sliding across the floor. "Sentimental Journey" came on.

"On Saturday nights," she said, "when the snow piled up and you couldn't go anywhere, my granddad put on a record and we'd dance around the living room. I was ten or eleven, a little girl full of dreams. He helped me so much."

"He sounds like a great guy."

"He was," she said. "He was."

"My kind of music."

"Yes."

There was no talking for a while. I was aware of her body, the long, solid thighs and the slight tummy pooch and above that the concave intake of her rib cage and the softness of her breasts against my chest.

I started to say something but she placed a cool finger on my lips. She touched my chin, my cheeks, my nose, my forehead. "You're sweating."

"It's the brandy."

"Very funny." She slipped a hand inside my shirt, ran it up my rib cage, under the arm, touching the bandage. She slipped the other hand under my shirt. I took a deep breath.

"Hmm," she said as she put her head on my chest. "Hmm."

After a while, I heard the needle dragging away at the wide inside grooves of the record, *swish a swish a swish,* and she led me by the hand over to the turntable and bent down to turn the record over. Then she came into my arms and we kissed. Not hard, not fierce. A testing kiss, light and easy. A getting-to-know-you kiss. Our dancing was closer now. We danced to "Volare" and "Love Is a Many-Splendored Thing" and "The Age of Aquarius." Dancing with her I forgot about time. There was only the music, our feet moving. There was only us.

After a while the music stopped and she did not start the record again. Instead, she led me into her bedroom. "Lie down," she said. I lay back against the pillows. She snuggled into my arms. We kissed, her face in close up, eyes open, probing my soul, lips and teeth and her tongue on mine, the weight of her leg across mine, my world a whirl of warmth and softness and the fragrance of her hair and her fingers on my belly inside my shirt.

She undressed me, giggling, tugging, pulling my jeans off.

"Come on, you. Come on."

"Easy. Damn."

"Did I hurt you?"

"No."

"I feel . . . strange," she said. "I feel okay. I feel as if I've known you before. Like we're not strangers at all."

"I feel that too."

"It's crazy. I like it."

"Me too."

She left the bed. In the pale shadowed light from the street I watched her slip out of her clothes, heard them drop to the floor, and then we were safe beneath the covers and I buried my face in her soft throat and she pressed herself closer, murmuring, touching, the feel of her hand on mine as she guided me to her secret places, opening, closing, clasping, soft brush of her lips, body slick as a water creature, nipping at my beard with sharp teeth, and then the long feel of her as she took both my hands in hers and we interlaced fingers and she whispered, "You're an angel in the snow," and lay on top of me, my arms out straight like a skydiver's in free-fall, her arms along mine, our mouths locked, bellies touching, hearts pounding together, and then she opened up like a flower, taking me inside, settling in, breathing together as she began drumming with her thighs, only her thighs moving in rhythm against mine, drumming and drumming, the sound of the drums pounding in my brain as I whirled with her, world within world, on our wild clinging trip out to the stars.

20

Hana served me coffee in bed.

"How about we stay here all day?"

"How about all week?"

"This is super good coffee."

"My own special blend, from Starbuck's."

"Seattle," I said, "is a wonderful place."

"My town," she said.

"Tell me about the painting," I said. "The nude with the death's-head."

"Homage to Georgia O'Keeffe."

"There's a painting at Rollie's place, signed St. Cl——. The death's-head is signed Lakota."

"Outer self, inner self," she said.

"Which one is real?"

"I seldom know. Both, I guess. I don't know."

"How long have you been an artist?"

She smiled, stretched, sipped some coffee. "I did my first drawing when I was three. Other girls bought dolls at the local K mart. I made my own dolls. Made them out of clay and sticks and papier-mâché. I scrounged for drawing materials, paper, crayons, pencils. I had a little friend in my head named Alicia Angel who told me what to draw. Alicia Angel got me through a lot of tight spots. In college, I devoured Greek myth and switched to a father-figure muse, an old Greek named Xanthos. After college, I studied with a woman who'd worked with Georgia O'Keeffe. That's when I did the death's-head."

"Where did you go to college?"

"Here. At the U-Dub."

"And high school?"

"In Bellingham. That's north of here. My father wasn't around much. My mother died when I was eight, so I lived with her sister, Aunt Harriet, and was raised mostly by my granddad. He had Indian blood and dark skin and black hair like me. I hated it when he died. That's the story of the education of H. L. St. Cloud. Now tell me about Matt Murdock. Where did you go to school?"

Neat change of subject. "Army bases," I said. "Or towns where army bases were. Three years in El Paso. Another three in North Carolina, at Fort Bragg. My old man was career army."

"As a soldier, you marched in his footsteps."

"The idea was to do better, ace him where it hurt. So I went to OCS and became an officer, just to spite him."

"What rank?"

"Captain, on my way to major."

"So you could order him around."

"You're sharp," I said.

"I know some veterans. They're very bitter."

"Vietnam was a dumb war. A writer I got to know over there called it a media war. I never thought about that until I got back, but he was right. The cameras were there, shooting, recording rock music as those kids went into the bush." I sipped some coffee. "Cameras miss smells."

"What smells?"

"Cordite. Mud. Blood smell like copper pennies. Rats and rat shit and jungle rot and jungle stink."

"The jungle," she said. "I think it's—"

She didn't finish because the phone rang.

Hana answered, then handed me the phone. "It's Louie."

"Hey, Louie."

"Sorry to bother you guys, but a Fed just spent a half hour bugging me about your whereabouts. They put a tail on me. I'm phoning from the QFC market on Twenty-fourth."

"What Fed?"

"His name's Feldman. He had a message from a guy named Loomis. That's your guy, right?"

"Right. Where is he?"

"Feldman gave me a local phone number. If you call it they can patch you through. Got a pencil?"

"Sure."

Louie read me the number. "What do you think is up?"

"He's after something," I said. "And it's not just bad guys."

"The elusive formula that we peddled to Big Daddy?"

"Maybe."

"These Feds are intense, man. And pushy."

"Being a Fed brings out the best in a guy. Are you staying put?"

"I can stick here for ten."

"I'll call you back when I know more."

I got dressed. When I went into the main room, Hana was at the cabinet making fresh coffee. She wore boot socks, Indian moccasins, and a heavy terry cloth robe. Her face looked worried.

Standing at the window, looking out, I blinked, stretched. What did Loomis want? I turned the dial on Hana's egg timer to three minutes—they couldn't complete a trace in less than five—and punched in the number I'd gotten from Louie Chen.

"Garcia," a voice said. "State your business."

"Patch me through to Agent Loomis," I said.

"Who wants him?"

"Murdock. From Newport Beach."

A pause, multiple clicks on the phone, probably the sound of activating their tracing apparatus. "Patching. Please hold."

More clicks on the line as the equipment routed my call through to Agent Loomis. I missed the old days when they'd hold a cupped hand over the phone and yell for whoever you wanted and you could hear conversations through cracks between grimy fingers. No more. This was the age of the electronic patch-through.

"Mr. Murdock. I was hoping we could set up a meet."

"You in town, Agent?"

"No. I meant with some of my people."

"There's nothing new at my end."

"Well, you never know about that. We have a couple of leads we might pass along, depending."

"Depending on what?"

"Depending on how you're doing with the Seattle police."

"What's that supposed to mean?"

"I have on the desk in front of me a report of a melee that took place yesterday afternoon in a parking garage in downtown Seattle. One dead, one hospitalized, a third man unaccounted for."

"Still nothing new at my end."

"The current carnage fits your MO, Murdock, and I thought my people might give you a hand when the police do arrive with a warrant. A meet would reconnect us, so to speak. We could pool our information and our insights and if we don't come up with answers, we might formulate keener questions. Good detective work, as you know, is a process of eliminating suspects."

"Thanks," I said.

"It's just after eleven now. Do you know Seattle?"

"Not well."

"Beautiful city. There's a view spot on the Ballard locks, it's called Hiram's. An agent named Feldman will meet with you there at noon. He has information I'm sure you'll find—"

The egg timer went *ding.* I hung up.

"What was that all about?" Hana said.

"Something cooking with our man at the CIA."

"Agent Loomis, right?"

"You've got a good memory for names."

"Thanks."

I phoned Louie Chen at the QFC market, told him to keep moving, try to shake that tail. I didn't want to meet with Agent Feldman. I didn't want to meet anyone, didn't want to leave the house. I wanted to climb back into bed with Hana.

We had $100,000, con money from Borklund. In Mexico, $100,000 would last forever. I forgot we had to split with Louie Chen. Maybe he'd come too, a happy threesome in Old Mexico.

While Hana poured coffee and served a plate of sweet treats, I recounted my two meetings with Agent Loomis of the CIA. When I finished, she asked a smart question: "So you don't trust him?"

"No way."

"Tell me why not."

"He's a fat cat in the making. He's young and well fed, a sleek look about the eyes, a smoothie always licking his own fur. His middle name is manipulator. He's found me in his computer and now he wants to use me as a probe."

"Probe into what?"

"Something to do with the case, all these killings."

"That's more like a cat's-paw."

"You're right." I sipped my coffee. "I had a buddy in Saigon who worked for the CIA. His name was Bruce and he was an ace recruiter. Lots of rah-rah talk about flag and country and apple pie and the minute you said yes he'd ship your ass off on Mission Impossible while he kept his cool in the air-conditioned splendor of the command shack."

"This Loomis, how did he find you up here?"

"Through Louie, I imagine."

"How did he find Louie?"

"Louie was on my answering machine."

"Oh." She bit into a pastry. "Are you going to that meeting?"

"No."

"Good thinking." She left me alone and headed into the bedroom. The phone rang again and I heard her answer. In a moment, she came to the door. "Matt, you'd better hear this."

I picked up to hear Hana talking to a guy with a Spanish accent. His voice sounded tired and weak.

"Who is this?" I said.

"*El hombre de* . . . It is the man from the parking garage. I am hurt, *señor*. I need your . . . *ayuda*."

Ayuda was Spanish for help.

"How did you get this number?"

"A black book, senor. *Un libro negro*. You have the debt with me. Will you help?" He stopped talking and went into a coughing fit, a burbly, watery, drowning man kind of cough.

"Matt," Hana said. "He needs help. Listen, he's really—"

"Yeah, but who the hell is he?"

"Matt, I have a feeling—"

"Okay, pal. Who is this and where are you?"

"I am called Eduardo. I have a doctor in the city, *el médico,* and . . . do you know the *apartamento* of Señor Chick Dickens? It is—"

"I know it."

"Oh, Matt."

"Ten minutes, Eduardo. No tricks or you're dead."

"Please, *señor.* Please to hurry."

21

WHILE SHE DRESSED, HANA INSTRUCTED ME ON the medical stuff we'd need: bandages, tape, hydrogen peroxide, homeopathic remedies. I gathered it into a red REI backpack. Louie called as we were leaving. The CIA tail was still on him. I briefed Louie on the latest development. If he could shake the tail, he said, he'd meet us at Hana's pad.

In Hana's Olds, heading for Rollie's place, Hana said, "That voice, with the Spanish accent. I think he's called before."

"When?"

"Friday, early afternoon. A man called, asking for Chick Dickens. He had an accent. I told him he had the wrong number. There was no Dickens here."

"Chick Dickens," I said. "As in Charles."

"Yes." Hana's voice was excited. "Then last night, when Louie and I got to talking, he told me about Gaspard, the name Rollie used in that motel in California. I filed it. I forgot it. Then when I heard that voice again, things started to click. Gaspard was a character in *A Tale of Two Cities.*"

"There was a paperback copy of the book in Rollie's U-District place. I picked it up."

"Do you have it?"

"It's at Louie's."

"I need to see the book."

"Okay."

"There's a connection, Matt. I can feel it."

"Dickens and Gaspard," I said. "Gaspard and Dickens."

"The man on the phone knew. But how? And how did he find me?"

"Reverse directory, is my guess. Did Rollie have a black book?"

"Of course, his bachelor fun book." She made a right turn and we were heading uphill. "If the man has the book, that means he killed Rollie?"

"It's a good bet."

"What's he doing here?"

"He's after that ice lab, just like everybody else."

"So he thinks it's here too?"

"That's the first question we'll ask him."

Her fingers dug into my arm. Her face burned with intensity. She kept driving, toward Rollie Nielsen's condo.

Hana rang Rollie's buzzer and stepped to the left of the door. I stood on the right side, holding the .45 muzzle up.

The lock clicked and the door opened and a man stood there, leaning against the door frame. He had wrapped his upper torso with a strip of yellow bedsheet. Blood had soaked through the bedsheet. His face was pale and he held a pistol in his right hand. He was a medium-built guy, five-eight, weight maybe 170 pounds. His face had a day's growth of beard. Light from the interior bounced off his bald head and I recognized him. He was the guy who'd watched me at Sea-Tac Airport. From this close, you could smell the wound festering.

"*¿Por favor?*" He sagged against the wall, dropping the pistol.

We lugged him into the bedroom. On the bedside table, next to an empty water glass, was a set of keys. A suitcase sat on the floor at the foot of the bed. It was leather, with a big silver buckle and wide straps.

While I secured the apartment, Hana stripped off the makeshift bandage. When I came back into the bedroom carrying a bottle of Chivas, the man's eyes were closed. Hana had the bandage off and you could see the bullet hole in his torso, an entry wound the size of a yellow number 2 pencil that had smashed the lowest rib on the left side. Around the entry wound was a rough circle, six inches across, of purple and green skin. Hana handed me a brown bottle with an eyedropper squeeze top. "Can you open that."

I opened it and handed it back. Bending over the man, Hana dripped ten drops of brown liquid into the entry hole.

"What is it?"

"Ledum. Good for punctures. There's nothing in the materia medica about bullet wounds."

"Did it go through?"

"There's no hole in his back. No bleeding. Help me get his mouth open."

While I pried his teeth apart, she popped in six Arnica pellets. Gunshot wounds are bad business. There's shock and bleeding and the danger goes up if an organ gets hit.

"He's burning up, Matt."

"That slug needs to come out. He mentioned a doctor—one who won't yap to the cops, I'll bet. If he doesn't come to and tell us, he's a goner."

"Harborview," Hana said. "We could take him there."

"Okay. Bandage him up and I'll get some fresh clothes."

Hana dropped more Ledum into the wound. Hana bandaged him while I checked out his suitcase. In it I found ammo for the pistol, a U.S. passport, a Florida driver's license, shirts, underwear, bundles of cash, and a vial of green pills. No label on the vial. The passport and driver's license had the same name: Eduardo de la Cruz. The address was in Miami. Eduardo's eyes popped open. He said something in rapid Spanish.

"Did you catch that?"

"Too fast for me."

"El Hombre del Saco, señores. He comes for me."

"Man with a sack?" I said.

"Sí, señor. He comes for me as a child and now in this life of a man grown he comes for me again, carrying a black sack with which to capture me to the land of *Los Muertos.* He wears a serape and sandals of straw and his face is—" He blinked. There was more color in his cheeks. The homeopathy was working. I gave him a shot of Scotch, for courage. He nodded his thanks.

"Where's your doctor, Eduardo?"

"In Magnolia." His eyebrows arched as he noted the black book. "Is that the *libro negro?"*

"Yes."

"The doctor is called Cortazar. Let us hurry, *señores.* Bring the *maleta,* the suitcase. This pain is *formidable."*

He groaned when we sat him up. Groaned again when we got him standing, face pale and sweaty now as I draped a clean shirt over his shoulders, and then a jacket. Old Eduardo was a tough guy, lasting this long with a bullet in him. In the elevator, he leaned against me, barely breathing. He had Rollie's keys, Rollie's black book. If he hadn't killed Rollie, he'd been in the motel room soon after. The packages of hundred-dollar bills could be Rollie's loot from his last ice deal. Question: If Eduardo had killed Rollie, then who had shot Eduardo?

In the Olds, Eduardo tapped the black suitcase with his index finger. *"Dinero,"* he said. "Money inside. Half is yours."

"You killed Rollie Nielsen, right?"

"He is known to me as Chick Dickens, *un comerciante* of the ice."

"But you did kill him?"

"Sí, señor. It was a necessity."

"For the formula?"

"No, *señor.* Because I am forced."

"Bullshit, Eduardo."

"He comes at me, *señor.* A strong man, he comes at me, forcing me to—"

"Bullshit."

"As a soldier, *señor,* I have too much of the killing. I am a professional. To kill him was not my job."

"Okay. What was your job?"

"To locate his lab, his *laboratorio.* Is there more of those *pastillas?* This pain is—"

I gave him more Arnica. He nodded his thanks. We were heading downhill, raindrops slanting against the windshield of the Olds. Hana was at the wheel, driving just over the speed limit. I wiped sweat off Eduardo's forehead. He nodded, wet his lips. I didn't believe him about Rollie. I kept on with the questions.

"Tell me about the job."

"Do you know a man called Loomis? Of the CIA?"

"We've met."

"I am *un investigador* in Miami, a *detective privado,* such as yourself. Before that I was a refugee. Before that, a soldier."

"Which army?"

"The army of Colombia, *señor*. In Miami there are many drugs and much fighting over the customers. In Miami I meet many agents of the government. One of them—Agent Loomis—has the evidence from the old days to use against me. Agent Loomis desires that I work for him. If I shall do this, he agrees to, how does one say, to push away the evidence."

"Suppress," Hana said.

"*Sí, señorita.* To suppress the evidence."

"What was the job, Eduardo?"

"A secret operation, he says, a thing against *los cocineros,* the cookers. It is my job to locate such cookers and from them I should also find the location of *la cocina,* the kitchen where they are doing this cooking. I must inform Agent Loomis, who takes over. Señor Chick Dickens was my first such."

Hana turned onto a bridge. We were heading west now, houses up ahead. I did not recognize the street names.

"When did you find out Chick Dickens was Rollie Nielsen?"

"It was on Friday," Eduardo said. "When I telephoned *la señorita.*" He indicated Hana. "Open the black book, *señor.*"

I opened it. On the first page was a column of *A*'s, each *A* followed by a ten-digit phone number. Some I recognized— 213 for Los Angeles, 714 for Orange County, 415 for the Bay Area, 818 for the Valley, 619 for San Diego, 206 for Seattle. The columns ran alphabetically. I flipped to a page in the middle of the notebook, initials *G, H,* and *I*. One *H* had a 206 area code. I read the number to Hana.

"It's mine, all right," she said.

"Okay, Eduardo. How does the book fit in?"

He paused, searching for the words. "It happens in this manner. Señor Dickens dies *en el sábado,* on Saturday, forcing me to depart the city. My *misión,* you understand, is not finish until the *laboratorio* is found. Agent Loomis raises the price to twenty-five thousand dollars. Before it has been only five. Señor Dickens says the *laboratorio* is in Loma Linda. I am not able to find it there. From the black book, I make the calls. Señor Dickens is in demand from his drugs. But, *que lástima,* after many calls I have nothing, and so it is that—" He broke off to cough. "And so it was that I am thinking perhaps it is possible to turn this one around. Do you see?"

"Not yet, Eduardo. Not yet."

"*Pues,* how to say it." He thought for a minute. "Here it is, *señor.* As I failed with those who knew him, perhaps the track is with someone who does not know."

"You mean people who didn't know that Señor Dickens was also Rollie Nielsen?"

"Not people, *señor.* Only the women. Only the ladies."

"That sounds like Rollie," Hana said.

"So you telephoned the *señorita.*" I indicated Hana. "And then what happened?"

"A simple matter, *señor,* as I know Seattle."

"How?"

"From business," he said, "on previous occasions."

"The detective business?"

"*Sí, señor.* Shall I continue?"

"Go on."

"*Bueno.* On following Señorita St. Cloud to the *apartamento,* I see you and another man, *un chino.* With the keys from Señor Dickens I can open the door. For me, this is a sign that I am near the end of my hunt." He coughed, a small one.

"Let's backtrack a minute."

"As you wish, *señor.*"

"You were in the airport on Friday, watching me."

"A thing done without the usual care."

"How come you knew who I was?"

"From the television. From the report of the shooting in Newport Beach. Then, too, I have seen you while I wait for Señor Dickens to make his deal. We have the same work, you and I. We are *compadres, señor.* Brothers-in-arms."

Eduardo, my brother. What a laugh.

"Okay, Eduardo. You killed Rollie by accident. You got this phone number from the black book. You followed the lady around a couple of days and then you got shot. How?"

A tired smile from Eduardo. "Agent Loomis is eager to find the *laboratorio.* Yet when I ask why, he does not say. I know now that he shall pay more."

"So you gouged him?"

Eduardo blinked. "Because of the death of Señor Dickens, I am now in need of money. I must leave the country. Therefore, when I do find it, I phone Agent Loomis. He is not happy, but we agree on a new price. Then, when I meet with his *gente,* his people, they try to kill me."

"When was this?"

"Last evening."

"Where?"

"In a *depósito, señor,* a warehouse that I know."

"What happened?"

"They did not bring money. I know one of them, a *mercenario* called Landsberg, from the old days. They shoot. I shoot. And then . . ." Eduardo shrugged. Pain contorted his face.

"They wanted these, didn't they?" I showed him the vial of pills.

"Ahh," he said.

"What are they for, Eduardo? What do the green pills do?"

He closed his eyes and shook his head slowly. "I do not know, *señor*. Truly I do not."

"Where's the lab then? Where's Rollie's lab?"

No answer from Eduardo. Up ahead, against the gray clouds scudding, I could see the edge of a park, bushes of deep green, wet shining grass.

Hana spoke from the front seat. "I think that's the doctor's house on the right, Matt." She swung into the driveway.

I stayed with Eduardo while she went to the door. "How did Rollie Nielsen die?"

"I desire him to take me to the *laboratorio*. He makes the agreement. The telephone rings. He comes at me. I see that his bravery comes from the ice. He is strong, *señor*. It is not my desire to kill him, not my job. I have killed before. Never do I find it the easy thing that is shown in the movies with the *pistoleros* in their sombreros in the sun."

I pointed to a spot behind the left ear. "You shot him here, right?"

"No, *señor*."

"Someone did."

"It was not I."

Hana jogged back to the Olds and climbed behind the wheel. At the same time, the garage door opened. Hana drove inside and the garage door closed behind us. Eduardo's doctor was a tiny little man with a sad face and small brown eyes behind thick metal-rimmed glasses. He spoke to Eduardo in rapidfire Spanish as we loaded him onto a gurney and wheeled him inside, down a hallway to the back of the house, where a room was fitted out like a miniature ER. Hospital smells here, alcohol and antiseptic, and over it a layer of heavy cigarette smoke. Light caught the gray hair of the doctor as he bent to examine the wound, muttering at Eduardo.

"*Señor,* in the *maleta. El doctor* wants his money."

"I'll get it." Hana left the room.

With a pair of blunt-nosed scissors, the doctor began snipping away at the makeshift bandage. Eduardo reached out a hand to me and I took it. "A favor, *señor.*"

"What?"

"Do you know a man, a *politico* who lives in Laguna Beach? He is called Carruthers."

"I know the name."

Eduardo nodded. "Three times I see this man together with Agent Loomis. At another time I see him, Señor Carruthers, with the dope dealer who showed Señor Dickens to me. It is my feeling"—he pointed to his heart—"that they are tied together as in a knot."

"This dealer, was his name Joel?"

"*Sí, señor,* a youth with the face of a rat. I am telling you this so that you can perhaps . . ." With his hand like a knife, he made a slicing motion across his own throat and gave me a savage look. I got the message: Eduardo wanted revenge. He figures he might not make it with a bullet in him, so he brings me in. I grinned. Loomis, Joel, Carruthers. I was closer to skinning my fat cat.

Hana came back with the black suitcase. Eduardo motioned for her to open it. She popped the latches and unbuckled and he tilted his head okay. The tiny doctor reached in a tiny hand. He brought out money packets. A smile broke through his doctor mask.

"You must go," he said. "Do me the honor of leaving my house."

"There is something," Eduardo said. "Something from Señor Dickens." He unfolded his fist to show me a rectangle of cardboard. It was mangled, sweaty, the edges stained with blood. He handed it to me, a business card: CHICK DICK-

ENS, INSURANCE ADJUSTOR, with a P.O. box in Loma Linda,
CA.

The sun came out as we headed east, away from Magnolia.

"You have to hand it to Eduardo," Hana said, "for his detective skills. He found me. He spotted you at Sea-Tac."

I was thinking of Shelby Carruthers. "What screwed things up was killing Rollie before he located the ice lab."

"You think he would have killed Rollie anyway?"

"Yeah."

"And those others? The ones who died before Rollie?"

"Maybe."

"He seems so helpless."

"One thing's for sure. He can really shoot. He hit that guy in the parking garage at seventy-five feet with minimum light."

"I see him as a victim. A refugee fighting for his life."

"Well, we helped him. Got him to his doc."

"I feel good about helping him."

"So do I. But what do I tell Rollie's dad?"

"The truth."

"Thanks," I said.

"And so now you have a name. Shelby something."

"Shelby Carruthers."

"What do you know about him?"

"Just the usual half lies you hear about politicians. He's a California boy, a rare native son. Born in L.A. to money, used his inheritance to parlay a fortune in real estate. Lives in a gated community in Laguna Beach. A liberal friend of mine who's pro-choice filled me in. Shelby's anti-abortion and pro-nuke."

"I hate politics."

"Keeps the creeps off the street and in the parliament."

"So. When are you leaving?"

"Today. Tonight. The first flight out."

"I'm going to miss you, Matt Murdock."

"I'll miss you too. Why not come for a visit? Work on your tan."

"I don't like California. I feel stifled down there. I feel caged."

"Well, you're invited."

Through the windshield, Seattle sunlight, a pale yellow, fought a losing battle with gray Seattle skies. Raindrops dotted the windshield of the Olds and I was aware of Hana, hands on the wheel, mood building like a dark thunderhead.

"Before you go, there's something I want."

"What's that?"

"Help with some unfinished business."

"What kind of help? What kind of business?"

"Big Daddy Borklund."

"We took him for a hundred grand. What else do you want?"

"Not money. I want to . . . squeeze him. I keep seeing that little girl in his bed. I keep hearing that silly marching band. He's a filthy man. He sent those men after me. He deserves to be punished. And—"

"And?"

"And since revenge is your trade, I thought—"

"Leave it, Hana."

"No. If you won't help, I'll ask Louie."

"You'll both get hurt. Leave it alone."

We stopped at a red light. Her eyes burned with emotion. "Why can't we do something with that lab? Trade it? Suck him in? Hatch a sting or something?"

"Great idea, but we don't know where it is."

"Eduardo knows. He found it."

"He forgot to tell us."

"He gave us the clues, Matt."

I stretched. I thought of California. "What clues?"

"Dickens, Gaspard, Rollie's paperback of *A Tale of Two Cities*."

"As clues, those are pretty thin."

"Okay, look. Why did Eduardo wait until the last moment before handing over that bloody business card?"

"He was shot. He was delirious."

"Maybe not."

"Okay. Chalk it up to Latino melodrama."

"Maybe not."

"I've covered that ground, Hana. Nothing there but a dead writer and more of Rollie's games."

"I have a friend," Hana said. "She's a prof at the university, a Dickens specialist. Let me call her."

"Waste of time," I said. "And fat cats don't wait around forever."

Hana put a hand on my leg. "Please?"

"Okay," I said. "Call your friend."

22

Louie Chen arrived just as Hana was wrapping up her call to her friend the Dickens expert. Happy grin as he walked past me, the physics major turned private eye. "I shook them, Matt."

"Good for you."

"Two bird dogs, and I shook them both." He danced a few steps on his way to the sink. He waved at Hana. Louie put water on for tea.

I was waiting for my turn at the phone. I had calls to make to California. I had my agenda.

"Thanks, Deirdre," Hana said. "I owe you, hon." She hung up and we all sat at the coffee table while she explained things to Louie. He loved it, the idea of clues taken from a novel by Dickens.

Louie opened the phone book and Hana gave him the first name: "Chuzzlewit."

"Long shot," I said.

"No Chuzzlewit." Louie traced his index finger down a column of names. "This is hard to believe, you know?"

"What's hard to believe?"

"Rollie. Here's a guy whose idea of light reading is *Scientific American* so he designs a code setup from Dickens? Jazzy, is what I say. What's the next name?"

Names from Dickens buzzed between them. Uriah Heep, Pickwick, Mr. Jarvis Lorry. The water boiled. I brewed tea. While it steeped, I made a call from Hana's bedroom phone to Webby Smith at the police station in Laguna Beach. It answered after the second ring. Webby briefed me.

Shelby Carruthers was connected, Webby said, local mayors, county supervisors, the sheriff, the lieutenant governor, key members of the coastal commission. In his run for the U.S. Congress, Shelby was ahead in the polls. Webby said he'd have the San Berdoo sheriff check out the Chick Dickens P.O. box in Loma Linda. Then he gave me the name of Sergeant Otto Rolfe, a contact in the Seattle PD.

That reminded me of my favorite policeman. "Things still chummy with Detective Giordano?"

"Something funny going on there, Sherlock."

"How so?"

"Seems he's called in sick for the last couple of days."

"Blue flu?"

"Maybe. Where did you pick up the skinny on Carruthers?"

"From a Miami private eye and ex-soldier for the army of Colombia who I suspect is a hit man for the CIA."

"Oh boy," Webby said. "Here we go again."

"What's that supposed to mean?"

"You leave town for a rest. A couple days later you've uncovered a conspiracy to bring down the government. A Colombian contractor with CIA linkage. You're something else."

"Thanks. Will you check this stuff out for me?"

"Sure. No problem." Papers rattled at Webby's end of

the phone. "Before you hang up, I got some news on that kid, Julio, the one you wasted."

My stomach swirled. Sudden taste of copper on my tongue. "What news?"

"Here it is. The autopsy report showed traces of ice in the bloodstream, on Julio and that other guy too. They were smoking and shooting, crazy on an ice high. Chemical courage, buddy. You had to waste him."

"Thanks, Iron Man."

"There was one way to go. You took it."

"It still doesn't sit still," I said.

"Bad dreams?"

"Yeah," I said.

"Hang tough," Webby said.

After we hung up, I phoned St. Boniface Hospital. Cindy was in Thor's room, watching TV. I spoke to her first. The pain was almost gone, she said, but there was still some swelling. Wally came in every day with "that medicine" and Cindy's attending doc was amazed at her progress. She had not been allowed to attend Phyl's funeral, but Phyl's mom visited every day. "She keeps saying she's sorry, like she's finally noticed about Phyl. Oh, and she asked me to apologize to you. She's sorry about that too."

"Thanks. Is your room still available at her place?"

"Yeah, but I'm not thinking about that. It's not home anymore. Here's Thor."

"Hey, Murdock," Thor Nielsen said. "Any progress?"

"Some." I didn't want to tell him about Eduardo. "I'll be back down there, maybe tomorrow. I'll tell you about it then."

"Can't talk on the phone, eh?"

"Right." I stared at the pattern of light on Hana's wall. "How are you feeling?"

"Stronger every day, eager to get back home. I sure like this Miss Cindy Duke. She's a sweetheart."

"Thanks for looking after her."

"Bright as a penny," Thor said. "Beats me at checkers, so I'm teaching her chess."

I said good-bye and rejoined Hana and Louie.

"No Oliver Twist," Louie said.

"How about Carton? Sydney Carton."

"We could have done this faster if we'd been alphabetized."

"Come on, Louie. Come on."

"Sidney was Rollie's middle name. I've got one. Carton, S. There's no address, but the number could be U-District."

I watched Hana punch in the number. I had dismissed the Dickens stuff, skipped over it, tossed it aside, and now I had this empty feeling in my gut because it was right there, Gaspard and the Dickens paperback, and I'd let it slip away.

"It's Rollie's voice." She shoved the phone at Louie. "Listen."

"It's him." Louie was doing an Irish jig, not an easy thing while you listen to the phone. "It's Rollie." She dialed again so they could listen a second time. "Sydney Carton had a double. Who was it?"

"Darnay," Hana said. "Charles Darnay."

"As in Chick," Louie said.

Hana dialed the number for Darnay. When the phone rang, they made me listen in: "Hiya," a voice said. "This is Chuck. If Myra or Helene or Bitsi calls, leave a number and I'll call you back. Gotta fly, so bye."

"That's Rollie's voice?"

"Yes. Of course it is. Okay? Are you with us now?"

"I'm catching up, guys. Carton in the U-District, Darnay on Queen Anne, but where's the lab?"

"Be patient, okay?"

"The father of the bride." Louie snapped his fingers. "The old guy in the Bastille, what was his name?"

"Manette," Hana said. "He was a doctor."

Louie was at the phone book now, flipping through. "Manette, right here." He dialed. He held the phone so we could listen, three ears straining together as we heard Rollie's voice saying: "Hi. This is Bob. I'm away from the phone right now, but if you'll leave your name, your number, and the time you called, I'll get back to you toot sweet."

"Oh, Rollie." Hana's ear was close to mine. "You poor sap."

"The number looks like north Seattle," Louie said. "Let me call my guy for the address."

While he called, Hana poured tea. "I told you," she said. "I told you."

"You told me," I said.

"It's in Bothell," Louie said. "A trailer park or mobile home court named Sammamish Shores Mobile Park. The address is 17 Emerson Lane."

"Well?" Hana was looking at me.

"Well what?"

"Well, what's the plan?"

"What plan?"

"The sting," she said. "The punishment to fit the crimes."

I exhaled. "We'll need the local cops."

"I thought you didn't like the police," Hana said.

"Only when I'm a suspect in a shooting," I said. "Otherwise, I like cops just fine."

"Murdock," she said. "You're a rascal."

∎

The sun was out, fleecy white clouds loafing across a blue sky as we motored north on Interstate 5 toward Bothell. Trees lined the interstate on both sides and Seattleites were zipping along the asphalt, their eyes on pleasure and fun.

"What are you thinking?" Hana asked.

"I didn't tell him," I said.

"Didn't tell who what?"

"Didn't tell Thor that I'd found Rollie's killer. Didn't tell him I'd let the guy go."

"You had your chance to shoot him."

"I thought about it."

"For how long?"

"Couple of seconds."

"He was hurt. He gave us the lab. He gave you Carruthers. Why not tell Mr. Nielsen you treated the man with professional courtesy?"

"He hired me to find Rollie's killer."

"You found him."

"I let him go."

"He made a deal with you. He also saved your life in that parking garage."

I said nothing as Louie turned off the interstate and we headed east, the sun behind us to the right.

A map of the area, courtesy of the Seattle AAA, helped us locate 17 Emerson Lane at Sammamish Shores, a verdant spot nestled between a grove of evergreens and a lake. The mobile homes were double units with postcard-size lawns and white picket fences and shrubs running along the fences, remnants of the American dream. Number 17, a single, was the last unit in a row that curved in a parallel track to the water. A hedge, five feet tall and bushy green, stood between number 17 and the nearest neighbor.

The afternoon sky was brilliant, the air washed clear by

rain, white clouds puffing along to the west. Gulls swarmed over the surface of the lake where a man in a powerboat was tossing them bread bits from a brown paper sack.

Playing the roles of newlyweds on a house hunt, Louie Chen and Hana distracted the neighbors while I scuttled around behind the hedge to number 17 Emerson Lane. Chilly in the doorway, out of the sun. I pulled out the lockpick, twenty-nine seconds before the tumblers fell into place and I was inside.

According to his dad, Rollie Nielsen loved to play. He played with ink, colored dyes, colored paper, colored modeling clay. With his first chemistry set, Rollie made gunpowder. As a kid, he loved Halloween more than Christmas. As an adult, he got high on ice. He put on a mask and a leather codpiece and became a pirate, a love slave, a naughty child begging to be whipped.

It was dim inside Rollie's mobile home lab there on the shores of Lake Sammamish. A long porcelain countertop ran the length of the room. Racks loaded with beakers and test tubes hung from the ceiling. A gas jet was mounted in the wall.

I squatted down and opened the cabinets. Inside I found king-size Bunsen burners and rows of plastic containers labeled with chemical formulas. In the cabinet to the left were metal rings to hold the beakers above the burners. I ran a finger along the countertop. A thin film of dust, but otherwise it was clean. The storage cabinets were neatly arranged. The narrow bed under the window facing the driveway was made, the Hudson's Bay blanket tucked in tight. I tried to picture Rollie Hansen working here, wearing a white lab coat and protective goggles, while the ice bubbled away in wide-mouthed beakers.

His raw material, the base for making ice, was stashed in the closet at the end of the trailer. Two dozen cardboard cartons, neatly stacked, wrapped in plastic. The labels faced out. They were three-color labels, bearing the name of a Fortune 500 chemical company.

EPHEDRINE the labels said.

The ice itself, the product that had started things rolling in the Rollie Nielsen case, sat atop the cartons of ephedrine. I'd heard about ice, I'd read about it. This was my first contact with the stuff.

In the light of the bare ceiling bulb, the ice looked colorless. I put my nose close. The smell was medicinal, like ether or rubbing alcohol, mixed with a faint perfume I could not identify. There were two kilos of ice packed in five sandwich Baggies, clear plastic, with Ziplock tops. Labels on each bag directed the ice to a delivery point in California: La Jolla, Newport Beach, Beverly Hills, Santa Barbara, Burlingame.

The California carriage trade.

In a drawer of the cabinet, I found two vials of green pills like the ones Eduardo had given me.

I dropped the green pills and the packets of ice into a plastic shopping bag from QFC market and locked up. Clouds roamed the sky, turning the day chilly and dark as I circled behind the mobile homes, pausing to let a dog quiet his barking. The man in the boat was gone from the lake. I saw no birds feeding.

Hana and Louie sat in the van, out of the wind.

I showed them the ice, described the interior of the lab. On the way back to town, they gave me a play-by-play of their interview with Rollie's neighbor. Using the name Robert Manette, Rollie had rented the space in May, had come back with the trailer in early June. Wasn't there much, according to the neighbor, mostly weekends. Rollie did not live high, no women, no loud parties. He drove a Chevy pickup, pretty beat up, and worked as a security guard at an industrial plant down in Renton. Rollie's reason for coming to the lake, according to the neighbor, was for rest and relaxation. He wasn't much of a talker. A nice fellow, the neighbor said. Kind of lonely.

"Good job, guys."

"It was fun."

"Hana's great at undercover."

"When did he see Rollie last?"

"Couple of weeks ago," Louie said. "Rollie came out, stayed overnight, and left early the next morning. Once when the neighbor got up to use the bathroom, he saw lights on in the trailer."

"Midnight cookery," I said.

"Poor Rollie," Hana said.

I told them what I had in mind for Big Daddy Borklund. Hana complimented me on my ability to plan, a real surprise, she said. We tossed it around for a half hour. Back at Hana's apartment, I phoned Sergeant Otto Rolfe, Webby's contact at the Seattle PD. It took a while to set things up because Sergeant Rolfe had to phone Webby and check me out. Then he had to check with the chief of detectives. It turned out the Seattle police were hungry for a piece of Big Daddy Borklund. They didn't like working with a stranger from out of town. In the end, however, they said they'd give it a shot if we played it by the book.

No cowboy stuff from me, they said.

So then Hana phoned Big Daddy Borklund and made a deal—just the two of them, she said—at a waterfront table at Hiram's on the locks for 8:30.

It was just after 7:00 when a female officer arrived at Hana's door, carrying a black attaché. Her ID said her name was Elena Lido. She was dark, mid-thirties, with eyes as hard as ball bearings. She and Hana went into the bedroom to rig the wire.

The door closed. Louie Chen nodded at me. We were ready. I phoned the number for Agent Loomis. Garcia answered, as before, and patched me through. With the cassette recorder going, I kept up my end of the deal by informing Agent Loomis of the location of Rollie Nielsen's lab. In Bothell, I said, at 17 Emerson Lane.

"Good work, Murdock."

"Thanks."

"How'd you do it?"

"Broke a secret code."

"Fantastic. What was it like inside?"

"Couldn't get in. It's locked up tight."

A chuckle from Agent Loomis. "Murdock," he said. "You live up to your reputation. I owe you one, friend."

"Yes," I said. "You do."

23

UNDERNEATH THE RED HUNTER'S CAPE, HANA wore black. Black cossack boots with sharp spike heels. A black skirt, full and swirling at calf-length. A black blouse, cut to show a deep V between her breasts. Over the blouse she wore a black jacket. Her hair was piled on her head, pulled tight at the temples to accentuate the Sioux cheekbones. The lipstick matched the red cape. The fingernail polish matched the lipstick. Around her neck she wore a thin gold chain with a locket attached. Inside the locket was a sepia photo of her maternal grandmother, Mary Hana Lakota.

Walking across the lighted lot at Hiram's, her head high and her back straight, Hana made two teens whistle and yell and lean on the horn. And a construction guy in a pickup ogled her so hard, he dented a Mercedes.

In a severe black briefcase, she carried a stack of chemical formulas Louie Chen had brought from the U-District gradpad and two kilos of ice from Rollie's lab.

Out on the water, a boat with running lights slipped free of the locks and eased west toward Puget Sound. It was dark now, and chilly as I tracked Hana with Louie's night scope. No amateur's last look over her shoulder as she walked down the short flight of steps into Hiram's. Beside me in the van, Louie kept rubbing his palms together. The time was 8:20, ten minutes until the arrival of Big Daddy Borklund.

"Calm down, Louie. Jesus."

"I'm worried. What if he brings his apes?"

"Apes?"

"I'm trying out my new PI talk."

"If he brings apes, she'll walk out. The cops have her covered."

"I hope so."

"She wants this, Louie. Her pound of flesh."

"I know. But I'm still worried."

Hana was inside. On our hookup to the police wire, we could hear the hostess, then a waiter's voice. Hana ordered Chardonnay, asked for the menu. The waiter left. In a low voice Hana asked if they were picking her up. Loud and clear, said the lady cop.

Louie rolled his window down. He rolled it up again. He jumped out and ran circles around the van. It didn't help control his nervousness. I knew the feeling. Action is easy. Sitting is no fun.

The dashboard clock inched along, 8:21, 8:22. I could feel Louie's nerves. I was edgy too. At 8:27 a big Cadillac eased into the parking lot and Louie's handset crackled and some cop said, "They're here."

A goon opened the rear door. Big Daddy climbed out. He wore a raincoat, a Burberry. His head was bare. The goon with him was the bozo from the beach house.

"No apes, Matt. That was the deal."

"Wait."

Long, breathless moment while Big Daddy made his way

inside. I didn't like what Hana was doing, but she'd insisted. Hana was a fighter, a lady who got her own way. She could handle herself and she wanted revenge.

"Well, well." Big Daddy's voice on the police pickup. "Aren't you something."

"The agreement was, Mr. Borklund, no second persons. Just the two of us."

"This is Julie. He remembers you."

"I'll count to ten, Mr. Borklund. If he's not gone, I'm going, taking the formula with me. One, two—"

"Hey, Julie, get yourself a beer."

"Boss?"

"Go on. Can he sit over there? Have an innocent beer?"

"All right."

"Order a Ballard Bitter, Julie. Leave the case with me."

Rustle of cloth and a clunk, sounds of Big Daddy getting settled. "Some day, huh. The sun comes out like this, it reminds me of Indian summer in Minnesota."

"Is that your home, Minnesota?"

"Yeah. Little town nobody ever heard of, north of Duluth. In the winter you could freeze to death between the house and the barn and they wouldn't move you until spring thaw."

Voice of the waiter, cutting in. "Can I bring you something, sir? While you study the menu?"

"Glenlivet on the rocks. No water. Got that?"

"Yes, sir."

"That kid's in love with you," Big Daddy said.

"I doubt that."

"The whole damned joint's in love with you. The way you look, black on red on black, I could fall myself."

"Aren't you clever with your compliments."

"You're tough. I like that. You got brass balls. I've seen grown men who couldn't handle what you handled out at my place on the island. I could have had you killed. Instead, because of the way you look, I'm here dealing."

"You're here because of Rollie's formula, Mr. Borklund. You're here because you want your hands on that lab. I trust your valise contains your two hundred thousand."

"My valise? I like it when you talk. Say something nice."

"Do you have the money?"

"I got it." Long pause here. "How about a hundred grand to spend a week with me in Paris?"

"The price for the formula is two hundred thousand. We had a deal."

"I meant above that. You get your two hundred thousand for the boys, the beard and the other guy. The hundred's all for you."

"I've seen Paris. It's not a place I need to see again."

"Okay. Tokyo. Tahiti. Timbuktu. Name the place."

"I'm not going."

"One-fifty."

"Sorry. I'm not for sale."

"I heard different."

"Here's the attaché with the formula. If you'll hand over the money, I'll be on my way, Mr. Borklund."

"Call me Bjorn, okay?"

The waiter's voice. "Your Glenlivet, sir."

"Yeah. Thanks."

"And are we ready to order?"

"Get lost. Split."

"Bring me another white wine," Hana said.

"Another Glenlivet," Big Daddy said.

"Yes, sir."

My palms were wet with sweat. Listening. Helpless.

"What if I raised the ante?" Big Daddy said.

"The ante?"

"For a week of your time. What if I offered you two

hundred thousand? A hundred now, a hundred when the week's up. No hanky-panky unless you say so, unless you give the word. I know people, bankers, government weenies, people who run things. I could pave your way to—"

"From those ladies I saw at your island citadel, Mr. Borklund, I'm twenty years too old for you."

He snorted a laugh. "My first woman was your age. I was a jerkoff kid of fifteen and we made it in the barn, with her old man not a hundred yards off. I love the ladies, any age, any color, and—"

"And I have an appointment waiting. The formula's here, along with a map to the lab."

"Let me see the map."

Crackle of paper. Then the sound of Big Daddy humming. "Bothell? You've got to be kidding."

"I'd like the money now. What Rollie made out there is very popular stuff. I have two other bidders."

"Nielsen tried that shit. Got his ass killed."

"He didn't have backup."

"Where are they, by the way?"

"Let go of me."

"Sit down, bitch."

There was a soft splashing sound, then Big Daddy growled, "You bitch. What the hell did you have to do that for?" A pause, a chair scraping. "Okay. Okay. Now that you've got the room staring at us."

The waiter's voice: "Everything all right, sir?"

"Get me some napkins. A half dozen."

"Yes, sir."

"The money." Hana's voice, resolute.

"Okay. Here. Take it. Two hundred G's. Christ, that's cold."

"It's been wonderful dealing with you."

"I've got your number. I own this town. I'll be seeing you, kid."

And then, over the hum of conversation, the sound of men shouting. Big Daddy cursed, *goddamn, goddamn,* and then a man's voice saying *This way, miss,* and Louie Chen and I were out of the van and inside the Hiram's entrance in time to see Big Daddy being handcuffed by a man wearing an apron and a cook's white hat. Off to the side, Hana passed Big Daddy's attaché to Sergeant Rolfe, a burly cop with red hair. He escorted her over to us.

"Good job, Hana. How wet is he?"

"To his creepy crotch," she said. "They were right. Revenge has a sweet, sweet taste."

Sergeant Otto Rolfe had a vise-grip handshake and bushy eyebrows. "Nice touch with the valise full of ice, Murdock. The Feds have been after this turkey for ten years. They'll hate it we nailed him first."

"Thanks for letting us sit in."

"No problem."

"Can I ask you a question, Sergeant?" Louie said.

"Shoot, Mr. Chen. Ask me anything. Anything at all."

"Someday I'd like a tour of the police station."

"Anytime. Bring your friends." He handed Louie a business card. Then we shook hands and the sergeant walked off.

In Louie's van, heading east, Hana couldn't stop shivering.

"Are you okay?"

"That man Borklund. He makes my skin crawl. He kept staring at me with those eyes. Did you hear him? He buys and sells, money money money! He's awful!"

"You got your revenge, though."

"Yes," she said. "And I'd do it again in a minute."

■

The earliest direct flight to Orange County did not leave until Monday evening. I paced. Hana and I went for a walk in the rain. In the aftermath of revenge, she said she'd do it again. Anything to trap Big Daddy. I did not remind her that he was not convicted yet.

I phoned Sergeant Rolfe Monday afternoon. He had news.

Bail for Big Daddy Borklund had been set for $1.2 million. A team of hotshot lawyers with offices in the Bank of California Building had worked all night calling in favors, but the judge, a hard-liner up for reelection on a war-against-drugs slogan, had not budged. A lot of people wanted Big Daddy put away. This time, because of the ice in the attaché, it might happen.

There was more. At midnight on Sunday, King County police on surveillance duty had intercepted two men attempting to break into 17 Emerson Lane at the Sammamish Shores Mobile Home Park. The men were Arthur Feldman, an agent of the federal government, and David Garcia, a private investigator from Tampa. Feldman's story was that they were there because of an anonymous tip and, like a good agent, he could not reveal his sources. They changed their story when they heard Louie Chen's tape of my voice telling Agent Loomis where the lab was. Feldman and Garcia were in custody.

The CIA had been notified. Agent Loomis was on assignment, undercover, the CIA said. An internal investigation would of course commence immediately.

Of course.

"You know what a catalyst is, Murdock?"

"Catalytic converter," I said. "Gives you a double burn on the exhaust."

"A catalyst is an agent that makes things happen. Since

you hit town, the bodies keep dropping. We've got solid IDs on all but one and I was hoping you could help me out."

"I could try, Sergeant."

Papers rustled at his end of the phone. "Okay. This stiff turned up on Sunday morning in a warehouse off Airport Way. Three slugs in him, matching three more we got from a stiff found in a parking garage downtown sometime Saturday afternoon. Can you help me out?"

"No, sorry."

"Where were you Saturday afternoon?"

"Shopping."

"And Sunday morning?"

"In bed."

"Alone?"

"No."

"The warehouse victim was blond, early forties, wearing a leather coat that's gotta be Paris. No ID. No driver's license, no plastic, no labels in the clothes. He looks European, German or Scandinavian. He's got powder burns on both hands and our lab people picked up twenty-three spent casings at the scene, all nine millimeter." The sergeant coughed. "Ring any bells?"

"Maybe he worked for the CIA."

"Very funny. Can you hold on a minute?"

"Sure."

A click at his end of the line and I was on hold. The sergeant's description, male, fortyish, European, sounded like the mystery hit man trotted out for me on the beach by honest Agent Loomis. Eduardo had called him Landsberg, a spook from the old days. With three slugs in him, he would freelance no more. Agent Loomis had offered me $500. Maybe the CIA paid more for hotshot mercs in leather jackets. The sergeant came back on. "Listen, Murdock, if you're not busy later, how about meeting me. I've got some photos I'd like to show you, more of the Borklund crowd."

"I've got a plane to catch. How about a raincheck?"

"Heading back down south?"

"Yes."

"The California Connection?"

"Maybe. I'll keep you posted."

"I'd appreciate that. This case has holes you could drive a truck through."

"See you around, Sergeant."

"Yeah. See you around."

24

HANA AND LOUIE FLEW SOUTH WITH ME FROM SEA-
Tac to John Wayne Airport. Louie came because he wanted
to continue his on-the-job training as a private eye. Hana
came because she wanted to keep an eye on me. "I like to
be with you," she said. "I like to be where you are."

"Good thinking," I said.

"Have you thought about the shape of the case?"

"Shape?" I said.

"At first it was a pinpoint. Then it became a line on a flat
plane, and then a maze."

"Speaking as an artist," I said.

"It feels like a Ping-Pong game to me," Louie said.

"Come on Louie. Sports metaphors are out."

"It fits," Louie said. "Rollie goes to California. Matt
comes to Seattle. We go to California. That's Ping-Pong,
Hana. Back and forth. Back and forth."

"It's a maze," Hana said. "And we are approaching the
monster at the center."

I left them arguing about the shape of the case while I

closed my eyes and tried to plot our Orange County strategy.

Joel and Bernie, the ice twins, might make stepping stones to Shelby Carruthers. Had to find them first. I had two vials of green pills, pills worth dying for. And in Rollie's black book I had found a *V* in Orange County, a number with a 714 area code. The same number appeared on a business card in Rollie's stack I'd found at the Queen Anne condo. The name on the card was Valerie Smith, real estate agent for Laguna Bell Realty. Valerie's home number was listed along with her business number.

It was 9:30 when the plane landed at John Wayne Airport. While Louie gathered the luggage and Hana rented a car, I phoned Webby Smith. Joel's last name was Stedman. He'd been arraigned a couple of times on drug charges. No trials, no convictions. His last known address was in Fullerton. He wasn't there when the cops stopped by. Hadn't been seen by neighbors for three or four days. Webby would not give me Joel's address.

Valerie Smith had a couple of traffic tickets, speeding, running a stop sign. She had a reputation for doing multi-million-dollar deals. There was nothing new on fat-cat Shelby. Before I hung up, Webby warned me to stay away from Bernie Dodds.

I phoned the hospital. Thor and Cindy were in Thor's room, watching TV. I told him about Eduardo. He said he understood, considering Eduardo had saved my life. What really hurt, Thor said, was Rollie's keeping secrets. That really smarted. "Here's Miss Cindy," he said.

She was glad I was back and if I wanted to visit her in the hospital I should hurry because she was getting out tomorrow. We chatted for a moment. Phyl's mom hadn't visited today. From across the terminal, I saw Louie Chen wave. Hana had the rental. There was work to do.

"Gotta go, kid. See you tomorrow."

"I miss you, Matt," Cindy said.

The Avis rental was a Lincoln town car, a white pimpmobile. Louie drove with Hana in the passenger seat and Murdock as backseat driver. It's ten minutes from John Wayne Airport to Geronimo's Burger Palace in peaceful Irvine. The scene had not changed since Thursday, the night of my last visit to Geronimo's: forty hot cars making a loose circle for break-dancers and gawkers and dudes desiring to hang, man.

"That Trans Am," I said, pointing out Bernie's vehicle.

Kids eyed us as we cruised the area. They looked at Louie. They ogled Hana. I spotted Bernie Baby leaning against a Jeep Wagoneer in deep and doubtless cosmic conversation with three hip dudes. Bernie wore gray. The dudes wore black.

"The fat one," I said. "That's Bernie Dodds."

"Cut him out of the herd, right?"

"Right. You still want to do this?"

"Three Musketeers, right?"

"Right."

"The A Team," Louie said. "Rah, rah."

She undid two buttons on her blouse. "My mission, if I choose to accept it, is to lure him to this garish white car. Right?"

"Right."

From the car, we watched as she walked toward Bernie Dodds and his *compañeros*. "She walks in beauty," Louie Chen said.

"Yeah."

"What do you think she's saying?"

"Doesn't need to say much."

"I wonder what would have happened if we'd stuck with my plan," Louie said. "The one where you fell."

I didn't answer. Across the parking lot, Hana nodded, put her hand through Bernie's arm, then pointed him toward the Lincoln. He was talking away, yap yap, his face working, his fat forehead gleaming with nervous sweat. It was too dark inside the car for him to see me. Louie's window was down and Bernie peered at him.

"Who the fuck's he?"

"Our driver, Peaches."

"I thought we'd be alone, hey?"

"Another hundred for the room," she said, "and we will be."

"Hey." His frown cleared and he passed her some money. "This is mondo. I dig it."

"Climb in the back, Peaches."

He opened the rear door and Hana gave him a calculated shove and Bernie's eyes got wide as he saw me sitting there. I grabbed his collar and coat lapel and hauled him in. Hana closed the door. Bernie Dodds took a swing at me and I dodged and his fist glanced off my shoulder and slammed into the metal frame. The pain took the fight out of him. Bernie moaned, tucked his right hand between his legs, and called me a dirty name. Hana's door closed. Louie took us north on Culver. Bernie was crying before we'd made the first traffic signal. By the second traffic signal I had a phone number for Joel Stedman.

From the phone outside Ralph's supermarket in the Heritage Shopping Center Bernie called Joel to set up a drug buy. Twenty minutes, Joel said, at cabana number 404 at the John Wayne Motor Hotel on Jamboree Boulevard in Newport Beach. On the drive over, Bernie admitted setting me up for last week's Thursday hit. After hearing from

Phyl's boyfriend about her visit to my place, he'd called Joel. Didn't like gang stuff, he said. Had never heard of Los Boleros before tonight.

In the lush lobby of the John Wayne Motor Hotel, Hana called cabana 404 on the house phone. "Hi," she said. "This is Val and I need some product. Uh-huh. Oh, yes. Hmm. I like the sound of that." She hung up smiling.

Cabana 404 was the last one in a row of cabanas, little fake Tahitian honeymoon huts with fake thatched roofs, which backed up to a fence that bordered the John Wayne Tennis Club, twenty-one lighted courts, open for play from seven in the morning until midnight. From across the fence you could hear the *plonk-whunk-plonk* of a solitary tennis match. Louie stayed in the shadows with Bernie Baby. I stood to the side of the door while Hana knocked.

"Who's there?" A tinny voice, sissy, from behind the door.

"It's Val, I just phoned. Open the door, okay?"

Click of the lock and the door swung open and I could feel him there, staring at her, taking her in. "You're not Val."

"I'm her cousin, from Ventura." She waved money in his face. "Phyl said you were cute. Can I come in?"

"Phil? Phil who?" He started to close the door, but Hana stepped forward, nailing him with karate knuckles to the Adam's apple. He grabbed his throat and dropped to his knees.

"You okay?" I asked Hana.

"I saw him moving, trying to get away. I didn't mean to hit him. I just . . . lashed out." Her face was white with anger. "It gets to you, doesn't it? The sleaze, I mean."

"Welcome to California."

We hauled him inside. Louie Chen brought Bernie along. Party time at the John Wayne Motor Hotel.

Eduardo had been right about the rat face. Joel Stedman had skinny arms and bony shoulders and long wrists that stuck out of the cuffs of his shirt. He wore black trousers held up by black galluses and a shirt of muddy green. His mouth was turned sideways in a frozen sneer.

I hauled him into the bathroom, where he lay on the floor, coughing, holding his throat. I sat on the commode lid, waiting. When he'd finished, I stuck the muzzle of the .45 under his nose. Eyes wide, he strained higher until he was on his knees, back against the wall. "Yow! Hey, dude, let up! Hey, easy, dude! Easy!"

"What I want, Joel, is a confession. Your ice dealing. The name and address of your boss."

"I work alone, man."

Taking my time, I cocked the hammer of the .45. Up close, the click was louder, making his big eyes go buggo. "If I don't get a confession, Joel, I'll beat the shit out of you. Then I'll dump you at the emergency room door and phone your room to wake you up and when you get out I'll be waiting and when you can walk again I'll beat the shit out of you again. Look in your rearview, I'll be there. Try a dope deal and I'll ruin it. Leave town and I'll track you down. Only two places you'll be safe from me, Joel. One is Siberia. The other is jail."

I shoved the muzzle higher. Tears dripped from his eyes. They were red around the rims. Okay, he nodded. Okay, okay.

I took him back into the bedroom and we got his words down on Louie's tape. He'd met Chick Dickens in June. Since then, he'd bought half a million in ice from Chick. His principal got interested. That was unusual, Joel said, because the boss usually kept his distance. After each Dickens deal, Joel had to report in to the boss, a real pain in the ass. When Dickens phoned to set up last Saturday's buy,

Joel reported to the boss, who told him to see a dude who wanted to make a deal with Dickens. What kind of deal, Joel didn't know. He just followed orders. Joel's description —a bald Latino with a chunky build and a "Mexican" accent—matched Eduardo de la Cruz.

"What did you tell him?"

"The time and place of the next buy."

"What did you get out of it?"

"A couple hundred is all."

"So on Saturday this Latino guy was on the pier?"

"Yeah. On a ten-speed."

"So what happened next?"

"I was out of town for a couple of days. I have this doll in San Mateo, see. And when I get back on Thursday, Bernie over there he calls with some news about two chicks. One of them saw me, he says, and my vehicle. So she tells her friend who knows a private dick who's just hassled Bernie. That's you, I guess. The boss says to sit tight. The next thing I know he's on the phone telling me to make sure the dick's at home around eight on Thursday. I get Bernie to check that out—I'm only following orders here, see—and the next thing I know is from the television." Joel shook his head. "Those fucking Boleros, man, they're crazy."

"Joel hired them," Bernie said. "He's in this, up to his eyeballs."

"Screw you, lardass."

"He gave them four hundred apiece," Bernie said, his teeth chattering. "He paid them. He told them what to do. All I did was see lights on and make a phone call. Joel and his boss set things up."

"Shelby Carruthers?" I said.

"How'd you know that?" Bernie said.

"What do you know, lardass?" Joel's voice was harsh.

"I know more than you think," Bernie said.

"You sold them ice, didn't you?" I asked Joel.

"Sold who?"

"Those Boleros. You sold them ice. The ice made them think they couldn't die when they came shooting."

"Fuck you, man."

It took twenty minutes to wear him down. When Joel refused to answer, I asked Bernie, who talked until Joel cut in, giving us the names of the two Boleros who'd escaped. He spelled names for us. Giordano was spelled Joradno. Carruthers was spelled Crowthers. He gave us the address of Carruthers's home in Jamaica Cove. He denied knowing any CIA agent.

I pressed the Stop button. We had enough now—even our local DA could make this stick—so we drove Joel and Bernie in the white Lincoln pimpmobile to the Laguna Beach police station, where Webby Smith locked them up. I signed the complaint—conspiracy to commit murder—and Webby said he'd have them transported to a county facility in the morning.

"What about Carruthers?" I said.

"Gotta go slow on that, like I said."

"Because he's buddies with the mayor?"

"That's one reason. I'll get to work on it. All the *t*'s crossed on this one, Sherlock. All the *i*'s dotted. I mean, this guy could be our next congressman."

"It's always the same old story, isn't it, Iron Man?"

"What story?"

"The fat cat eats the mice. He sits up high, above it all, cleaning his fur, and when he's hungry or bored he grabs a mouse, chews off its head, laughs. No one touches a fat cat."

Before we left, I asked Webby about ballistics on the slugs that had killed Rollie Nielsen. He said nothing had changed. I told him to check the slug from the neck against the slugs from the torso. He'd try, he said. But it wasn't his case.

"You look tired, Sherlock. Go home. Get some rest. You did good tonight. Might have stretched the law some, but that's what gives you kicks. You did good. Why not save the rest of the world mañana?" He indicated Hana on the other side of the glass partition. "That is some trophy you bagged up north."

"She's the hunter, Iron Man. I'm the trophy."

"Better straighten that out," Webby said. "Before the situation gets out of hand. Now go home."

25

I DID NOT TAKE WEBBY SMITH'S ADVICE. I DID NOT GO home. I should have gone home. Weariness made my bones ache. My brain was frozen. I sat in the back of the white Lincoln and told Louie to head north on Bluebird Canyon Drive to Robin's Egg Lane, a dead-end street built in a long S-curve. Valerie Smith's house was the last one on Robin's Egg, a two-story architectural statement, glass and decks, an attached three-car garage. We parked the Lincoln in a cul-de-sac and walked up. Lights glowed in the house. The time was almost midnight as I rang the bell. No answer.

"Can you believe this weather?" Louie said. "Balmy October?"

"It feels too close for me," Hana said. "Here, there's only the fast lane."

"I see why Rollie came here," Louie said. "Sun, sand, surf."

"There's no one home," Hana said. "Let me try this lock."

"Go."

While Louie waxed poetic about southern California,

Hana took her turn with the lockpicks. She was faster than Louie, ninety-two seconds before the tumblers tumbled into position. The alarm was not armed. I hadn't realized I'd been holding my breath until it came out in a whoosh. Mother Murdock, hovering over his trainees.

A curved staircase led upstairs. Hana and I took the second story, leaving Louie with kitchen, library, and living room.

Three bedrooms upstairs. One for the mistress, a second one for guests, a third converted into a study. Valerie kept her house neat, like a model home ready for viewing.

Hana checked Valerie's walk-in closet while I searched the study. Mostly real estate stuff in here, clean desk, everything organized into files in three steel cabinets. In a Rolodex in the lower right-hand drawer I found three numbers for Shelby Carruthers. The phone was programmable. The name beside the third little auto-dial button was "Shel."

I carried the Rolodex into the guest bedroom, where I found clothes for a man. Chinos and jeans with a crease and two jackets, raw silk, with labels from men's specialty shops in Miami. Four of the shirts were long-sleeved, green, like the shirt worn by Agent Loomis for his bartending job at the Inn of Cortez.

In the top drawer of the bedside table I found a clear glass tube with a tiny little bowl on one end and a plastic sack of ice crystals.

Hana called me into the master bedroom. "Look at this closet, Matt."

The walk-in closet was twelve by fourteen, big for this size house, with racks of clothes and built-in shelves marked by labels according to activity: *Evening Wear, Office Togs, Beach and Water Sports, Aerobics, Lingerie, Fun Stuff.*

Fun Stuff meant garter belts, see-through bras, and crotchless panties.

"This Val Smith is organized."

"Lots of energy," I said, "to have all these interests."

I was showing Hana the Rolodex when a shout from Louie Chen took us to the window that looked out across the deck. A car was coming up the dark street. As we headed downstairs, I heard the hum of the garage-door opener.

"What's the plan, Matt?" Louie's face was excited.

"Let her come inside. Let her see me first. Maybe I can scare her into instant confession."

"That neatnik?" Hana said. "She'll be cool."

"You have another suggestion?"

"Some girl to girl. Maybe try some hypnosis."

"My way first," I said. "Is the recorder ready?"

"The tape," Louie said, "is ready to roll."

They hid in the shadows while I stood in the kitchen just inside the entry door. The door opened and she came in. She was tall and athletic, a classy blond lady with lean lines and a designer wardrobe. She flipped on lights and her eyes got wide with fright. "What do you—"

I kicked the door closed. The shoulder bag slid off her shoulder, hit the parquet floor with a clunk. She backed away from me, her hand guarding her throat. She kept backing until she slammed into a glass-framed print, knocking it loose from its hook. Sound of glass cracking. The frame snapped open at the corner and the print flopped out.

"Who are you—" She coughed, braced herself, palm flat against the wall. "What do you want? Drugs? Money? What?"

"Remember this guy?" I showed her a photo of Rollie Nielsen.

"Him. Oh shit. Damn. Not him. Oh—"

Valerie Smith stumbled to a chair and sat down. Her pale skirt, something silky, hiked up above her knees. The jacket looked expensive. The blouse was closed at the throat with a gold butterfly latch. The eyes of the butterfly, bright green stones, glinted in the light. Tight smile as she looked from Rollie's photo to me. "I know you. I've seen you on television. You're that—"

Louie came out, followed by Hana.

"Who are these people?"

"Friends of the deceased," I said. "Tell me about Shelby Carruthers."

"Shelby?" Sharp tone of surprise. "I hardly know him."

When Hana showed her the Rolodex cards with Shelby's phone numbers, Val's face clouded and the tears started to roll. I laid her business card on the table. "Found this in Chick's collection."

"So?"

"So tell me what you know about Shelby Carruthers."

"I don't know anything." She buried her face in her hands. "I feel really sick and—"

"You've got his number on automatic dial on your upstairs phone. You're the link between Shelby and CIA agent Terry Loomis."

She gasped. She coughed. Strain dug deep furrows in her tanned forehead. "I'm calling the police."

"Good idea, Val. The head cop in town is a pal of mine. When he gets here, I'll tell him to do a DNA match of your pubic hairs with the samples they found in room 203 at the Inn of Cortez. In case you forgot, that's where Chick Dickens died. Since they don't have a killer yet, they might like nailing you for it."

"Killer? You think I could—" She folded her arms, and then her eyes rolled and her face turned green and she threw up, urped right onto her stockinged knees and onto the pea-green rug. Vomit smell filled the air.

Hana put a wet washcloth on the back of Val's neck. In a couple of minutes, she took a deep breath and sat back against the chair and I showed her the vial of green pills Eduardo had passed to me. Val looked at them. She looked away. Putting a hand to her chest, she coughed, a hollow sound. Finished, she gave a short nod. "What will happen to me?"

"You didn't kill him?"

"No."

"But you're an accessory."

"He made me do it. You'll never catch him."

"By *he,* you mean Agent Loomis?"

"Yes. He has this plan—to market those pills—and whatever gets in his way makes him furious. He's like a crazy man. He scared me to death. I was not . . . myself."

"Tell you what, Val. You tell us about Chick and Shelby and Agent Loomis. We'll let you pack a bag and slip out of town. You've got emergency money tucked away, I'll bet."

"Some," she said.

"For a rainy day," I said.

"Yes," she said. "For a rainy day."

Speaking low, bent over, her jacket tight, her elbows propped on her knees, Val Smith gave us her story. She'd met Agent Loomis in March at a kink party at the home of Shelby Carruthers. After that, she engaged in threesomes with Shelby and Jerry, three consenting adults just having some fun, she said. It was harmless. There was no rough stuff.

In June she'd met Chick Dickens, who'd been referred to her by a banker friend of Shelby's because Chick had $200,000 in cash in his possession. He wanted a house on the beach in California. He did not want a loan or a mort-

age. "The regulators are pouncing on all cash transac-
ions," Val said, "because of the dope money coming in. So
he banker said he'd handle the cash."

"He laundered it, you mean?"

"He didn't exactly say as much, but yes. I suppose."

"So then you and Chick went house hunting?"

"Yes."

"And when did you hop into bed?"

"We became intimate in July. Jerry . . . recruited me. I
vas his favorite operative. I'd never done anything like that.
t was really . . . exciting."

This was the routine: She'd see Chick for a weekend of
iouse hunting. Then she'd report in to Agent Loomis. In
August, they found a house with an asking price of
650,000. She bargained the owner down to $500,000. In
ieptember, Chick came up with another $200,000. The last
100,000, he said, would arrive in October.

"Did he give you the money on Saturday?"

"I saw it. He was going to give it to me. Then he . . .
lied."

"Tell us about that night, Val."

"What do you want to know?"

"You were in the room. Why did you leave?"

"A phone call," she said. "From Jerry."

"How long were you gone?"

"Three hours or so. Some guy wanted to talk to Chick,
erry said. When I got back, Chick was on the floor by the
ied. The money was gone. So were the green pills."

"What do they do?" I asked. "What's so great about
hose pills?"

"It's an ice antidote," she said.

"How does it work?"

"They bring you down easy." She looked up at me. "You
ver smoke ice?"

"No."

"Ice is great, especially if you're up to here stresswise and have to keep going. The smoke takes you up and for twenty-four hours you feel strong as Wonder Woman, like you can do anything. Then you crash. That's bad, so Chick comes up with the antidote. One little green pill and you float down. No strain, no pain. A landing soft as a fleecy cloud."

"So Loomis sent you after the green pills?"

"Yes. Jerry knows people everywhere. Thailand, Colombia, the Middle East. He said we'd all be rich."

"*We* meaning you and Loomis and Shelby?"

"Yes."

"Who was the guy who wanted the meeting with Chick?"

"Some agent connected with the operation."

"Did the operation have a name?"

"Yes."

"What was it?"

A long pause before she said, "Operation Ice Cap."

"Where is Jerry now?"

"He's around."

"Is he coming back here?"

"He said so."

"When?"

"Maybe tonight. Maybe tomorrow. With Jerry, a girl never knows. One minute he's not there. The next minute, there he is."

"How do you feel about Chick?"

"I'm sorry he died. I'm sick about that. No one said anything about anyone dying."

The session was over. Hana took Val upstairs. Louie went outside to scout for Agent Loomis. I lay down on the sofa in the living room and closed my eyes.

The sound of the garage door opening woke me up. My

head whirled as I sat up. My eyes felt bleary. A sliver of light came under the door from the kitchen. I was halfway across the room when I heard voices from behind the door. Then the door opened and there stood Agent Jerry Loomis, with Louie Chen behind him, holding the .45.

"Murdock?" he said.

"Come on in, Agent. There's a tape I want you to hear. And then maybe we can deal."

"Deal?" he said. "What would you say to twenty years in Leavenworth? For interfering with a federal officer?" He pointed at Louie and Hana. "And you people are included."

Louie flipped the wall switch and the light came on. Agent Loomis wore a sport coat of raw silk, a pale blue shirt with no tie, and blousy slacks. His cheeks were newly tanned. His eyes showed uncertainty. He sat in a chair while we played him the tape. It was after four in the morning when we finished.

"Christ," he said. "How could Val—"

"I want a face-to-face with Shelby Carruthers," I said.

"What for?"

"I want to see his face when I play him this tape."

"What's my end?"

"Introduce me to your buddy. Then you walk."

"How much lead time?"

"Couple of hours. Time to grab your stash and split for Mexico."

A smarmy smile from Agent Jerry Loomis. "It's a deal."

26

FAINT COLOR IN THE EAST, A MILKY BLUE. THE DASH-
board clock said 5:45. A delivery truck with its headlights
on crawled along Pacific Coast Highway, heading south toward Laguna Beach.

I sat with Agent Jerry Loomis in his vehicle in the deserted parking lot of Le Club of Newport Beach. His vehicle was a Ford, a green late-model four-door equipped with
a cellular phone and a police scanner. The tape recorder
sat on my lap and we were parked here at Le Club because
Shelby Carruthers and Agent Loomis had a date for six.

A squash date.

"Eduardo sends his regards," I said.

"Are you taping this?"

"I've got him on tape, if that's what you mean."

"That royal Colombian fuckup. You wasted him, I hope."

"Nope."

"What?" He turned to stare at me.

"I left Eduardo with a doc. When he gets patched up,
he'll come hunting for you."

"Thanks a lot, Murdock."

"He nailed your boy Landsberg."

"Landsberg. He's been over the hill for a year."

"Eduardo was pissed, Agent. He couldn't get to you himself, so he recruited me."

"You're so righteous, aren't you? So squeaky clean? Mighty Matt Murdock, charging in to rescue the sob sisters?"

"You're pretty neat yourself, throwing in with the drug pushers and the fat cats."

"It's better than saving sheep, my friend. Better than ending one's days with a gold watch made in Korea and a government pension that won't keep up with inflation." He drummed his fingers on the steering wheel. "You could still throw in with me. I've got enough for two."

"Give it to Val. She worked for it."

"Sheep are for shearing, Murdock. For every one you save, a hundred die. That's what they're here for, you know, that's their raison d'être, simply to die. They gather in herds and bleat and wait to die. They—"

He didn't finish because a Jaguar had just pulled into the light, a sleek animal of a car with only the fog lights burning. It parked three slots down from the Ford. The driver's door opened and a man climbed out. He wore white. As he came toward us, I saw he was a big man, a solid citizen, a man of presence and substance, a true American headed for Washington, D.C.

Shelby Carruthers, ready for squash.

He rapped on the window and Agent Loomis lowered the glass. The tape recorder sat on my lap. In it was a copy of Val Smith's tape. Two copies had been made by Louie while I slept. The original was with Webby Smith. A copy was safe with Hana and Louie, who waited for me in the rented Lincoln, parked out on Coast Highway.

"Jerry?" the big man said. "You're not suited up, boyo!"

Then he stooped down and saw me in the passenger seat. "Who's this?"

"Tell him to get in," I said.

"Better get in, Shel."

"What's up, Jerry? You know my schedule with the election coming up and—"

I pressed the Play button to start the tape so he could listen to Val's voice.

"Who's that?"

"The voice of Val Smith," I said. "She fingered you as a playground pusher."

"Ridiculous."

I pressed the Stop button. "We've got Joel, too. And his pal Bernie. They're turning state's evidence to save their butts."

The dome light came on as he climbed into the backseat. The door closed, but not before he got a look at me. "Arrest him, Jerry."

"Can't help you, Shel. Sorry."

"Rats leaving the ship, is that it?" He turned to me. "I know you. You're that private dickhead, the one who's sticking his nose into places it doesn't belong. Murdock, right?"

"Right."

"What do you want? Money?"

"Not money."

"What then? A favor? Drugs? Girls? Boys? What?"

"I want to bring a little girl back to life. Since I can't have that, I'll take a pound of flesh. And you've got lots of that."

I pressed the Play button and we listened for a moment to Val's voice on the tape. Then I tossed him the tape recorder. It hit him on the chest and kept going, Val's voice, my voice, Val's voice telling all.

Carruthers cursed. Agent Loomis laughed, a high-pitched cackle, man on the edge. I climbed out of the car and left the two of them alone. They belonged together, in a cage with Bernie and Joel and maybe even Eduardo. Let them claw for food. I checked my watch. The time was 6:01. By now Webby's cops from the Laguna Beach PD would be at Shelby's house in Jamaica Cove, armed with a search warrant.

It was all over for Shelby Carruthers.

A car door slammed. I heard footsteps running. I turned to look. Shelby Carruthers, 220 pounds of California political candidate in a fancy white warm-up suit, came running at me, brandishing his squash racquet.

I turned my back on him, kept on walking.

The footsteps came closer. When he was close enough to swing, I dropped to my hands and knees, fingertips spread on the tarmac like a sprinter in the starting blocks. The swinging racquet cut the air at what had been eye level before I hunkered down. He cursed, calling me a dirty name, and I chopped at his kneecap.

He yelped. The racquet fell to the tarmac. And Shelby assumed the Bruce Lee martial arts fighting stance, huffing air through his nostrils to scare me, making that battle yell they make in the Ninja movies, a sound pitched halfway between a horse's whinny and the cry of a rooster with a hemorrhoid.

We fought it out there on the tarmac, with Agent Loomis watching through the windshield. Shelby was younger and heavier, but he was a bad guy, a dope pusher and a turd, and I had right on my side. I had moral force. He nailed me with a kick. I hit him in the nose, in the sternum, in the gut. He aimed a kick at my privates. I took it on the thigh, felt a numbing sizzle. We traded punches, his fists shod with iron. He hit harder than I did. I dodged better than he did. He wound up on his knees, red in the face, breathing hard. My gut ached. My right eye was starting to swell.

"See you in jail, Congressman."

I heard the squeak of tires on tarmac as I walked past the traffic control center with the striped traffic bar in an upright position. It was Agent Loomis, trying to run me down with his Agency Ford. I turned. I waited until the headlights were on me, and then I leaped to the left and he followed. The left front fender grazed my pants leg and plowed into the yellow automatic gizmo that raises and lowers the candy-striped bar. The Ford died. I jerked his door open. I grabbed the lapels of his raw silk jacket. I pulled him halfway out of the car and punched him twice, once in the gut, once in the face. He sagged.

In the parking lot, Shelby Carruthers crawled to his Jaguar.

Louie parked the Lincoln under the NO PARKING sign behind my house. He and Hana helped me up the stairs. My knee was swollen, there was no feeling in my right thigh.

Zeke Amado had been busy. New front door, new lock, new picture window. The tumblers were the same, so my key worked.

Louie sacked out on the sofa. Hana gave me homeopathy and then we slept. It was good to have her beside me. It was marvelous. When I woke up to a sunny afternoon, the leg was worse. No feeling, a sense of impending doom. Hana helped me dress. They drove me to Lake Forest, to see Dr. Mal, Wally's chiropractor friend and sometime doubles partner. A half hour for X rays. A half hour on his adjusting table, getting torqued. Dr. Mal had good hands.

"You'll live," he said. "You'll have some numbness off and on. But the leg will come back."

"What happened, Doc?"

"An old injury," he said. "With some scarring. The nerves are inflamed. When you start to hurt, you'll know you're on the mend. You're lucky."

"How's that?"

"At your age, it could have been a lot worse."

"Thanks, Doc."

I was sitting on my deck in the sun when Sergeant Rolfe phoned from Seattle. Louie brought me the phone on a twenty-five-foot line.

Big Daddy Borklund was still in custody, the sergeant said. His lawyers were having trouble raising the $1.2 million required for bail because the ambitious judge had signed a search warrant and local police in conjunction with federal officers were pawing through the records of Borklund Import and Export, Inc., and bankers had shut down the Borklund Industry credit lines. The trial would be a long one.

"Just wanted to keep you up-to-date," said Sergeant Rolfe. "How're things at your end?"

"The fat cat is in custody. His lawyers are assembled. He'll be out on bail before dinnertime. The DA is getting testimony in return for immunity. It's the same old song and dance."

"You sound tired, Murdock."

"I am. Did you find your mole?"

"We've found him. Hard to nail a fellow officer, though. Really hurts me, really hurts the department."

"Hang tough," I said.

"Will do."

We hung up.

Later that day, I sat with my friends on my deck and tried to pretend the world was back to normal. Drinking helped.

I was on beer number five and feeling only minor pain. I'd been knifed and battered, but not shot, not killed. The leg was still numb. Cindy was inside with Hana, working on a meal. Thor Nielsen was healing. He and Wally were busy discussing the flora and fauna of the Sea of Cortez, down in Mexico, where Agent Loomis was headed with his stash. I wondered how much he had tucked away. A hundred thousand? Two hundred? Five? With the Rollie Nielsen green pill ice antidote, Agent Loomis could have ruled the drug world.

At the railing, Louie kept sniffing the air.

"Why do you keep sniffing the air?"

"Whiffs of Murdock Country," he said. "Sucking them in."

"What?"

"The smell of Murdock Country. Like Raymond Chandler Country, which is up in L.A." He sniffed again.

"Okay," I said. "What does it smell like?"

"It smells like romance," Louie said. "Like green waves and beach glitz. Like diamonds and palm trees and green money and suave ladies and men who lust for power. It smells like hot suntan oil on sizzling flesh. It smells like—"

"The Planet Mondo," I said, hoisting my empty can.

"Mondo is an adjective," Wally said. "A modifier. Stretches the boundaries of language to use mondo as a noun."

"Murdock Country smells rad," I said. "It smells bodacious."

"Isn't he great," Cindy said from the doorway.

"He's unreal," Louie said. "Because he's at the center of Murdock Country. How about another beer?"

"Good for my leg," I said. "Never walk again, you can bring me beers forever. Deliver me unto beers."

"You're drunk, Matt." Cindy's face frowned at me.

"At least," I said, "I'm not a fat cat killing sheep."

"No more beer for you," Wally said.

"It's beer beer beer that makes you want to cheer," I said.

"Stop," Cindy said. "Stop it." She went away from the door.

I stared around at the sky, at the beach, at the faces of my friends. My eyes were wet. I was home.

27

LOUIE CHEN HAD BUSINESS WAITING SO HE FLEW back to Seattle on Wednesday evening. Thor Nielsen flew back on the same flight, taking his boy's body in a wooden box. Hana phoned a teacher friend to take over her classes at the Art Institute so she could stay in town and take care of me. She and Cindy got very chummy, walking on the beach, laughing with the waves as a backdrop. After their beach walks Hana quizzed me about women. Who was Teri? Who was Kelly? Who was Kathy? Who was Roxanne? Who was Meg? Who was this Senator Jane with the ranch in Texas?

On Friday I appeared at a preliminary hearing held at Harbor Court as the defendant because Shelby Carruthers, the plaintiff, had charged me with aggravated assault. I walked in on crutches. Dr. Mal, my loyal chiropractor, produced X rays verifying damage to my body. Shelby had a broken nose, but he looked tough and tanned and rich and mean. The charge did not stick. On advice from the Newport Beach PD—for hassling Bernard L. Dodds, Junior—the judge suspended my PI license for six months.

Have no gun, will travel.

On Fat Tuesday, Shelby Carruthers, free on bail, lost the election by 2,100 votes. Up in Seattle, Big Daddy Borklund was out on bail too. It's tough to keep a fat cat behind bars.

My scorecard on the Rollie Nielsen case didn't look so great. Phyl was dead. Cindy could have been dead. So could Thor. I'd killed a guy named Julio, a Latino sucking courage from an ice high. On the Dickens clues, I'd dropped the ball. Thanks to Hana and Louie for picking it up again. Agent Loomis was loose. Rollie's killer was loose. My Turf War scenario—Medellín coke versus domestic ice cookers—was a figment of my imagination. A pain quivered down my right leg, a reminder I wasn't as young as I used to be.

Not a great score for Murdock.

But I'd found Hana. And when she walked into the room my heart went wild. I liked being with her. I liked watching her cook, sketch, walk, smile, comb her hair. I liked her strength, her gentleness, her feminine intuition. I liked it that she knew what I was thinking. It meant something.

The question was, what to do now?

One afternoon we had drinks at the Inn of Cortez. There was a new waitress working, and no trace of Agent Loomis lurking undercover in his green shirt behind the bar. On our way out, we rode the elevator upstairs and stared at the door of room 203, where Rollie Nielsen had died.

"What an awful way to die," Hana said.

"Are there any good ways?"

"In nature," Hana said. "So that you can be recycled."

"In the woods," I said. "In a rain forest."

"The desert would be okay. Or the ocean. They're nature."

"Less waste when you're recycled," I said.

"It's better than here in a room on the beach."

"Dying is dying," I said. "It's never better than."

"Let me teach you," Hana said.

"There's nothing to teach," I said.

A week with the chiropractor brought painful tingles to my leg. The leg was alive. So was I. To celebrate this historic event, Hana invited people to dinner. Cindy, she said, was bringing a new friend with her. His name was Mike.

I was waiting for them, leaning on a shillelagh borrowed from Wally, when they rode up around five.

"Hey Cindy!"

"Hi, Matt!" Cindy Duke, wearing her biker's outfit, waved as she came toward me. Her new friend was a skinny guy with endless energy. They locked their bikes and romped up the stairs. She hugged me, then introduced Mike. He was older than Cindy, seventeen or maybe eighteen, a lean, rangy kid with a topknot hairdo, shaved clean from the ears to the crown, topped with a bush of curls. Cindy went to help Hana. Old pals now, they hugged.

I asked questions and Mike answered in monosyllables. He called me sir. He wanted to be a forensic pathologist, but would serve his country with the marines first. I said I'd put him in touch with some people at the county lab.

Wally St. Moritz and Leo Castelli joined us for dinner. Wally and Mike discussed surfboards. Leo, playing Italian lothario, flirted with Hana. Hana and Cindy waited table like sisters, smirking at each other, trading secret looks. I sat there drinking wine.

Hana leaned close. "Cindy has something to tell you."

"Okay, shoot."

"Not here." With a tilt of her head, she indicated Cindy, waiting by the front door.

"Where?"

"Outside. On the deck. Are you sober enough to listen?"

I levered myself up from the table. Hana handed me the cane. The room swirled. Hana watched me move to the door. It was chilly on the deck in the wind. Cindy, staring out to sea, crossed her arms and shivered.

"How are things with you and Phyl's mom?"

"Pretty sad, I guess. Every time she sees me, she thinks of Phyl."

"I like Mike. Seems like a good guy."

"He's sweet." Cindy ran her index finger along my railing. "I'm going to Texas, Matt. To live with Jane. There's a great school there. I need to get . . . out of here."

"Yeah," I said.

"I know you'll be sad but Jane asked me and I thought it over and really meant to talk it over with you, I really did, but things got in the way, sort of, so I'm talking about it now, okay?"

"Okay. Sure."

"Jane's lonely. I love her. Not love her like a mother, I mean, but more like a friend. There's no way I can take Heather's place, and she's not really my mom, and she's sort of been waiting around, carrying the torch, she says, for you, but now that you and Hana—" Cindy stopped talking to take a deep breath. "I like Hana, Matt. She's beautiful and smart and she's been really nice to me. Like a sister, I guess. She's so . . . real."

"Real," I said.

"Will you come to visit me in Texas? Visit us, I mean. Jane and me?"

"Sure."

"When?"

"Soon."

"How about Thanksgiving? Or maybe Christmas?"

A quick flutter in my heart, like a dying bird beating one weak wing. "Maybe."

There was a heavy silence and then she gave a little sob and came into my arms. From inside my house came the buzz of conversation. Friends in there, good solid stalwart friends.

"Will the dreams stop someday?"

"What dreams do you mean?"

"Dreams about the shooting, the killing, the night when Phyl died. I dream about it, and I try to run, only it's in slow motion and I can't outrun the bullets and there's all this blood."

"They'll stop," I said. "When you get to Texas."

"I'm glad," Cindy said.

"We were lucky."

"In the hospital, lying there, I wanted to kill Bernie Dodds. And not just for that, either."

"Then you'd have been in jail."

A shiver. She pulled away from me. "It's complicated, isn't it? Hitting back, I mean."

"Yeah. It's complicated."

"Hana said you beat that man up, Matt. That Carruthers. I'm sorry you got hurt."

I said nothing.

"See you before I leave?"

"When do you leave?"

"Week from Saturday. The noon plane."

"Let's have dinner."

She nodded. "Can I bring Mike?"

"Sure," I said. "Bring old Mike."

Later, after the good-byes and the dishes done and the long, hot shower, Hana lay snuggled close, her mouth close to my ear. We'd made love and I could feel the strength she was giving me, that earth mother force flowing through me

like warm spring sap. I was planning my debut workout at
Wally's health spa when Hana turned serious.

"Cindy's sweet," she said. "And very pretty. She's been
through a lot for a kid."

"Yeah."

"She's the kind of girl who asks you to wait for her. Wait
until she grows up."

I patted Hana's flank. "I like my women already grown."

A silence, then she said, "I've got to go back, Matt."

"Jesus. When?"

"Tomorrow."

"Wait a week. Wait a month."

"I have to go. My students are there. I want you to visit
me."

"Stay here where it's warm."

"I can't breathe here, Matt. It's too close, like a lid was
down tight, the smog heavy, holding me down."

"Dammit, Hana. Don't go."

"I have to." She kissed me. "What will you do?"

"Now that I can't work, you mean?"

"Yes."

"Rest. Work out. Drink beer. Sleep around."

She pinched me, her fingers like vise grips on my bare
belly. I pried her fingers apart. Her face was filled with fury.

"Just joking," I said. "Just kidding around."

"Look." She spoke through tight teeth. "I fell for you
that day in the parking garage when you charged out of the
dark to rescue me. You didn't know me, didn't know who I
was. But here you came, anyway, to save me. I've been in
love. I've been hurt. I don't like the feeling. It scares me to
need anyone this much. I don't know how to handle it. All I
know is I like having you around. It's weird."

"Thanks." My heart thudded like old gray concrete under the jackhammer.

"So when are you coming?"

"We can get to know each other here," I said. "Where it's warmer."

"It feels dead here. I hate it. The people are rude, an entire state on a fast track to blitzville. The air is unbreathable. That merciless sun."

"My friends are here, my contacts. My cop connections."

"And I'm in Seattle."

And then she turned her back to me and I could feel the chill, like a deep-freeze, where the warmth had been.

28

EVERYONE WAS LEAVING. HANA AND I HUGGED IN the crowded terminal at John Wayne Airport. Final imprint of her body, pressing close, people passing by, frequent flyers, eyeballs on us, the old guy with gray in his beard and the gorgeous earth mother from the Pacific Northwest, and then it was time and she kissed us both, Wally and me, and moved to the door with tears in her eyes.

I leaned on my borrowed cane, watching the big jet waddle out to the runway. It was a smoggy afternoon in Orange County, the air thick with gridlock grunge and burned-out California dreams. My heart was heavy as a beached mama whale as I watched the takeoff.

"Diana the Huntress," Wally said. "Juno, Hera, Aphrodite, Latona, Terpsichore, Morgan le Fay."

"Babble, babble," I said.

"Mythic female," Wally said. "An earth goddess straight from the castles of Otherworld. Demeter, Persephone, Halcyone, Helen of Troy, Galatea, Dante's Beatrice, Merope, Penelope at her loom . . ."

He was still muttering about ladies of legend as we

walked to his Saab. It was forest green, with matching upholstery and four-speaker sound all around. Wally buys in
August, when the car dealers jettison old iron from their
lots to make room for new iron in September. Behind the
wheel of his Saab, Wally drives like Andy Granatelli.

We didn't get far. Gray sky lowering, Newport Boulevard
clotted with vehicles. Trucks, buses, pickups, cars. Horns
honked in anger and people flipped fingers at each other
and up ahead two husky construction guys were having a
slugging match in the center lane.

Wally checked his watch. "*Merde.* I've got tennis at four."

"Drop me off at a phone. I'll get a cab. You can zip to
your match on the side streets."

"But your leg, Matthew."

"I've got your shillelagh." I patted the cane. "Maybe I'll
hitch a ride with a blonde in a miniskirt."

"Hmm," Wally said.

So he drove off and I phoned for a taxi at the corner
Exxon station. I was a mile from home. A month ago I
could have walked it. Or jogged it. Today, with the traffic on
Newport Boulevard, it took the taxi an hour to reach me
and another hour to get home.

And when I got there I had bills to pay.

I talked with Hana on the phone. Phone talk felt empty.
My voice sounded dead. I needed to touch her, watch her,
admire her, lie with her. She was busy painting, she said,
busy with her teaching. Big Daddy Borklund, out on bail at
last, had skipped the country. Louie had installed a lovely
security system at Hana's place. No one had bothered her.
She'd finally checked Rollie's P.O. box and found money.
What should she do with it? Save it, I said. You earned it.

Louie called from Seattle. A client had a security problem that involved bodyguarding and could I advise him? A

local corporation needed personal security for their annual meeting of the board and could I advise him on that? How about coming up for a weekend and helping out? The money was good, he said. I'd think about it, I said.

I mailed the green pills to Professor Lindstrom at the University of Washington. Maybe she could write a scholarly paper and save the world from the next ice age.

A day dragged by. A week. Attorneys for Shelby Carruthers worked hard to get ready for his trial.

I saw Cindy off at the airport. She hugged me. She kissed Mike on the side of the mouth. He was planning to visit her in Texas for Thanksgiving. I couldn't remember Mike's last name. I had no plans for Thanksgiving.

Webby Smith dropped by my place, bearing official news. With him was Jeannie, his old flame. They were back together again. They were heading for Mexico for Thanksgiving. They did not invite me to come along.

Webby's news was cheery: There was a warrant out for the arrest of Detective Nick Giordano, who was wanted for questioning in the case of California versus Shelby Carruthers. According to the neighbors, Detective Giordano had not been seen for a week.

There was no news about Agent Loomis.

At Castelli's for Sunday dinner, Leo announced he and his wife were flying to Italy the day before Thanksgiving. Visit the Old Country, he said. Visit the relatives before they get too old.

Old, old, old. Age in the air. Age in my beard, age in my skin, my bones, my semibenumbed leg.

While I was chewing lasagna, Wally told me he planned to spend Thanksgiving back East. In his other life, away from the beach in California, Wally had two ex-wives and half a dozen kids. He talked about them only on New Year's Eve, when he drank too much, what he called the

Too Full Cup of Academe. I'd known him eight years. This was the first time he'd paid them a visit.

"I feel old," Wally said. "It's time."

The grand jury probe into the crimes of Shelby Carruthers got under way. People were angry about drugs and drug dealers so the DA shoved the low-profile stuff aside to make room. I was not asked to testify, but in return for diminished jail time, the DA got good stuff from Joel and Bernie Baby. Shelby's plans for marketing drugs to tots and teens made a nice media splash. Channel 3, down from Los Angeles to film the courtroom fun, gave Shelby top spot in a documentary called "Drugs for the Nineties." The centerpiece of the documentary was a series of plot maps of southern California, maps that showed a detailed network of drug distributors from San Ysidro north to Bakersfield, from Santa Barbara to Fresno, from San Diego east to the Imperial Valley.

The hot market niche for drugs was kids, ten to sixteen. Drug pushers hooked ten-year-olds on marijuana, moving them up to horse and coke. Joel, Shelby's prince of the playground pushers, had been test-marketing ice, probing for price barriers in his customers, when he'd met ace ice maker Chick Dickens in the heat of the summer.

Squirming on the stand, Joel tried to slide away from the DA's questions. A piece of their dialogue was reprinted in the *Orange County Tribune:*

D.A.:   When did you know Mr. Dickens was dead?
JOEL: When I read it in the paper.
D.A.:   How did you feel?
JOEL: Crummy.
D.A.:   Did you see Mr. Dickens on the day of his death?

JOEL: Like I told you, he sent a mule to do the deal. She had the stuff in that backpack. I gave her the money.

D.A.:   And what role did Mr. Carruthers play in all this?

JOEL: He told me to deal with Dickens. Then, later on, he told me to talk to some guy.

D.A.:   What guy is that?

JOEL: A guy on the phone.

D.A.:   What did Mr. Carruthers say to do, Mr. Stedman?

JOEL: He said I should tell the guy on the phone about the next meet with Dickens.

D.A.:   May I ask why?

JOEL: Teach Dickens a lesson, he said.

D.A.:   Why?

JOEL: Dickens was boosting prices.

D.A.:   For the ice, you mean?

JOEL: Yeah. It p——— him off.

D.A.:   And you never saw the man on the phone?

JOEL: That's right. I never saw him.

D.A.:   Did Mr. Carruthers threaten you?

JOEL: He said he'd have me killed if I told.

D.A.:   You're under police protection, Mr. Stedman. Let's proceed.

The DA was after old Shelby. Maybe that was why he didn't follow up on the voice on the phone. There was no percentage in chasing after Eduardo. There was no mention of Valerie or the ice antidote or Agent Loomis or the Seattle connection. Like most DA's, this one had political ambitions. Nailing a fat cat like Shelby would get him headlines that would get him farther up the ladder of politics.

In a sidebar next to Joel's dialogue the paper printed a

recipe for cooking ice. The recipe came from the witness who followed Joel on the stand, a chemistry student from a local college who identified Joel as the person who paid him $1,000 in cash to cook up a test batch of ice.

A courtroom artist's sketch showed Joel in the witness box, tears coursing down his rat-face cheeks. The caption under the sketch said: *I'm sorry for what I've done. When I get out, I'm walking the straight and narrow, for sure.*

Lies.

Webby told me, on the QT, that Joel had changed his testimony because the DA had played him our cassette tape recorded in cabana number 404 at the John Wayne Motor Hotel.

"Great job on that tape, Sherlock," Webby said.

"Doesn't square," I said.

"Doesn't square with what?"

"With what I learned up north, from old Eduardo. Doesn't square with what Joel said on tape. Doesn't square with what I extricated from Shelby baby."

"Sherlock, Sherlock, you know the law. What you got is either hearsay or inadmissible."

"It's true, goddammit. I put it together."

"That's not the point," Webby said.

"What is the point?"

"To nail the bad guys. The fat cats. Isn't that what you always say?"

"Is it?" I said. "Is that what I always say?"

"You feeling okay, Sherlock?"

"Oh, sure. I feel great."

"When you're out of the dumps, boyo, you still owe me a lunch."

"Lunch?" My voice sounded dead. "Oh, sure, lunch."

"It's that woman," Webby said. "The eccentric artist from Seattle. She's gotten under your hide. I see the signs."

"Thanks, Iron Man. I really appreciate your insight." I hung up.

Is killing the only way? The law courts are jammed. The jails are jammed. DA's across the country have clearance quotas instead of conviction quotas. What the hell's going on with society? The fat cats get rich and the sheep get butchered and maybe I could have saved everyone pain and saved the state some court costs if I'd taken direct action. Maybe I should have kidnapped old Shelby, motored him down to Mexico, and hammered him to death with a squash racquet. Maybe killing's the only way.

But I'd killed Julio the Skateboard Assassin and I'd pushed people around—goons and kids and women—and I was tired now. I was tired of reporters, tired of postmortem should-have-beens and after-the-fact what-ifs. I was tired of the trial so I stopped reading about it. I worked out at Le Club, sponging off Wally's membership. I cut my beer intake down from a six-pack to four beers a day, then three. I stumped along the beach and felt sorry for myself. And then I got this letter from Hana:

Dear Matt—

You are a stubborn man. I miss you. I love your voice on the phone. I should play hard to get, but it's not me. Come to Seattle. Louie has a job for you. My building has an elevator for your leg. The weather was gorgeous today, a pale yellow sky against those gray clouds, with an orange streak glowing at sunset. When I make soup, I think of you. When I paint, I think of you. Phone me when you get this. I want to talk to you, hear your voice.

It was signed "Love, Hana."

In a dream that night I was a little kid again. Wearing my Dr. Dentons, I climbed into my bed. It was my last night in this house. The Sergeant had his marching orders. Tomorrow, we would move again, out of this house to another house in another army town. I cried in my pillow because I did not want to move again.

I woke sweating.

I picked up the phone. I put it down. I walked around the room. My leg hurt. I thought of Hana's elevator. I thought of her moods. I thought of her curves, cheekbones, moisture beading her upper lip, waterfall of dark hair, those eyes reading me. My heart pumped along, thud, thud, and I remembered our early-morning dance, those old records. I picked up the phone. The time was 5:01 A.M. In a rusty voice, I made a reservation to Seattle.

And then I phoned Hana and told her and there was joy in her voice, joy thrumming through the phone, joy rushing at me, torrents of joy, joy enough for both of us, joy to the world, and when we finished talking I hung up and brewed a pot of Murdock Blend and packed my Eddie Bauer backpack, red with black straps, for the long trip north.